PENGUIN EBURY PRESS

POLICE AFFAIRS

Amit Lodha is an IPS officer currently serving as assistant director general of police. He has been awarded the prestigious Police Medal for Gallantry and the Internal Security Medal, as well as the Utkrisht Seva Medal and the President's Medal for meritorious service. He has previously authored *Bihar Diaries* (2018) and *Life in the Uniform* (2022). This is his third book.

ADVANCE PRAISE FOR THE BOOK

'An entertaining, thrilling read. So much more than just another cop story!'—**Akshay Kumar**

'Amit is a master storyteller of the crime drama genre. *Police Affairs* is yet another example of that. Gripping and fast-paced, one gets drawn to their flawed characters, shadowy conspiracies and a mystery. This is Amit at his best!'—**Amish Tripathi**

'Full on masala screaming for an adaptation'—**Neeraj Pandey**

ALSO BY THE SAME AUTHOR

Bihar Diaries: The True Story of How Bihar's Most Dangerous Criminal Was Caught
Life in the Uniform: Adventures of an IPS Officer in Bihar

POLICE AFFAIRS

BEYOND THE CALL OF DUTY

AMIT LODHA

EBURY
PRESS

An imprint of Penguin Random House

EBURY PRESS

Ebury Press is an imprint of the Penguin Random House group of companies
whose addresses can be found at global.penguinrandomhouse.com

Published by Penguin Random House India Pvt. Ltd
4th Floor, Capital Tower 1, MG Road,
Gurugram 122 002, Haryana, India

Penguin
Random House
India

First published in Ebury Press by Penguin Random House India 2025

10 9 8 7 6 5 4 3 2 1

ISBN 9780143473244

Typeset in Adobe Caslon Pro by MAP Systems, Bengaluru, India
Printed at Thomson Press India Ltd, New Delhi

www.penguin.co.in

MIX
Paper | Supporting
responsible forestry
FSC® C010615

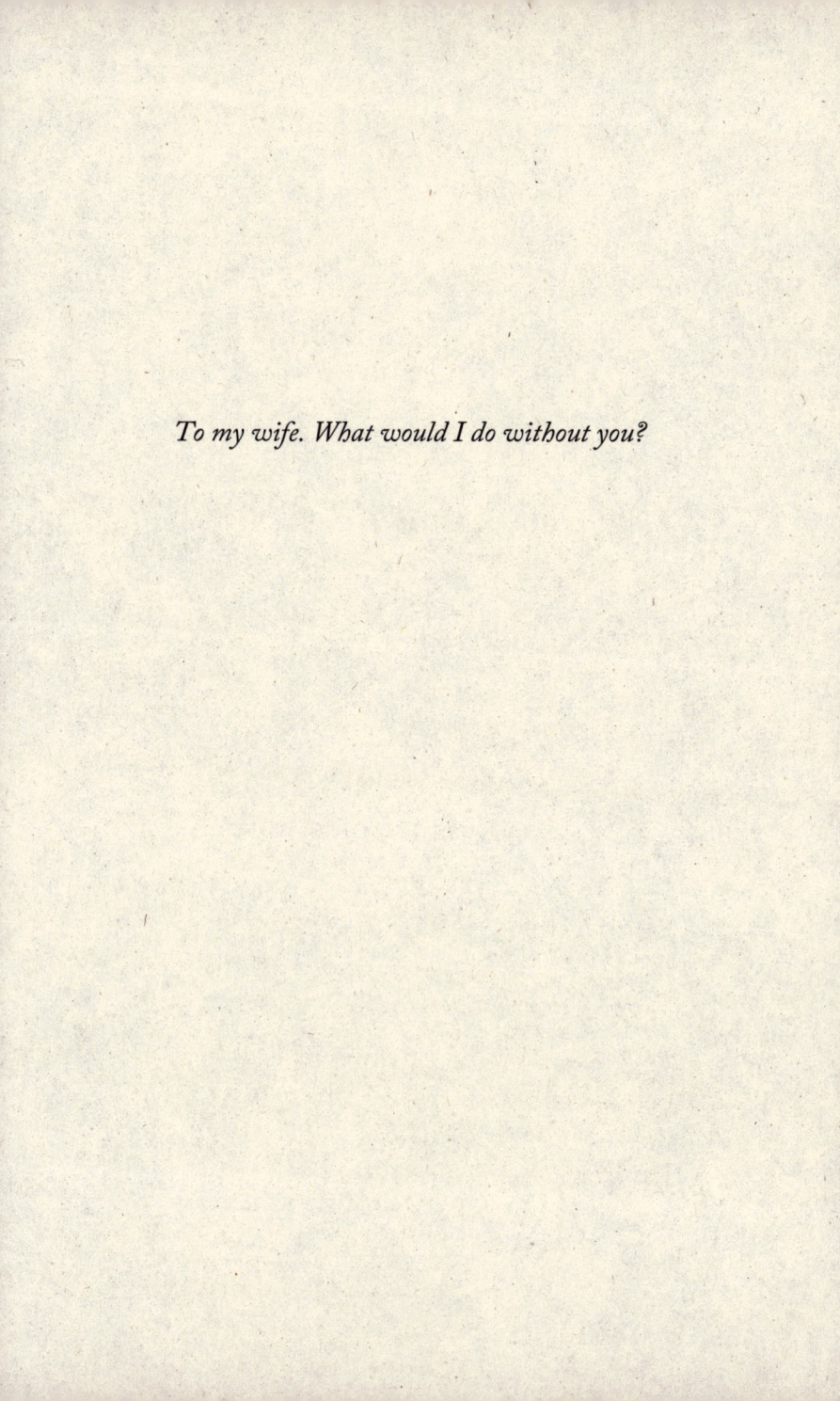

To my wife. What would I do without you?

Author's Note

'We all have both light and dark inside us. What matters
is the part we choose to act on. That is who we really are.'

—J.K. Rowling

I wrote this book with contradictory feelings—apprehension and confidence.

Apprehension because it marks a significant departure from my earlier works, which reflected the life of an 'ideal' police officer. This time, I have chosen to tell the story of a morally ambiguous officer—someone who appears to be ideal but is, at his core, a flawed human being.

Confidence because this story is relatable. All of us have shades of grey.

My first two books, *Bihar Diaries* and *Life in the Uniform*, were based on my real-life experiences in the police force. The love and appreciation I have received for them over the years have been overwhelming—especially when young readers tell me how these books have inspired them. It deeply humbles me to receive messages from people across the world, remarking how my books have helped change the often clichéd perceptions of an IPS officer.

I have always been meticulous about my conduct, both in my personal and professional life, and I go the extra mile to uphold the dignity of my service. As many young people look up to an IPS officer as a role model, I strive every moment to stand by my principles and core values that define selfless service.

Over the years, I have often been told that I am too idealistic, unwilling to indulge in the so-called 'pleasures' that life offers. At times, I wondered—what if I had given in? What if the balance between duty and desire tipped in the wrong direction? That thought experiment led me to this book—an exploration of how a momentary lapse of reason can change a life forever, especially for someone bound by the highest ethical standards. I imagined how devastating the consequences of unchecked pleasures and temptations could be—particularly for an IPS officer.

The protagonist of this book is a successful and brilliant officer driven by a mix of duty and desire, and, at times, not immune to temptation. Instead of portraying an idealized hero, I wanted to present a complex, deeply human character—one who struggles with difficult choices and, sometimes, crosses the very boundaries he once upheld. At the end of the day, an officer is also human—with the same vulnerabilities, conflicts and imperfections as anyone else.

This book is a work of fiction. It is in part inspired by personalities I have met, situations I have encountered and the moral dilemmas I have pondered in my own life. However, no character in the book is to be read as a portrayal of an actual person, living or dead and no incident in the book as a recounting of a real-life event. The story is a product of my imagination as coloured by my life experiences, both personal and professional.

I am eager to see how my discerning readers respond, as they may have certain expectations based on their experiences with the themes of my earlier books. It has been both thrilling and unnerving to etch a character who is more flesh and blood than perfect. I believe it will make for an intriguing study of human fallibility and, in some ways, serve as a cautionary tale.

I hope you enjoy reading this book as much as I enjoyed bringing this story to life.

Foreword

When you think of an IPS officer, you imagine a tough, disciplined and duty-bound individual who spends their life fighting crime and upholding the law. But what happens when such an officer also happens to be a storyteller? You get someone like Amit Lodha—a man who has not only served the nation with dedication but has also ventured into the world of fiction, this time bringing us a cop thriller that blends his first-hand experiences with the power of imagination.

Amit Lodha and I go way back—to our days as batchmates at IIT Delhi. Back then, we were just young students with dreams, figuring out where life would take us. While I ventured into writing, Amit took the tougher road, dedicating his life to public service as an IPS officer. Yet, despite the pressures of his duty, he kept his passion for writing alive.

Amit's journey from an IITian to a top cop and now an author is truly inspiring. Writing a novel is no small feat, especially when your day job involves tackling real-life crime. But Amit has managed to do it, bringing his knowledge and experiences into a cop thriller that only someone in his position could tell with such authenticity.

I congratulate Amit on this incredible achievement and wish him all the best. May he solve many more real crimes and write many more stories.

Chetan Bhagat
March 2025

List of Abbreviations

ADG	Additional Director General
AOR	Area of responsibility
BSF	Border Security Force
CP	Commissioner of Police
CRPF	Central Reserve Police Force
DC	Deputy Commandant
DIG	Deputy Inspector General of Police
IED	Improvised explosive device
IFS	Indian Foreign Service
IG	Inspector General of Police
IPS	Indian Police Service
MHA	Ministry of Home Affairs
NSG	National Security Guards
SOG	Special Operations Group
SP	Superintendent of Police
SPG	Special Protection Group
TNF	Tumour necrosis factor
UPSC	Union Public Service Commission

Prologue

8 July 2020
Pathankot, Punjab

'Sir, security is on maximum alert. All your instructions have been carried out. Is there anything else we need to do? Have I missed anything?' asked Vikram, Pathankot's young superintendent of police. His expression was calm, but his eyes betrayed his stress.

It was not every day that the Prime Minister of India visited a town on the Pakistan border. Naturally, all the security forces and intelligence agencies were on their toes, but Vikram couldn't help feeling that the PM's overall security was ultimately his responsibility.

'Vikram, a PM visit is always a big challenge for any SP, but I'm sure you'll manage this VVIP visit very well. Just follow the instructions in the Special Protection Group's Blue Book on proximate security for the PM. The BSF jawans will ensure that no terrorist infiltrates the border,' I said.

Though I was Vikram's senior, I too was nervous. All my experience in the police and the paramilitary forces would soon be tested. The PM faced strong threats from terrorists. As the IG BSF, Punjab Frontier, I had to ensure that no terrorists crossed into India from Pakistan. This was one of the biggest challenges I had faced in my career—of the 3000 km of India's border with Pakistan the BSF patrolled, around 550 km was under my area of responsibility (AOR).

On the Western front, the BSF had to contend with vast deserts, salty marshes, hills and mountains. Though the jawans and officers maintained a 24/7 vigil at the border, it was not impossible for any desperado to cross over. Sometimes, terrorists sneaked into India while enemy forces distracted the BSF with intense shelling. Natural riverine gaps and tunnels made by smugglers, spies and terrorists to infiltrate the country made the BSF's task even more challenging.

'Sir, this is my first VVIP visit! And the circumstances are so trying. The Intelligence Bureau has alerted us about terrorists from the Liberation Front trying to cross into our border to carry out an assassination attempt on our PM. There is a clear danger, and yet the PM insists on coming here,' said Vikram.

'Vikram, I have specially come from Jalandhar for the PM's visit,' I said. 'I have alerted all my commandants to keep an extra vigil on the border, particularly in the vulnerable areas. We are scanning for tunnels and searching all the houses on the bordering villages door to door.'

I took a breath and continued, 'Normally, it is not the BSF's job to secure the route of a VVIP, but in view of the grave threat to the PM, the MHA and the state government have given us that responsibility. We will cover the complete route of the motorcade, so you can relax.'

'Thank you, sir. Jai Hind,' said Vikram, saluting as he got up to leave.

'Jai Hind, Vikram. Best of luck,' I replied.

The assassination threats made by the Liberation Front had given the BSF a lot of stress. The onus of this fell directly on my shoulders as the head of the BSF, Punjab Frontier, and the senior-most IPS officer in the area.

In the course of my duty, I had often visited the borders of Pathankot, Amritsar and other towns to supervise the BSF battalions under my command and meet the local SPs and intelligence officers. And as a Punjab-cadre IPS officer on deputation to the BSF, I had mentored younger officers as well. But I had a special fondness for Vikram, the young, dynamic IPS officer posted as the SP of Pathankot.

Punjab had become a hotbed of narcotics smuggling of late and Pakistan's intelligence agency, the ISI, had been supplying weapons and counterfeit Indian currency to terrorists through these smugglers. Though the Pakistan government was working on improving the nation's relationship with India, the ISI was bent on reviving militancy in Punjab. And of course, the enemy agency was still fighting a proxy war in Kashmir, following its doctrine of bleeding India with a thousand cuts. Terrorists were ready to infiltrate India at any time, particularly from the Punjab border, as the BSF and the army had managed to keep them at bay in Jammu and Kashmir after Article 370 of the Indian Constitution was abrogated in 2019.

Of all the terrorist organizations aiming to destroy India, the Liberation Front had vowed to avenge the deaths of many of its members in surgical strikes carried out by the Indian Army. It had attacked a few military camps and convoys recently, and the PM was its new target.

I looked at the map on my desk. Pathankot bordered both Jammu and Pakistan. Thousands of dedicated BSF personnel guarded the Western front. But all it took was one opportunity for terrorists to sneak into India.

Recently, the BSF had detected a 150-metre-long tunnel along the Pakistan border in Jammu's Samba district, and a 265-foot-long pipe near the tunnel that was used to supply oxygen. Were there any tunnels secretly like this in my AOR? Had we detected all the tunnels constructed by terrorists? If we hadn't . . . I shuddered at the thought of the consequences.

* * *

BSF jawans patrolled the roads with their eyes and ears alert for sign of any suspicious activity. The PM's motorcade was supposed to arrive early the next morning, but from the security point of view, it was necessary to keep the roads sanitized days ahead of any VVIP movement.

A few days earlier, in Srinagar, a roadside hawker had left his cart on the road. The cart had been laden with IEDs that exploded when a CRPF convoy passed by. The CRPF had lost thirteen jawans in that blast. So no chances could be taken with the PM's security. The district police and the BSF had cleared the entire route of all vendors and carts. No vehicles were allowed parking anywhere on or near the road. Security forces were deployed at a number of buildings along the road and at other vantage points. Hundreds of jawans moved about with mine sweepers, scanning for hidden IEDs. And, of course, all traffic would be stopped when the PM's motorcade came by the next day.

Asif Sheikh, the deputy commandant of the BSF, felt fairly confident as he monitored the security arrangements from his Tata Sumo. He could not have done anything more, he thought. Perhaps he could stop soon and enjoy the view of the stream flowing beside the road.

As he looked around for any suspicious activity, he saw a cyclist in the distance, pedalling laboriously down the road. Nothing to worry about, the DC thought. The jawans at the check point a little further away would stop the cyclist and check his credentials.

The weather was turning nippy and the DC rolled up the window of his Sumo. Perfunctorily, he looked into the rear-view mirror again. But there was no sign of the cyclist. Where had he gone? There was no hiding place on the road, no turning to duck into. He grew alarmed. Something was wrong.

'*Roko, gaadi roko*. Stop the car,' he ordered the driver and jumped off even before the Sumo came to a halt, calling frantically to his men, '*Ek cyclewala tha, dhoondho usse.* There was a cyclist here, find him.'

How could he vanish into thin air, the DC wondered as he ran to the spot where he had last seen the man. Suddenly, he caught sight of the cycle hidden in the bushes by the road.

'He must be nearby. Keep up the search,' shouted the DC. Looking closely ahead, he spotted footprints on the wet soil along the stream.

'Here, come here,' he called for support, following the footprints to a culvert. That was when he saw the man and the explosives vest he was wearing, grenades dangling from the front. Before the DC could react, the man scurried off like a rabbit.

* * *

I rushed to the BSF's secret interrogation site, my heart pounding. As I entered the room, BSF DIG Madan Singh, SP Vikram, DC Asif Sheikh and several IB officers sprang to attention.

'What has he revealed so far? Give me all the details,' I said.

'Sir, the IG Intelligence of Punjab has learnt from his sources that this man might be a part of a *fidayeen* attack on the PM's motorcade. We're trying to get more information about the terrorists' plans,' said Vikram.

'That's obvious. Has he told you anything about his partners? Any accomplices?' I asked.

'No, sir. He's a tough nut. We've tried all our tricks, but he won't open his mouth. Here, let me show you what we recovered from him,' said the DIG Madan Singh.

I looked at the explosives vest, two grenades, a walkie talkie and a pistol, all laid neatly on a table.

'And these are some of the documents we got from his bag, sir,' said Asif.

There was an Indian passport, most likely fake, a picture of an infant and a few other papers. As I rummaged through the pile, I stopped suddenly, when I saw a crumpled ticket with the word 'Faisalabad' printed on one side.

The man was almost certainly a Pakistani who had crossed over into Indian territory. As the IG BSF, I was squarely responsible for this failure. I swallowed, feeling sick. But this was not the time to panic.

'What kind of a terrorist is he? Tell me, DIG Saheb, why did he not blow up his vest? And did he exchange fire with our jawans?' I asked.

'It was just our lucky day. The guy panicked at the sight of the checkpoint and the DC's car and tried to hide. Surprisingly, he did not put up any resistance when he was surrounded by Asif Sheikh and his men. He just surrendered meekly after an initial attempt to run,' replied Madan.

'Our bomb disposal squad then opened the belt and removed the explosives,' Vikram added.

My shoulders relaxed. We really had been lucky. But then luck plays a part in every aspect of life and death. In 1984, when the Irish Republican Army had narrowly missed killing the then British PM Margaret Thatcher in the Brighton Hotel bombing, it had issued a statement that read, 'Today we were unlucky, but remember we have to be lucky only once. You will always have to be lucky.'

I thought about reversals of fortune. Today seemed to be our lucky day, not the terrorists'. Once in a while, thankfully, even security forces have fortune smiling on them.

When I was escorted into the dank, nondescript interrogation room, I looked at the man huddled in a corner, fear written large on his face. He seemed poor and uneducated. Many such illiterate, impoverished people had been radicalized by the ISI and terrorist organizations to fight in the name of *jihad*. The man in our custody reminded me of Ajmal Kasab, the Lashkar-e-Taiba terrorist hanged in India for the 2008 Mumbai terror attacks.

'Clearly, he was not willing to die and meet the seventy-two virgins in paradise. Becoming a martyr is not easy. Most of us love our lives,' said Madan.

'Maybe he wants to live for someone else. His family perhaps,' said Vikram.

'Vikram, DIG Saheb, we need to interrogate him properly. I'm certain he's not the only one to have crossed the border. Maybe he even has local support. Come on, let's start,' I said.

After a good three hours of police treatment and different interrogation techniques, the man in our custody broke down.

'*Bas*, stop sir. I cannot take it anymore. I will tell you whatever I know. Just let me go back to my family. I have a three-month-old son. I want to see him,' he wept.

The man was a wreck. If he hadn't been trained by the militants, he probably would have broken earlier.

'Where are you from? How did you cross over?' I asked.

'It is not easy to sneak into our country. Our BSF jawans work 24x7, 365 days in all kinds of weather and terrain. How did you get in?' asked the agitated DIG BSF. He was a proud man who knew that his jawans guarded the nation's borders with the utmost devotion.

DIG Madan was right, of course. The India–Pakistan border is fully fenced and constantly patrolled by BSF constables and officers. Though it is not like the demilitarized zone between North and South Korea, which has millions of landmines. But even there, some people do manage to cross over, I mused.

'Sir, my name is Kamran. I am a poor man from Faridkot in Pakistan. I was trained at a camp in Faisalabad. We crossed from one of the tunnels near the border. We were helped by the drug smugglers in your country,' said the terrorist, scrubbing his face with his hands.

Every officer in the room jolted.

'We?' It was a collective cry of horror.

'Yes, we were four people,' said Kamran.

'Names? Description?' I yelled.

'Bashir Khan.'

'And?' I shouted again.

'A mysterious man. I never heard him talk, but I'm sure he was hard of hearing. *Thoda bhenga bhi tha*, he had a squint in his left eye,' he said.

'And the fourth person?'

'Timur Ali,' he replied after a pause.

My heart skipped a beat.

'Timur Ali. Are you sure?' I asked.

'Yes, sir,' he replied.

Timur Ali was the chief of the Liberation Front. The TLF had claimed responsibility for the attack on the Srinagar Convention Centre a year ago. If Timur Ali had infiltrated India, something disastrous was imminent. We knew this for sure.

Madan Singh grabbed the terrorist's collar and shook him.

'What exactly were you trying to do when we caught you?' he asked furiously.

'I was just doing a recce of the route and looking for a place to hide for the night before your PM arrived. I was supposed to blow myself up near the BSF camp to divert the security forces' attention, but I panicked and ran,' he said.

'What is the plan of the other terrorists?' I asked.

'Sir, I am a small pawn in this game. Timur and the other guys never discussed anything in front of me. But I could gather that they were planning something big. Maybe they would blow up your PM's motorcade.'

Beads of sweat ran down my face in the chilly night.

* * *

'How much time do we have before the PM arrives?' I asked.

'Sir, he'll be here in ten hours from now,' said Vikram, glancing at his watch.

'Can we not cancel his trip?' I asked the IB officer.

'No way, sir. This is an international meeting which took months to organize. The PM will not hear any such suggestion,' the IB man replied.

'So, can we change the route or the venue instead?'

'Unfortunately not, sir. There is no other route to the venue. Our town is too small for an alternate route. And there is no other place where we can hold such a high-level meeting,' said Vikram.

Then we have no option but to go ahead with the programme. 'Put all the forces on the highest level of alertness,' I directed him. 'There is only one way we can keep the PM safe.' I said, turning to the other officers, 'We have to find the three other terrorists.'

I turned to Kamran and glared at him. 'Where is your hideout? Where are your accomplices?' I shouted.

'Janab, I don't know,' he said. We could tell that he was bluffing. Vikram slapped him.

'Don't you dare lie to me!' he thundered. Kamran quivered as Vikram raised his hand again.

'*Soch le*, think about it. If you help us, we'll release you and let you go to your son,' said Madan Singh, flashing the photograph of Kamran's son. The DIG was experienced enough to know that emotions could melt even a hardened terrorist.

'*Batata hoon*, I'll tell you. But promise me you'll let me go back to my family,' Kamran replied, reaching for the picture of his son.

I smiled faintly at Vikram and DIG Madan Singh's good cop-bad cop act.

'Yes, we will see that you are united with your family. But only if you help us,' I said, reiterating our promise.

'Saheb, I am an utterly dispensable person for Timur. The other guys never discussed their plans in front of me. All I know is our hideout. I'll take you there. It's the only place I know in Pathankot,' said Kamran, tears rolling down his cheeks as he caressed the picture of his son.

We knew it wouldn't be easy to catch the other terrorists. Nevertheless, we jumped into our vehicles with a glimmer of hope.

* * *

'That's the house, sir,' said Kamran, pointing to a beautiful cottage at the end of the lane.

'Tell the jawans of the BSF and state police to cordon off the house. The commando team will enter for the search,' I ordered.

Normally, senior officers like me were not directly associated with operations. Operations are the job of the people in the field, but considering the grave danger to the PM, I needed to lead from the front. I had already spoken to the state DGP and state IB chief about the alarming situation. All security forces were on full alert.

The commando team carefully entered the house, looking for booby traps and ready to take on any terrorists within, but the house was vacant. Even after a thorough search, they found no one.

'Sir, *kya mazaa se rahte hain, yeh* terrorist! How much fun these terrorists have!' said a jawan looking at a huge flat screen TV mounted on a wall.

Less frustrated by the good life the terrorists were apparently leading than the fact that he and the rest of the security team had been unable to nab them, the jawan slapped the wooden wall on which the TV was mounted. There was an ominous creak and then the TV slowly fell forward. Even though the jawan instinctively leapt to save it, it crashed to the ground.

The other jawans came running at the sound. One of them was staring at the wall where the TV had been mounted. There was a slight gap in the woodwork that looked like an open panel.

The jawan stepped forward and pushed the piece of wood aside. He peered inside to see a compartment about 6X3ft big. There was no one in the room but inside, they found a cache of arms large enough to fight a small war.

* * *

'Sir, we're running out of time. This Kamran fellow doesn't know of any other hideout. We need to find the other three men. This huge recovery of arms shows how prepared they are to face anything. What do we do now?' asked Vikram.

I looked at the officers around me, seeking answers.

'We should look for the owner of the house. He will definitely know something about the terrorists,' said the IB officer. 'After all, it is his house. And he must have had the secret chamber constructed.'

In less than forty minutes, the owner of the cottage, Farooq Ahmed, was in front of us.

'Farooq, for the first and last time, where are the terrorists who were hiding in your house?' Vikram said menacingly.

Farooq's shoulders drooped; he knew there was no point in feigning ignorance. The security forces were smart enough to guess that he was an accomplice of the terrorist's, at least an indirect one.

'Janab, I do not know where any terrorist is hiding. I don't live in that house anyway. The Liberation Front bought the house and registered it in my name. I had no option but to accede to their diktats. I also got greedy. Who would not want a house in their name?' Farooq stammered. It was not surprising that a poor man like Farooq could be lured into becoming the owner of a house that was beyond his means.

'Who did you commission to make the secret chamber?' I asked. 'The chamber looked like the work of a professional, someone really skilled.'

'I was asked by those people to find an expert carpenter. There is only one carpenter in our locality who is as good at his work. His name is Waqar and he lives nearby,' replied Farooq.

'Sir, I know this carpenter very well. He had come to the BSF campus to help with the construction of the gurudwara,' said the DIG BSF.

'Then we can get him easily. This Waqar guy will be our key,' I said.

Guided by Farooq, the SOG team quickly located Waqar's house and quietly whisked him away. Two slaps and a thunderous tone was all it took to make Waqar sing like a canary.

'Sir, I don't know anything. I am just a poor carpenter. Some dangerous men, fully masked, knock on my door once in a while. They ask me to make secret chambers for them, well concealed from the naked eye,' said Waqar.

'How many chambers have you made? Take us to every house in which you made a secret chamber,' I commanded.

'Janab, I made five more such chambers but I can't take you to any of those houses. I was always blindfolded and then dropped off at an isolated place. You don't ask questions or act smart with these dangerous people. I just get my money and keep my mouth shut,' said Waqar.

'Another dead end. Will we never get lucky?' I slapped the wall in frustration.

'But sir, I know the location of the last house that I was taken to,' Waqar added suddenly.

'Where is it? Tell us, man,' I snapped.

Waqar gulped.

'After I made the secret chamber in the house, I was dropped by the masked men near a wooden bridge which is quite a popular spot in that area,' he said. 'I removed my blindfold and out of curiosity, I climbed a little hillock. From there, I could see a house at the edge of the forest. That must have been the house I had been taken to. Maybe the men became a little careless after numerous visits and let me out early.'

'How are you so sure about the house?' asked Madan Singh.

'Janab, that is the only house there,' replied Waqar.

* * *

Within an hour, we were at the house.

The commandos leapt out of their bulletproof gypsies, their Israeli X95 guns at the ready and night vision goggles already on, as the BSF troops and the policemen quickly moved to cordon the three-storey house.

The house was dark and silent. Either it was vacant, or all its occupants were fast asleep. Suddenly, a light flickered from the top floor.

I looked at Vikram and Madan. We nodded at each other and signalled the commandos to enter. There was no time to lose. This house was our only chance to find the terrorists. Even if we failed to find them here, at least we could find some more clues to their plan.

With a single blow, the commandos broke down the door. In the spartan hall ahead of us, an elderly woman startled awake. A young boy next to her looked frightened. Neither said a word as the commandos signalled them to remain quiet.

The commandos scanned the ground floor and then moved to the first floor. There was not a soul in sight. The second floor was also vacant. The exasperated team leader signalled us to come up.

'Sir, *yahan toh kuchh nahin hai*, there is nothing here,' said the DC leading the commandos. He entered a room and switched on his torch. The room appeared to be empty. There was just a large mirror, almost covering an entire wall, with a narrow counter in front, on which some toiletries were placed.

'This is the place from where we saw the light,' I said, my gut tightening as I sensed danger.

Vikram looked at his reflection in the mirror and sighed resentfully. 'There is no one here, sir. We are not getting anything, not even a clue. And who uses this hearing aid?' he said, picking it up from the counter.

'Call the carpenter,' I said. 'He will show us the secret chamber at least.'

One of the commandos escorted Waqar into the room. The carpenter looked fearfully at the large mirror on the wall, as though death was staring him in his face. He nudged me delicately. Before I could react, the staccato sound of an assault rifle almost burst my eardrums and splinters of glass flew at my skin. As I fell back, shielding Vikram with my body, I saw two people firing at us indiscriminately. One of them suddenly fell down in a heap. I looked back to see Madan Singh firing his pistol. In that moment, a hail of bullets hit him on his bulletproof vest and he slumped. Another volley from the terrorist's AK 47 shattered his arm.

As I lay on the floor, my head down, I glanced at the man still firing at us. It was Timur Ali. There was no doubt about it. As the most wanted terrorist of the Liberation Front, I had seen his pictures countless times.

Just for a moment, his weapon jammed. The Kalashnikov rifle rarely malfunctions because the clearances in its moving parts are much larger than those in standard guns. Perhaps the terrorist's AK 47 had not received enough pressure to blow the bolt carrier of the rifle back. Whatever it was, it had given me an opportunity and I took it. I leapt at him, aiming my elbow at his solar plexus. He fell, grimacing in pain. Before he could react, Vikram was at his throat. Together, we kept the terrorist down till the commandos arrived and overpowered him.

With Timur Ali gone, I looked into the concealed cavity behind the mirror. It was a two-way mirror, I noticed. When the terrorists heard our vehicles, they must have quickly entered the cavity. There were a few pairs of night vision glasses in the chamber, a CCTV monitoring the area around the house, two AK 47s with hundreds of rounds and a few grenades. A map lay crumpled in a corner; when I picked it up, I noted that the route of the PM's motorcade was marked on it.

Beneath the map was a diary. I flipped through the pages, but the notes appeared to be in code.

'Here, Vikram, keep this carefully,' I said as I handed him the diary. I hoped that the IB sleuths would decipher the code and find a minefield of data. Though, by now, I was more keen to learn which locals may have helped the terrorists. Three police uniforms and a few false beards were also found in a bag.

DIG Madan Singh was lying in a pool of blood. The commandos carefully lifted him and carried him to a vehicle. I fervently prayed he would survive as I could not imagine losing the extraordinarily brave Madan. I remembered the brave BSF DIG N.N. Dubey who had led the encounter that had killed Ghazi Baba, the terrorist responsible for the Parliament attack, in a startlingly similar operation in 2003, and cursed myself for not asking the carpenter about the hiding place before we entered the house.

When I returned to my vehicle, Timur Ali was being handcuffed. Looking disdainfully at the nameplate on my chest, he said, 'Arjun Kumar, you will pay for this someday.' He spat on the ground, his eyes bloodshot.

* * *

From a hillock not far away, a tall man watched as Timur Ali was placed in a vehicle by the commandos.

He put down his night vision monocular. The squint in his other eye made it uncomfortable for him to focus for long, even with his good eye.

'The plan will have to wait, but it will be executed, come what may. Vengeance will be mine,' he vowed.

1

'I Am Young!'

22 February 2021
Jalandhar

'Charu, come on, *yaar*. Hold the gun properly. Treat it as an extension of your arm,' I shouted.

'*Arre, kar rahi hoon na*, I'm doing it. You concentrate on your own target,' my wife said, irritated by my constant directions. 'Really, Arjun, why do you insist on me coming for firing practice at the shooting range? You know I'm good with pistols.'

'You know our family has been under constant threat since I arrested Timur Ali. He has vowed to come after us. Even the State Intelligence Bureau has reported threats of terrorist attacks against us. Why do I need to constantly remind you?' I complained.

'You arrested Timur and killed a few terrorists in the line of duty when you were on deputation to the BSF. Why would they make it personal? And now you have returned to your cadre and are posted as IG Jalandhar. I don't think you need to be so paranoid,' Charu replied.

'Those terrorists targeted the PM of our country, Charu. That means they are certainly capable of harming an IGP and his family. Do you really want to argue about this?' I glared.

Her expression turned serious. She was aware of the threats that are part of an IPS officer's baggage. She took a deep breath, grasped the Glock firmly and fired. The staccato sound of the shots pierced the silent sky. The armourer by Charu's side held out her cap to collect the empty shells as they ejected from the Austrian-made pistol. We finished firing our quota of ten rounds and proceeded to check our hits. Charu had hit the bull's eye seven times. The three remaining shots were also quite close to the bull's eye.

'*Huzur, gustakhi maaf,* pardon me, but madam's shooting skills are definitely better than yours,' said the armourer as he examined the targets.

He was not wrong. I had not hit a single bull's eye. In fact, I had literally sprayed the target with bullets, two of my shots missing the cut-out altogether! So much for my police training.

'It seems the pistol is defective, *ustaad.* Have it checked,' said the sergeant to the armourer, hoping to salve my bruised ego.

I was amused by the way subordinate officers do their best to inflate the pride of their senior officers.

'Oh, no, no. Madam is actually a good shot, much better than me. I'm trained to fire, but I'm not a natural with small arms. I'm better with rifles and carbines. Maybe putting the butt of the gun on my shoulder stabilizes the gun and improves my shooting,' I replied.

I was very proud of Charu. She was fit and energetic and loved sports and horse riding. As the daughter of a police officer, she had been groomed for an adventurous life. Now she enjoyed every bit of being the wife of an IPS officer. And she loved me like crazy.

'Saheb is also excellent in everything. He is such a fine officer,' said Charu, hugging me.

'Okay, okay. Thanks for the compliment, Charu. Save it for later when we have a fight!' I replied, embarrassed by Charu's PDA in front of so many policemen.

'*Saheb aur memsaheb ki Ram milae jodi hai*, your match is made in heaven. You are the perfect couple,' said the sergeant. Charu and I looked at each other and smiled.

'Let's go, Charu, or I'll be late for tennis. Vikram should be near the CRPF campus now. Siddharth and I must beat him and his partner today,' I said, getting into the car.

'Please, you father and son will just fight on the tennis court. Siddharth always complains that he doesn't want to play with you because you're getting old and slow,' said Charu, entering the car from the other side.

'I'm like old wine, getting better with age. Look at Roger Federer,' I replied.

'Wait, wait. I've forgotten my NSG cap!' shouted Charu, ignoring my foolish comparison with the legendary tennis player.

The armourer ran up with the lovely military green cap and gave it to Charu. She caressed the NSG monogram and smiled. The cap was special to her. She had got it when we won the prize for the best dancing couple during my three-day training at the NSG campus, Manesar, even though I had danced like Sunny Deol. The cap was worn out, but it had great sentimental value for Charu.

I held her hand, caressing it with my thumb and feeling the softness of her skin. Gosh, she looked as gorgeous as ever. I was madly in love with the mother of my two children.

* * *

'Jai Hind, sir! I hope we get a good game,' said Vikram.

'Yeah, sure. Siddharth, meet Vikram uncle, the SSP,' I said.

'Papa, of course I know Vikram uncle, he was the SP Pathankot. He used to come to our house in Jalandhar

often. I didn't know you had been transferred here, uncle,'
said Siddharth, bouncing the ball on the clay. Vikram's
doubles partner, the CRPF commandant smiled as he
waited patiently for the game to start.

'Please don't call me uncle, Siddharth. It makes me
feel so old,' said Vikram. 'By the way, I must say that
sir has done me so many favours. He's been my mentor.
He's a role model for so many youngsters like me. And he
saved my life!'

'Chalo, let's play,' I said, putting a stop to the
conversation. Though I tried to act humble, I was really
quite vain. I had been awarded the President's Medal for
Gallantry for arresting Timur Ali and saving Vikram's life,
which was a rare distinction, and I knew that if Vikram
continued to sing my praises, it would go to my head.

Buoyed by Vikram's flattery, I played quite well and
won both the sets. Of course, I also had the advantage of
having young Siddharth as my partner.

'You're quite fit for your age, sir,' Vikram commented.
'You look very young too.'

'I am young! I'm just forty-seven years old,' I replied,
outraged. I had been selected for the IPS at quite a young
age, and exercise and good genes helped me maintain a
youthful look. I had always been a sportsman and took
great pride in my agility and endurance.

'Apologies, sir, you certainly don't look forty-seven,'
said Vikram, flattering me again.

'Thanks, Vikram.' Basking in the adulation, I promptly
started doing push ups to impress him and the ballboys.

'Enough showing off, Papa. Let's get home in time for
dinner or mom will be angry,' complained Siddharth.

'These new generation kids, they don't understand
the hard work we did in our time. They hardly have the

strength and fitness we had when we were young,' I smirked as I finished my reps.

* * *

'When do you think the meeting will take place?' asked Ravi Bhushan, my dear friend and a batchmate from the IPS.

'Yaar, it all depends on the approval of the chief minister. But I think a few months from now,' I replied.

'Then congratulations in advance. Becoming the commissioner of police of such a big city is fantastic. You've had the best postings in the state and worked in the paramilitary too. This will be another feather in your cap,' said Ravi.

'Come on, we've both been in service long enough to know that transfers and postings are not in our hands. They depend on a lot of factors. In fact, at times the appointments and postings are quite arbitrary,' I replied.

'But you're the most deserving of the lot. You've had years of experience in the field. And of course, your reputation is impeccable,' said Ravi.

'Then you stand an equal chance of becoming the commissioner of police,' I said.

'I would, if not for you. You're number one in inter-se seniority and you're the government's favourite. Whereas I'm always sidelined.' Ravi smiled but couldn't hide his disappointment.

I looked the other way, feeling a little guilty but thinking about the possibility of becoming the CP. It was a dream for almost all IPS officers and would certainly be the crowning glory of my career. I was almost sure that the committee headed by the CM would choose me for the coveted post. But I had to stop myself from thinking too much about it. As I had just reminded Ravi, postings depended on several factors.

'Enough now, both of you. Stop talking about policing all the time. Dinner is ready,' said Charu, gesturing for us to move to the dining table.

'Cheers to both of us!' I said, raising my glass of nimbu paani.

'I'll be the happiest person if you become the CP, my friend. Cheers to you,' said Ravi, raising his glass.

Once again, my mind turned to the possibility of being given the post. I had had a stellar career so far. God had really been kind. Of course, I worked very hard, but luck had also played an important part in my career, I thought. There are so many touch-and-go situations in a policeman's life. I had been the SP of many challenging districts and even held the post of IG of the BSF. I had successfully faced many crises ranging from terrorist attacks to communal tension. I had always made decisions that were ethical and professional but also suited to the needs of the establishment. In fact, I had been fortunate so far that I had never antagonized the powers that be.

Ravi's career had been the exact opposite of mine. Even the best of his decisions had often not gone well with the ruling authority. Soon, he had been permanently relegated to the sidelines, almost becoming a persona non grata.

I looked around me. I was living in a majestic bungalow, surrounded by staff and guards. I had certainly come a long way from my humble background. But I did not waste much time thinking about these external embellishments of my life. Instead, I focused on tasks that required my immediate attention. A recent kidnapping and murder of a businessman had caused much unrest locally. And the PM could visit at any time. After all, it was the election year, and the stakes were high.

2

Desi Miss Marple

'Charu, did you read the newspaper today?' I asked, poring over the headlines.

'What is it? Tell me. You know I can't read the paper,' replied Charu, putting a paratha on my plate.

'I've told you so many times to have your eyes tested and get reading glasses. One's eyes become weak with age. And why have you put such little ghee on the paratha?' I complained, looking at my absolutely dry meal.

'IG Saheb, don't bother about my eyesight. I can still read between the lines. And you're also getting old along with me. You have flab on your stomach. You see, it happens as a man becomes middle-aged.'

'It's impossible to argue with you! Anyway, help me solve this murder mystery. I'll read you the details,' I said, surreptitiously reaching for the butter. I couldn't eat such a dry paratha.

'A labourer found a shapeless bundle in a plastic cover, burnt in some places, lying on open ground. He alerted the police who arrived within minutes.

'Here's what the police found: an inflatable air mattress that contained a naked human torso and a bed sheet containing arms and legs. Both were partly burnt. The head was missing.'

'Go on, the case sounds interesting,' said Charu, snatching the butter from my grasp.

'Our forefathers ate everything—ghee, oil, rice. God knows who comes up with all these low-fat, gluten-free, zero-sugar, no-carbs, fad diets—keto diet, General Motors diet! I'd rather die than have such tasteless food,' I said, annoyed.

'*Mote ho rahe ho*, you are getting fat,' she replied.

'Arre yaar. Then you should have married Hrithik Roshan. He has those washboard abs.'

'*Ab meri kismet me aap hi the*, you were the one in my fate,' she smiled sarcastically.

'I am sure you'd have found some flaws in Hrithik too. Wives can never be satisfied.'

It was futile to protest since I knew she was genuinely concerned about my health, but I tried anyway.

'One has to adapt to the times. Our elders did not while away all their time on mobile phones; they were active throughout the day. Now don't digress, tell me more about the case. It reminds me so much of the murder of that TV producer, Neeraj Grover, whose burnt body parts were found dumped in a forest. The police later arrested Emile Jerome, a naval officer, for allegedly murdering Grover after the producer had spent a night with his fiancée, the actor Maria Susairaj,' said Charu.

'How do you know so much about every murder in the world?'

'Continue. I need clues,' said Charu with a deadpan expression.

'The torso was wrapped in a black "Relax King" single bed mattress. And interestingly, one ankle had a medical grade metal implant.'

'Hmm. First of all, the police need to check the footage of all the CCTV cameras located in the vicinity to see how the mattress was dumped in that area. I am sure there were at least two people who carried such a big mattress. And of course, they must have used a vehicle. Also, that medical implant must have a unique serial number. I'm sure you can find the manufacturer from that. You can then check the hospitals that use those implants on their patients. And naturally you'll find the names of the patients, particularly those living in our city,' said Charu, giving me another dry paratha.

'Very correct line of investigation, Charu. What else do you suggest?'

'Once you find the names of the patients, check their whereabouts. The one who is missing is probably the person who has been murdered. Then, you can find out if he had had a property dispute or an affair. Next, corroborate the facts with the deceased person's call records. My intuition says that this is a case of an illicit affair gone wrong,' said Charu matter of factly.

'Excellent surmise! I will tell the SSP to investigate along these lines,' I thought how of I missed being at the helm of affairs like the SSP but as an IG, I was more of a supervisory officer. Moreover, we will also find out the list of possible buyers of the 'Relaxking' mattress from the local retailers. We will certainly find some clues there. I smiled, marvelling at my wife's intelligence.

'Hopefully, the killer will be arrested. I assume that the wife and her paramour killed the husband and then tried to hide the identity of the body.'

'Wah, Charu, you're my desi Sherlock Holmes. I think you've been reading too many detective novels and watching programmes like *CID* and *Crime Patrol*,' I said condescendingly.

'There you go again. Why Sherlock Holmes? Why not Miss Marple? You will always be a chauvinist,' replied Charu. 'And yes, I love reading Agatha Christie and the like. I am fascinated by the world of crime. Do you have a problem with that?' She glared at me.

'Okay, *baba*, just see that you don't inflict your wrath on me,' I said, raising my hands in surrender.

'Don't give me a chance to,' she said coldly.

3

Mills and Boon Hero

'Have you done your packing yet?' asked Charu.

'I thought you'd do it for me like always,' I said as I shaved.

'*Ha*, I have to take care of you always. You act like a baby,' she said.

I stepped out of the bathroom and hugged her tightly, rubbing my cheek against hers.

'What are you doing? Someone will see us,' she said, wiping the shaving cream off her face.

'Can't a senior IPS officer be romantic with his wife? Have I committed an offence under the IPC?'

'Keep your romantic instincts under control, IG Saheb,' said Charu as she folded my clothes.

'Don't forget to pack some protection,' I said, going back to the bathroom.

'Yes, of course. Your Glock. Arjun, I think you're worrying too much. You don't need to constantly carry a gun everywhere. After all, you're just going to Delhi for a meeting and then we'll catch up with your friends,' said Charu.

I came out of the bathroom.

'I'm not worried, I'm just being careful. And by protection I meant contraceptives, not a gun! Unless you want another kid,' I said with a twinkle in my eye.

'You scoundrel! That's why you're taking me on this trip!' said Charu, throwing my clothes at me and walking

10

out of the room. I ran after her, chuckling, loving the sound of her laughter as she skipped away.

As we drove to Delhi, listening to old Kishore Kumar ditties and gossiping along the way, I looked at Charu and shook my head.

'How lucky am I!' I thought. 'How much I love this woman!'

My life was perfect. A wonderful career, a beautiful wife, two adorable children and plenty of friends. But it hadn't always been like that.

I grew up in an average household in Bihar, my father was a teacher in the government school. He didn't have much money but managed to ensure that my sister and I received the best possible education. I worked hard and managed to clear the JEE. But just as I got admission to IIT Delhi, my father died, and our world collapsed. My mother had to sell the only piece of land we owned to make ends meet, and we survived on a day-to-day basis, hoping desperately for a better tomorrow.

'Beta, you should become an IAS or IPS officer,' my father had always told me. Getting a government job was the ultimate dream of millions of Indians and the IAS and IPS were the pinnacle of all government jobs. To fulfil his dream, I started preparing for the civil services exams while in college. After I graduated and could no longer live in the IIT hostel, I found a one-room accommodation in the squalid lanes of Jia Sarai. This urban village near the IIT campus became the fertile ground for quite a few future civil servants. But it also became the graveyard of many, many more aspirants, who spent years of their youth preparing for the UPSC exams only to fail them time after time.

To pay my rent and at least have a plate of the cheapest idlis for breakfast, I joined an NGO called Sambhav, which was run by the wife of one of the IIT professors. The stipend was meagre, and I was not interested in my job, which consisted of tedious filing work. In any case, I was a misfit among the elite Delhi crowd that staffed the NGO. Most of them were the bored housewives of wealthy businessmen who had joined the NGO to while away their time and add some substance to their inane conversations at the soirees of the rich and famous. They looked down on me. You can well imagine how a dark brown, scrawny boy with a funny accent must have been ridiculed behind his back. Sometimes that ridicule hit me straight in the face, like when an auntie tried to explain the difference between latte and mocha to me.

Practically unemployed, living in a toxic environment, with no money to join coaching classes or even buy pirated textbooks from Pandit Book Depot, I knew my civil services exam preparations were going nowhere. And with my family facing a very difficult financial situation, I stared at a dark future.

But then one morning, like a ray of light, Charu entered Sambhav's office, her radiant face reflecting her inner beauty. People rushed to greet her, and she chatted with them cheerfully, while I, too shy to even look her in the eye, settled in a corner to continue my mundane work.

'Hi! I'm Charu. I'm a final year student at LSR college. I thought I would make use of my summer holidays to do some good. So here I am, a part of Sambhav,' she said, extending her hand to me to my surprise. I hadn't expected her to come and speak to me.

I was totally dazed. Having come from a simple background, who attended IIT at a time when the college only had a few female students, I had rarely spoken to girls in my life. Now here was this lovely girl straight out of the movies, trying to start a conversation with me. I really thought I was dreaming.

'Hello! I am Arjun,' I replied, feeling awkward about my looks and accent. 'I do the filing work here.'

'Why are you dusting the files in the office? Let's go out and do some real work,' she said.

And off we went to the *bastis* (settlements) around IIT. I could not believe that there could be so many slums right in the middle of Delhi.

'We'll come here and teach these kids every day,' Charu said, distributing sweets to the children jumping around her.

I followed her every day, almost in a trance. But then I realized that I was just wasting my time. There was no doubt that my heart always skipped a beat when I saw Charu, but my dream had been to become an IPS officer, and I needed to focus on academics. So, I started borrowing books from my friends and studying in a corner while Charu taught the children.

'Oh, civil services,' Charu said with her million-dollar smile as she peered into my book over my shoulder.

'How do you know?' I asked, feeling a little embarrassed at being caught doing my personal work during the NGO's working hours.

'Arre, a lot of my friends are preparing for the civil services, so I know all about these books. And besides, my father, who is an ADG-rank IPS officer, is also after my life to appear for the exams.'

'Really? Your father is an IPS officer?' I exclaimed.

'What's the big deal? He's a normal person who qualified after an exam and is doing a government job,' replied Charu nonchalantly.

'For me, an IAS or IPS officer is a big thing. Whenever the SP came to our locality, we felt as if a movie star had come. We crowded the streets for a glimpse of him. He looked so dashing in his uniform, surrounded by his guards, moving around in his beacon fitted Gypsy!' I blurted out, unable to control my excitement.

'If this glamour and power is your inspiration for the civil services, then I am very disappointed in you. There is much more to an IPS officer than all these embellishments,' Charu said seriously. 'I hope you become a responsible officer, one who is passionate about his work. Remember, it is a service to the nation.'

'You're right, Charu. I'm sorry. But why don't you take the exam too?' I said, feeling guilty about wanting to join the IPS for the sake of power.

'*Nahin*, baba, first of all, I am not very hardworking. I cannot study so much for an exam whose results are totally unpredictable. And more importantly, I am an old-world romantic. I can't see myself working in an office surrounded by stacks of files and an endless stream of visitors. I'd rather be the wife of a Prince Charming and a loving mother to cute kids. And being a homemaker is not a small deal. It needs effort and sacrifices. I want a life straight out of a Mills and Boon novel,' Charu said.

'Yes, I've seen how hard mothers work,' I agreed. 'What is your definition of a Mills & Boon hero?'

She looked at me for a second too long, mischief in her eyes.

'Someone like you,' she said finally, with her dazzling smile.

I was stunned.

Charu leaned in and gave me a peck on my cheek. I just sat there, frozen in shock.

'Arjun, I really love you. You have all the qualities of my ideal life partner. You know what attracted me to you?'

I remained quiet. I was totally clueless about any quality I might have that would attract any girl, let alone someone like Charu.

'You will be a very loyal husband, unlike my father,' continued Charu, her voice breaking. 'My father is not a faithful husband. It's because of him that my mother is not normal anymore. Though he loves me a lot and I also love him, I can't ignore his affair. Maybe my father and mother were not meant for each other.'

She was crying now.

'My mother loses control of herself and sinks into depression. She has a hereditary mental condition and it's triggered by my father's adultery. She turns violent at times too. You can't imagine the pain and humiliation I feel every day because of my mother's abnormal behaviour. And my father is squarely responsible for it,' Charu continued, weeping profusely.

I gathered up my courage and hugged her tightly.

'Don't worry. I'll always be loyal to you,' I said, wiping the tears from Charu's beautiful eyes.

* * *

I had never imagined that anyone could fall in love with me, much less someone like Charu. But then it is impossible to understand girls! Initially our love was a typical young romance: we dressed up for each other, watched movies and talked for long hours about all kinds of things. But soon, Charu changed gear.

'Okay, Arjun, now listen to me. We have to stop all these activities and get serious about your exams. You have to clear the UPSC exams on your first attempt. Just work hard, put all your energy into the preparation. I'm with you on the journey, whether we reach the destination or not. I will always stand by you,' she said.

True to her commitment, Charu brought me notes and books from her friends and got food for me and my roommate, Ravi Bhushan. Ravi was also from Bihar and had already appeared for the exams twice but failed both times. Charu encouraged him to study as well. She massaged my head lovingly when I rested and carefully removed my glasses when I fell asleep while studying. Within days, Ravi, Charu and I had become inseparable, enjoying every moment of our friendship.

* * *

'*Suno*, Arjun, it seems Papa has learnt that I am seeing you. He wants to meet you and is coming in his car to pick you up,' said Charu.

I put the phone down and walked out of the PCO. So, this was my D-day. I was about to meet my future father-in-law, a man who was a senior ranking officer of the police. I had butterflies in my stomach. A lot of them.

After about an hour, a smart constable called me down from my room and ushered me to an Ambassador fitted with a beacon. The entire student community of Jia Sarai flocked around the car, deriving vicarious pleasure from my 'success'.

With great trepidation, I sat down. It was a surreal feeling to be seated in the ultimate symbol of power of those days. I wished Charu's father who just nodded in acknowledgement. He had a strapping personality, the same hazel eyes as Charu, the same fair complexion. He did not say anything and just stared at me, probably thinking how unfit I was for his lovely daughter.

It was only after we reached the main road that Charu's father spoke.

'So you want to marry my daughter. Pardon me, but like every other father, I want my daughter to be happy. I don't think you're capable of taking care of my daughter's basic needs. And there is no compatibility between the two of you. You both come from opposite backgrounds,' said Charu's father, not mincing his words.

He was not rude at all, but his words hit me hard.

'Yes, sir, you're right,' I said, clenching my fists. That was the end of our conversation.

I asked the driver to stop the car and let me off. On a DTC bus back to my accommodation, I ruminated over the things Charu's father had said. He had been absolutely correct. Who was I? Just a nobody with no past and no present.

But I did have a future. Things could change if I became an IPS officer. My resolve to succeed in the UPSC exams became even stronger.

I climbed the stairs of the dingy Jia Sarai apartment building, only to see an annoyed Charu outside my door.

'I told you I will always be with you. *Ab jiyenge bhi saath aur marenge bhi saath.* Now we will live and die together,' she said. 'Why did you not come back in the car? *Itna* ego?' She reached for my hands.

'It's not ego. It's self-respect,' I said, unlocking the door to my room.

My recollection stopped as the car came to a halt. I smiled. I had certainly come a long way.

4

Friendly Affairs

We checked into the lavish St. Tropez Hotel located in Chanakyapuri in Delhi.

'Good evening, Mr Kumar. Ashutosh Sir has asked us to provide you with the presidential suite. Let me escort you there,' said the lady at the reception.

The elevator took us to the twelfth floor.

'Wow. This is amazing,' I said, looking at the Delhi skyline from the large glass windows of our suite.

'I still don't understand why you had to accept such a huge favour from an unknown person. We could have stayed at the BSF mess,' Charu said, clearly not happy with me.

'It's not a favour, Charu. Somveer arranged this for us. He was adamant that we either stay at his farmhouse or at a hotel rather than a government guest house,' I said. 'Moreover, you know that Somveer is wealthy enough to easily organize anything for his close friends like me.'

'Remember, there are no free lunches,' Charu replied. 'And you know I don't get carried away by material things.'

'Okay, *meri maa*. Enough of the lecture for the day. It is very rare that we stay somewhere other than the government guest houses so let us enjoy a hotel this time,' I said, exasperated.

'Yes, yes,' said Charu, unpacking her mystery novels, absolutely unfazed by the magnificent room.

'Please Charu, not your novels now. Get dressed, we have to meet Somveer and Ashutosh for dinner. Abhishek and Verun will be there too.'

* * *

'Arjun, good to see you so happy in your *sarkari naukri*. It's difficult to believe a government officer can be happy with his meagre salary,' said Somveer, sipping his favourite Japanese whisky.

Somveer, Abhishek and Verun were my best friends from IIT. All three had become successful businessmen after graduation and were quite wealthy. I was the only one from my friends' group to have taken a government job.

'Let's not start this discussion again, Somveer. I'm happy with my life and my salary is comfortable,' I retorted.

'Remember, this is a choice Arjun made. Some of you went abroad and some of you continued with your family business. To each his own,' said Charu in my defence.

'By the way, meet Ashutosh, my friend and the owner of this hotel,' said Somveer introducing me to the suave man who had just joined us.

'How do you find your room, sir?' asked Ashutosh.

'Ashutosh ji, please don't call it a room. The suite is bigger than my house! Of course we love it,' I replied.

'I know you'd never have stayed in this hotel if I had not insisted, Arjun,' Somveer said as he looked at Ashutosh. 'Ashutosh is like a brother to me, so this hotel is as good as home for me too. And mind you, he is not looking for any favours in return. He's a clean guy and sufficiently well-connected on his own.'

'Okay, okay. What did I say to bring this on? *Aur main koi galat cheez ke liye* favour *karta bhi nahin hoon*. I never exchange favours for something personal anyway. And

I'd still prefer to stay in the government guest house,'
I protested, looking at Charu.

'You and your stupid ethics. Anyway, if you have any
problems, stay at my farmhouse in Westend next time. The
only issue is that it is not very well maintained. There's only
one caretaker-cum-cook as I'm in London most of the
time,' said Somveer.

'Why should I stay in your farmhouse?' I asked, irritated.

'Arre, it's my farmhouse and better than your government
messes and guest houses. Whenever you come to Delhi you can
stay at my farmhouse! What are friends for?' retorted Somveer.

'Somveer and Arjun, let's not fight. I know you
genuinely care for each other. It's just that you have different
principles,' said Abhishek.

'Sir, I have to leave. Please feel free to come here any
time. Treat it as your home in Delhi,' said Ashutosh, clearly
embarrassed by our friendly fight.

'That's very gracious of you. Thank you,' I said.

After Ashutosh left, we talked for a while and then
Somveer veered to his favourite topic—women.

'Tell me, guys, which of you has had an extramarital
affair?' asked Somveer, pouring himself another drink.

'*Kya kar raha hai, yaar*, what are you doing? Bhabhi is
sitting with us,' said Verun, looking apologetically at Charu.

'It's all right, Verun. I've known Somveer for ages now.
I know he has a great heart but loves his philandering ways.
I'm an adult. Let him speak. I want to hear his point of
view,' interjected Charu.

That was typical of Charu. She was fiercely independent
and also non-judgemental.

'Okay, then listen. My argument is that all married men
have an affair at least once in their lifetime,' said Somveer.

'Why do you say so?' asked the normally reticent Abhishek.

'The first reason is that we are genetically engineered
to produce more and more offspring, so we look for

multiple partners. And, of course, we enjoy the process. Our grandfathers, ancestors, everyone has done it,' said Somveer, clearly inebriated.

'Secondly, we tend to get bored in our marriages. Imagine spending time in the bedroom with the same person for fifteen, twenty years. How monotonous!'

I thought Charu would slap Somveer for his stupid and disgusting arguments, but it seemed she was in a different mood today.

'What do you think, guys? Do you agree with Somveer?' asked Charu, looking at Abhishek and Verun. They stared at each other, nonplussed.

'Of course not, Charu Bhabhi,' they said in unison.

'Please don't give me this shit. I could very well reveal your secrets,' said Somveer, banging his fist on the table.

'Yeah, okay. I've had one or two flings. Everyone makes mistakes,' said Abhishek sheepishly.

'Me too. But that was in the past. Now I am loyal to Suchita,' said Verun.

'But Arjun can never be like us. He's the epitome of a faithful, dedicated husband. Gosh, you're too perfect, Arjun. That's why I hate you sometimes. You don't make money, nor do you enjoy the company of women. And you don't drink. I don't even know how we're still friends,' said Somveer, almost delirious now.

'What do you think, Charu? Could Arjun fall for someone outside your marriage?' asked Verun curiously.

'Of course not! I'm proud of my hubby. He will never betray me. I trust him absolutely,' said Charu, smiling at me.

I smiled back at her.

'What if he has an affair someday?' asked Abhishek mischievously.

'Oh, Charu will kill Arjun,' laughed Verun.

'Better still, I'll kill the woman and send him to jail for her murder,' said Charu without batting an eyelid. My smile vanished.

5

'You Have a Wonderful Wife'

'Charu, I'll have lunch with Ravi, so don't wait for me,' I said as I got in the car.

'Looking smart in your uniform,' said Charu, giving my water bottle to Bhajan Singh, my loyal bodyguard. She always saw me off whenever I went out.

'As if you're seeing me in uniform for the first time,' I said, smiling at her.

The guards at the gate saluted as the car drove out of my bungalow. It was good to be back home. I always felt much happier in a small city than in the chaos of a metropolis. But this idyllic life would only last a few more months. After all, the post of a big city commissioner of police beckoned.

* * *

'Wow,' I exclaimed as my car approached the swanky, new, ultra-modern building where my batchmate, Ravi's office was located.

As I was escorted down the corridors by the guard, I could see Ravi surfing TV channels through the glass walls of his chamber. I knocked on the door and entered.

'What a nice workplace, Ravi Bhai! Very corporate and quite unlike our *sarkari* (government) building,' I said.

'Yeah, I know. Unfortunately, only the building has changed, not the work culture,' said Ravi. 'And to make things worse, my posting is quite inconsequential. I have practically no work.'

'I know, Ravi. But you'll get what you deserve. You're very much in the race for the CP post.'

'*Ab kya*, what now? I'm almost at the end of my career. I've never had good assignments in spite of working so hard,' he rued.

'Sometimes, brilliant officers like you get their due a little later. You still have a few years of service left,' I said, trying to assuage his feelings. 'But what is this? Why do you have the picture of that fraud god-man Maharaj on your table?'

'Please, Arjun, I don't want to hear a word against Maharaj,' said Ravi, tapping his fingers on the table furiously. I looked at the colourful rings on his fingers.

'Ravi, yaar, you're an educated person, an IPS officer. And you're wearing all these rings just because Maharaj gave them to you. Do you really think they can change your fortunes?'

'Enough, Arjun. Please don't question my faith. Maharaj Saheb is the reason I'm still sane.'

There was no point arguing. If Maharaj provided Ravi with some solace, so be it.

'Apart from my professional woes, you know my personal life is screwed,' Ravi said, sounding dejected.

'Yes, I know your marriage is in shambles and you can't do much about it. But professionally, you're very much in the race to become the CP,' I said, trying to get him out of this mood.

'No, you'll be the next CP. You know very well that I'm on the list of candidates only for formalities,' said Ravi brusquely.

We finished our lunch quietly. Life had been quite unfair to Ravi, both professionally and personally. While one could somehow accept the vicissitudes of professional upheavals, there was little one could do about a tormented personal life.

Ravi and Shweta were both my batchmates. Theirs was a marriage of convenience—Ravi had wanted a change of cadre to a 'better' state and Shweta had wanted an 'equal' in social standing, meaning that she wanted to marry only an IAS or IPS officer. Their massive egos and incompatibility had soon led to bitter fights, and their marriage spiralled into disaster.

'Why don't you separate from Shweta and marry someone else?' I asked him. I was close enough to Ravi to discuss personal issues.

'She's not willing to give me a divorce. She's threatened to make my life hell because she thinks I'm responsible for her unhappiness. And she knows that if she divorces me, I will remarry. She doesn't want to let that happen. She simply cannot see me happy.'

'Then maybe look for someone outside your marriage. At least you'll get some emotional support, or even physical,' I said with some hesitation.

'You mean I should have an affair? *Itni aukaat nahin hain*, I don't have the guts! And how come you, of all people, are suggesting an extramarital affair?' scoffed Ravi.

'I'm sorry. I just said it because it is quite common nowadays. I mean, my friends keep nudging me to have one,' I said.

'Arjun, please don't forget that you are very lucky to have such a wonderful wife. Don't you even think of such a stupid thing,' said Ravi as he ushered me out of his office.

6

'Oont pe baithe ko kutta kaat jaata hai'

'Charu, please pack our stuff for two days. Somveer is launching a new company, and he wants us there for the celebrations at his farmhouse in Delhi,' I said.

Charu was curled up on the sofa, reading a murder mystery as usual.

'You go alone, Arjun. I met your friends just a few days ago and Tani has her exams next Monday,' said Charu, putting her book down reluctantly.

'Come on, Tani is a seventeen-year-old now. She can manage on her own. And we'll stay at the IPS mess this time, not that fancy five-star hotel,' I said persuasively.

'Tani will always be my baby. I'm concerned about our daughter's academic performance. Go by yourself and have some kind of a bachelor party with your friends, the boys who refuse to grow up.'

'That's unfair, Charu. They're my friends. They just talk shit sometimes. I'll go alone but it's not that I don't care about Tani's studies. Please don't say things like that.'

* * *

'You have a lovely farmhouse!' I exclaimed, surveying Somveer's huge property.

'Thanks, Arjun! Come guys, grab your drinks. I'll show you around,' said Somveer. 'Bhola! Get some snacks by the poolside,' he called to his cook as we picked up our glasses.

'Arre, Arjun, I forgot to tell you. Bhola is also from Bihar and a big fan of yours. He must have heard about your achievements against criminals and terrorists,' Somveer added.

'*Ji* sir, *pranam*! *Bahut naam sune hai*. I have heard your name a lot,' said Bhola, pleased to meet me.

I was amused. We Biharis may work in different parts of the country, but we still take great pride in the success of fellow Biharis, particularly those in the civil services.

'Bhola, if ever Arjun Saheb comes here, take care of him. Arjun, note down his number,' said Somveer.

'Thanks, Somveer. But why would I come to your farmhouse without you?' I said.

'Bhai, you can enjoy the solitude. There is just Bhola here to take care of the property and the gardener comes two or three times a week. That's all. Since you don't have girlfriends like me, you can come with your wife. You and Charu can have a romantic vacation,' Somveer winked.

I smiled and added Bhola's number to my phone. The caretaker was grinning from ear to ear. He now had the personal phone number of a senior police officer.

'So Somveer, how's your love life going?' asked Abhishek. Verun nudged Somveer to reply.

'Fantastic! New girlfriends every few days. God has given me one life. Why not enjoy it?' said Somveer victoriously.

'How do you manage to keep these secrets from your wife?' I asked. I was not jealous, but certainly intrigued by my friend's sexcapades.

'Ha ha, Arjun, don't be childish. I take quite a few precautions. And I also keep my phone password protected so there is no question of Deepali reading any of my chats,' replied Somveer.

'Why do you do it? Deepali is beautiful,' I asked curiously.

'Just for thrills. It's exciting to have new flavours in life, isn't it?' Verun said on behalf of Somveer.

'*Itne gire hue log ho tum. Dar nahin lagta*? You guys are disgusting. And aren't you scared of the consequences?

'First, we will never be caught. And also, we know our wives. They'll never leave us. For them, family comes first. They love their husbands and won't destroy their kids' lives.' Somveer's smile was like that of a shark—all teeth.

'What about you? Don't you love your wives?' I asked Verun and Abhishek.

'Don't be silly. *Biwi ko hi toh pyaar karte hain*. Of course, we love our wives. Who do you think we work so hard for? For our wives, our families. We give them expensive gifts, take them on exotic holidays. It's just that we need some excitement. And we have our needs too,' replied Verun.

'And, I'm telling you, *Jisko mauka mil jaye who nahi chhodta*, whoever gets an opportunity doesn't ignore it. We are all the same,' said Abhishek as we sat down by the pool.

We sipped our drinks and snacked silently for a while, gazing at the expansive garden, only to be interrupted by a reverberating sound. Somveer had dozed off and was snoring loudly.

'So, Arjun, you've achieved so much in life. You're probably going to become the commissioner. All possible medals, the best postings and a great family. What's on your bucket list now?' asked Verun.

'Me? There's nothing left to achieve except an affair!' I said, laughing at my own joke.

Somveer woke up, rubbing his eyes. 'What are you guys talking about?' he mumbled.

'Yaar, Arjun is talking about having an affair,' said Verun, laughing. He looked at me, then looked at Abhishek. Suddenly, they became serious.

'Look, pal, that's a path to self destruction. It sounds fun but there's a very heavy price to pay for those few moments of hedonism. We seem to be having fun but deep in our hearts, we know that we are wrong. We can lose our families, our careers! It can simply end our lives,' Abhishek said.

'And be careful. You're at your peak right now and you could have a very nasty fall. "*Oont pe baithe hue ko kutta kaat jaata hai.*" A dog can even bite the one sitting on a camel,' added Verun.

'What was that proverb! *Jai baba* Verun *dev ki*. You sound like a guru now,' Abhishek said, laughing.

'*Abe, itna serious hone ki kya zarurat hai?* What is the need to be so serious? Enjoy life as it comes,' said Somveer before he started snoring again.

* * *

'Papa, come home quickly. Mom is behaving in a very erratic manner. She is acting violently all of a sudden,' said Tani. She sounded tense.

'Is this some kind of a prank, Tani? I have a lot of work at the office,' I said.

'No, Papa, I'm not joking,' said Tani, crying.

Within ten minutes, I was at home.

As I entered the bedroom, I saw a doctor checking Charu's BP. She was lying on the bed, the floor littered with the shattered pieces of a few of our trinkets. The glass of my favourite centre table was cracked.

I opened my mouth to speak, but Siddharth and Tani indicated that I should remain quiet.

'She's resting. The doctor has given her some pills to make her sleep. You should have seen her half an hour ago. She was really agitated,' Tani whispered.

The doctor got up and asked me to accompany him outside the room.

'Sir, does madam or her family members have a history of unnatural violent behaviour?' he asked.

I was quiet.

'Please don't be embarrassed. You can share the facts with me,' the doctor said.

'Yes, Doctor Saheb. Her family has had incidents of violent behaviour,' I replied.

'Don't worry, sir. I have given her some tablets to calm her down. Mental disorders are often genetic. Just ensure that madam is not emotionally disturbed in any way,' said the doctor.

I lay down next to Charu, caressing her hair. She opened her eyes after a while.

'It's okay, Charu. You're fine. There's nothing to worry about,' I said lovingly.

'I'm sorry, Arjun. I don't know what came over me. I can't believe I got so agitated,' she said, her voice trembling.

'What happened? What made you so angry?'

After a pause, Charu replied. 'Sandhya called me. My sister. She was crying and was in a murderous mood.'

'Why?' I asked.

'Because she caught her husband cheating on her,' replied Charu. Her expression twisted in rage and her eyes grew bloodshot.

7

The Ghost

He awoke at 4 a.m., fully aware of his surroundings in an instant. He could see in the dark and hear a pin drop. The months he had spent in isolation in gruelling jungles had heightened all his senses.

He sat in the lotus position and closed his eyes to meditate. After nourishing his soul, he began working on his body temple with an hour of various exercises and the practice of *Kalaripayattu*. The ancient Indian martial art had made his already rock-solid body even harder.

He looked at himself in the mirror. His 6'2" frame, gleaming with sweat, looked formidable. He was pleased by how well he had maintained himself, even under great duress.

The Ghost, as he was known to the few people he chose to be known to, moved to his terrace. Ahh, he loved fresh air. This was absolutely pure, quite the opposite of the polluted atmosphere of Delhi. He valued his freedom for he knew how it had felt to be confined in a rotten, dark cell for years. He had lost everything. His friends, his family, his reputation. His life. He was desperate to get everything back. He deserved a second chance.

The Ghost checked his cell phone. His number was known only to a very few chosen ones, but he waited for that one call. The call would come from a person of immense power, not a king but a kingmaker. He was the one person who could help the Ghost get what he desired. His family, redemption and retribution.

He closed his eyes. His little son wrapped his hand around his finger and walked his baby steps. His wife ran behind them, playing a game of *chor*-police. He was the happiest man in the world. And then everything blurred. As he opened his eyes, tears trickled down and merged with his sweat.

Suddenly, he was a man possessed, exercising with every fibre of his being. He must be fighting fit, fit enough to kill a person with his bare hands. Killing was the only thing he knew. And he was good at it. He had already done 200 push-ups, 100 sit-ups and fifty pull-ups. Now was the time to practise Krav Maga, the self-defence and fighting system of the Israeli security forces.

Though he had been an expert marksman, the Ghost hated guns and had vowed that he would never use them again. After all, guns were the reason for all his grief.

8

'You Are Married!'

14 March 2021

'The IG CRPF has invited us for dinner tonight. I'll see you there at around 8.30 p.m.,' said Ravi.

'Ravi Bhai, I don't think I'll come. I'll get bored. You know I don't drink, and how long can I eat peanuts and snacks till dinner is served?' I replied.

'Please come for my sake. And bring Charu. The card clearly says Mrs and Mr Ravi Bhushan. I'm sure you must have got a similar one for both of you,' said Ravi.

'Yes, the invitation is for both of us. Are you also coming with Shweta?'

'*Kahe zakhm kured rahe ho*, why are you rubbing salt in my wounds? Don't you remember the scene Shweta created at Niranjan's party? No bhai, I don't want to be humiliated at a public function again. But I'll certainly enjoy your company and Charu's,' said Ravi.

'Chalo, let me ask Charu,' I said, smiling faintly for I knew that Ravi really liked Charu, sometimes bordering on infatuation.

Always a sociable person, Charu immediately agreed, though I was still not in the mood for a party.

'Don't sulk. You'll meet officers there from the CBI, R&AW and so on. At least you'll have something important to talk about. Think about us ladies. We mainly discuss our family lives and all these wives' associations,' said Charu.

'Yeah, I'll meet the same set of people I've met at so many meetings where the agenda is when to hold another meeting to discuss the agenda of the previous meeting,' I said sarcastically.

'You're impossible! Why are you so cynical? Those meetings are certainly not useless. Please give credit to the good work done by the police and other security organizations,' said Charu.

'I'm sorry. I think I'm having a mid-life crisis. I've never felt so bored and grumpy before,' I said.

On the way to the party, I thought about my life. It was perfect. So, what was I missing? Why was I so bored? What would bring some thrill into my life?

Maybe the talks with Somveer and my friends had ignited some hidden desires all of a sudden.

After being received by the IG CRPF and his wife as the CRPF band played lovely music to welcome us, I greeted the usual set of people, picked up my nimbu paani, found a corner for myself and immediately took out my phone. Like everyone else, I was addicted to the internet.

'And now, ladies and gentlemen, please welcome the Shubham Orchestra. They'll play some old numbers from the 1970s for your entertainment,' said the compère. I noted idly that his suit was ill-fitting; he had probably had it made for his wedding many years ago.

'Not more torture,' I muttered. I hated it when people murdered old songs, particularly those by Kishore Kumar and Lata Mangeshkar, my all-time favourites.

I looked at my phone again, trying to avoid the cacophony that was about to start.

'*Aapki aankhon mein kuch mehke hue se khwab*,' started the male singer.

'Not bad,' I thought, my head still bent over my screen.

And then the female part started. The voice was mellifluous. It was almost as if Lata Mangeshkar was singing live. I looked up at the stage and was struck by the singer. Gosh, she was quite good looking! A young woman in her early thirties.

I put my phone in my pocket and concentrated on the singer rather than the song.

When the performance finished, everyone applauded the orchestra. But the star was definitely the female singer. A number of people stepped forward to chat with her. Some of them even took selfies with her. I was amused. Senior officers, people of whom the public is scared even today, were posing like school kids with somebody who was not even a local star!

'Heck, men will be men. A beautiful woman will have any man swooning over her,' I thought.

The woman was enjoying the attention, even making videos with her admirers on her cell phone.

'Sir, can you please present a small token to the orchestra on behalf of the CRPF? You're the senior-most officer here,' said the IG CRPF.

'Sure,' I said, buttoning up my jacket. 'Why don't you ask Mr Ravi Bhushan to join me? He's my batchmate and equally senior.' I pointed to Ravi who was chatting with Charu. As always, he had come to the party alone and was enjoying the company of my gorgeous wife.

Onstage, Ravi chatted with the members of the orchestra as he presented the mementos, but I was looking for someone else.

'You sang quite well. I'm a diehard fan of Kishore Kumar and you made me really happy,' said Ravi to the lead singer.

'Sir, can we have a group photo with the orchestra?' requested the singer.

I ignored him, looking around for the female singer.

'Ah, there she is, talking to Charu of all people,' I mused, turning to stride towards the table where the two ladies were chatting animatedly.

'Hey, Arjun! Come, meet Madhushree. I told her she sings fantastically well. I'm sure you agree,' Charu said cheerfully.

I smiled at Madhushree.

'Sir, it is such an honour. I have heard so much about you,' said Madhushree.

'I hope you have heard only good things about me,' I replied.

'Of course, sir. You are the Singham of our police,' said Madhushree.

'Oh Arjun, please stop talking about yourself. You're so vain,' interjected Charu.

'Nahin madam, sir is quite a popular officer. And what a great personality he has,' Madhushree replied with a dazzling smile. Her face was lovely. Her features were those of a typical Indian beauty.

Gosh, she's even more attractive up close, I thought. And then I saw the vermillion on her head, in the parting of her hair.

'Oh, you are married! You have *sindoor* on your head,' I said stupidly.

'Yes, sir, I'm married,' she nodded. But there was sadness in her eyes.

'Arjun, please stop asking her personal questions. Just compliment her for her amazing singing,' Charu said gruffly.

'Arjun Saheb is a fairly good singer too. He loves singing Kishore Kumar songs,' said Ravi, patting my shoulder as he joined the conversation.

'Uff, you guys just can't get over Kishore Kumar! Madhushree, let's exchange numbers. I'd like to invite you for a programme for the IPS Wives' Association,' said Charu, nudging me out of the way.

* * *

'Mr Arjun, I hope you were not too flattered by Madhushree's compliments,' Charu said on our way back.

'Na, na. Not at all,' I replied nonchalantly. I was always full of myself and needed someone like Charu to keep me grounded.

'You could not resist asking her about yourself. You're always looking for compliments. And you were concerned about her marital status. Seriously!' said Charu angrily.

'It was just an observation,' I said casually.

'Did you observe Madhav's haircut? His suit?'

'Who's Madhav?'

'The guy who sang the Kishore Kumar songs!' said Charu, glaring at me.

'Why would I bother about him? I am only interested in beautiful women,' I laughed and kissed Charu on the cheek.

'Not in the car, you fool. Bhajan Singh, *aage dekho*,' she commanded my bodyguard who dared not look back. But we could see a faint smile on his face in the rear-view mirror and Charu couldn't hold back a smile herself.

9

Madhushree

'I'm organizing a cultural programme for the IPS Wives' Association. So I won't be having dinner at home,' said Charu, putting on some lipstick.

'Okay, sweetheart,' I said absently as I watched the IPL game.

'We've invited Shubham Orchestra to perform. I think the ladies will enjoy the old songs and become fans of Madhushree. Even that male singer, Madhav is quite good.'

'Wait, wait. This is not fair. That orchestra is great! Why do you want the men to miss it?' I protested, muting the TV.

'Are you telling me you want to come? Really? I thought you hated those official parties and meeting the same people over and over again,' Charu asked, surprised.

'Yeah. But that orchestra is too good. Invite the husbands for dinner too. We'll all enjoy the music,' I said, switching off the TV.

* * *

Bathed in the multi-coloured fluorescent lights, the IPS mess looked beautiful. And Madhushree seemed even more attractive than the last time I saw her. She picked up the mic and started crooning '*Rajnigandha phool*', mesmerizing everyone with her dulcet voice. As the applause continued, Ravi Bhushan leapt on the stage.

'I invite my dear friend Arjun to sing a duet with Madhushree. Please put your hands together for our own Kishore,' he announced, pointing at me.

I was taken aback. I had a good voice but my singing was average at best. Though I wanted to refuse, my feet began moving of their own accord and I didn't even realize I had reached the stage until I got to the steps.

My throat dry and my pulse racing, I stepped up and watched Madhushree as she started singing '*Kya ye hi pyar hai*'.

'Sir, now you have to sing. This is your cue,' she smiled, turning to me.

My heart skipped a beat as I began to sing, and I skipped a few beats of the song too. My singing was bad, I knew, but I could not bring myself to leave the stage, not with such a striking young woman beside me.

We sang a few duets together, even though I went totally off beat time and again.

'Sorry for spoiling the songs. You sing very well though,' I said as I finally left the stage.

'And you look very handsome,' replied Madhushree. I stopped in my tracks. We looked at each other for a moment and she smiled, watching as I walked away.

'Hello, sir, I am Bhanwar Bagaria,' said a portly, balding man, his bloodshot eyes clearly displaying his intoxication. I was taken aback by the sudden appearance of this disgusting man in my path.

'Excuse me,' I said ignoring him. How could they let a drunk civilian enter the IPS mess, I wondered.

'Arre sir, you just sang with my wife but you are not willing to talk to me. I know. This always happens to me. People ignore me but flock to my wife,' Bhanwar slurred.

'What? You mean you're Madhushree's husband?' I asked incredulously.

'Yes, I know what you're thinking. How did an ugly man like me manage to marry a woman of her beauty,' he said thickly.

I didn't answer but he was right. I looked at him again. His shabby, unkempt clothes spoke of his modest means, he probably just lived day-to-day. And he was the antithesis of beauty.

'Here, take my card,' he said as he stumbled away.

'Bhanwar Bagaria, Insurance Agent,' the card said. I threw it in a wastepaper basket immediately, bumping into Ravi as I turned.

'Are you enjoying the singing or the beauty of the singer?' he asked in a teasing manner.

'Come on. You, of all people, should not say such things,' I replied.

'It's natural to be attracted to beauty, whether in a painting or a woman,' he said mischievously.

'Ravi, cut out this nonsense. Let's get our wives,' I said, annoyed.

'Yours. Not mine. I always come alone,' he said in a dejected tone.

I moved towards the crowd, looking for Charu, but my eyes stopped on Madhushree. She was posing with the ladies for a video that was being shot by Madhav. Everybody seemed to be in a boisterous mood, except Madhav. He returned the phone to Madhushree with a sullen expression, cursing as he headed to the bar.

* * *

'This Madhushree is really talented. But poor girl, she hardly gets her due. She just performs at weddings for a very modest fee or at official events like ours where we don't even think of paying her,' said Charu, taking off her bangles.

'Hmm, that's true. Her husband can't even support her. It seems she has a difficult financial situation,' I replied.

'Yes, she told me that Bhanwar Bagaria is a parasite. He treats her like a slave and takes all the money she earns from these shows. It's unfortunate that she's married to that rascal. The marriage was much against her wishes, but she had to do it because of some promise her father had made to Bhanwar's family. Imagine, such things happen even in today's world,' said Charu.

'How do you know all this?'

'Arre, girl talk. We've hit it off quite well. We seem to like each other,' smiled Charu.

'Really? So quickly? I mean you've just met her a couple of times and you already know about her personal life. I hope you haven't revealed any of our secrets,' I said.

'Women bond fast. I actually do like her. She's a very simple person. The purity of her soul is reflected in her singing,' Charu mused. 'And why would I talk about you? But yes, the lady seems to have a crush on you. Sir *toh ekdum hero lagte hai*, she told me today!'

'That's nice of her. At least she understood my worth,' I grinned.

'Don't get any ideas, old man. It's just a young woman's minor infatuation with a man who is successful and in a position of power,' said Charu as she switched off the lamp.

I tossed around in bed, unable to sleep. I did not understand why I was attracted to Madhushree. I had a stunning wife and generally remained unaffected by any other woman's beauty. But Madhushree kept creeping into my mind. As my restlessness continued, I quietly picked up my cell phone and tiptoed to the drawing room, opening Instagram to find her account.

There were six or seven Madhushrees on the app, but my eyes found the one I was looking for. Her account was public, though she did not have many followers. It was obvious that she wanted to be popular; she was quite active on Instagram.

'She posts a video of her songs or a philosophical message practically every day,' I mused as I scrolled through her posts. 'Ahh ... this is so banal. Or is it that she's unhappy with her life? Obviously, her husband is a jerk, how could she be happy?'

She looked very attractive in the pictures and videos. Madhushree was not a stunner like Charu, but there was something strangely alluring about her. She was smiling in all the pictures, yet I could see that she wasn't happy.

* * *

I was changing into my sports attire after a busy day at the office when I heard my mobile buzz. It was Charu.

'Listen, Madhushree is here at our house. She's desperate to get out of India and start a new life. She has a few offers to perform for the Indian diaspora in Canada. Can you help her get a visa? She has to leave in around a month,' said Charu.

'What can I do about it?' I said, a bit irritated. Perhaps, I didn't want Madhushree to leave. I would be very disappointed to not see her any more.

'Talk to your batchmate in the IFS. Come on, this is a small thing. I don't always ask you for favours,' said Charu.

'But—,' I tried to protest, only to be cut off.

'No ifs and buts. I'm giving your number to Madhushree. She will send you her details,' Charu said and disconnected the call.

* * *

The next morning, as I went through some routine files, my phone started buzzing. It was an unknown number. I answered the call reluctantly.

'Hello, sir, this is Madhushree. Sorry to bother you. Madam must have told you about my request,' said Madhushree in her saccharine voice.

'Yes, yes, madam told me. Why do you want to go abroad?' I asked, deliberately sounding indifferent to hide my excitement on hearing her voice. I was the IG, after all, I had to sound officious.

'Sir, I earn hardly any money here. And nobody bothers about my talent. Most people just want to dance to the latest pop songs after a few drinks. There are very few people like you who are connoisseurs of old music,' she said. 'At least I'll make good money in Canada. I have an offer from a Punjabi businessman living there. If I enjoy the experience, I will try to settle there.'

I paused, disappointed by her plans.

'Okay, let me speak to my batchmate in the Indian Foreign Service. Getting a visa should not be a problem,' I finally said. 'In the meantime, I will try to get a few events for you where you can sing and make some money.'

'Thank you so much, sir!' Madhushree sounded elated.

10

The Nightmare

'You are responsible for the death of our baby. It's because of you that our family has been ostracized. Children refuse to play with your son because they don't want to be friends with a murderer's child. Please leave us alone. Don't show us your face ever again,' said his wife.

'But I did it for our family. For us! Please let me speak to my son. Don't turn me away,' pleaded the Ghost.

'You'll have the right to your wife and son the day you're absolved of all your sins. Redeem your honour, get your job back and then come to us. That's the only way,' said his wife.

The Ghost woke up with a shudder. He had been having the same nightmare for the last eight years.

He had tried his best to convince his wife to let him return, but to no avail. The last time he had seen her was when he had been out on parole for his father's cremation.

After that, she had never come to see him. Nor would she allow him to meet his son. She and his son had even changed their surname. They were the only people he had ever loved, but they had disowned him.

He wanted to cry in frustration, but he had to have patience. His fortunes would change. He knew they would.

'I'll ask you for some work at an opportune time. I'll call you,' the kingpin had told him.

The Ghost waited for the call.

11

A Song a Day

'Sir, thank you so, so much. I've got my visa for Canada and it's all because of you,' said Madhushree. She sounded extremely happy.

'You're welcome,' I said, hiding my disappointment.

'What can I do for you in return, sir?' asked Madhushree.

'Nothing, just send me a song every day,' I replied, disconnecting the call. I felt quite bad that Madhushree would be leaving soon.

'Your order has been complied with, ma'am. Madhushree has got her work visa,' I said to Charu, who smiled. Charu always liked helping people, even if it meant going out of her way.

As I got into bed, I received a WhatsApp alert.

'Madhushree has already sent a song. That's fast,' I told Charu as I opened the audio file.

'*Aap ki nazron ne samjha pyar ke kabil . . .*'

'She has sung it very well. I think she has dedicated it to me,' said Charu.

'Hey, I'm the one who got her the visa. And she sent the song on my cell phone,' I said, cuddling Charu.

'Enough of your cell phone. Let's sleep,' she said, snatching away my phone.

For the first time, I sensed a little jealousy in Charu's voice.

* * *

44

Over the next few days, we organized some programmes for Madhushree and her orchestra to regale the audience with their splendid songs. I had started enjoying parties now, for the songs. And the singer. I met Madhushree at every party and was growing fond of her.

Lost in thought one afternoon, hoping I would be appointed the CP after the meeting chaired by the CM, which was to be held soon, I was disturbed by a WhatsApp notification. The message was from Madhushree.

'Sir, thanks once again. I hope you liked the song,' the message read.

'Yes, it was beautiful,' I texted back.

'And me?' said the next message.

I was taken aback. My heart started beating faster. How should I react? I had always been shy with ladies. And I was a very senior police officer. I was not supposed to flirt with anyone apart from my wife.

Still, I could not resist sending a smiley to Madhushree.

* * *

'Where are you off to, Ravi?' I asked as I dropped in at his office to meet him.

'I'm going to Maharaj Saheb's ashram for the weekend,' said Ravi, packing up his stuff.

'God, I can't believe how an educated person like you can follow such a fraud. His ashrams are dens of prostitution and drug peddling. There are allegations of rape and murder against this Maharaj of yours. There's even a rumour that he's involved in money laundering for terrorists,' I said with contempt.

'Arjun, when somebody like me loses hope from all sides, only spiritual gurus can lift us from the abyss of dejection and misery. It's become fashionable in our country to make allegations against God-men. Nothing has ever been proved against Maharaj Saheb,' said Ravi.

'But Maharaj? Of all people?' I asked.

'You don't understand the pain and suffering I go through every day. I have no family life and a lousy career. But at Maharaj's ashram, I feel alive again. And not just me. Millions of his devotees feel the same,' Ravi said as he literally slammed the door in my face.

I was a little worried for him as his devotion for an unscrupulous person like Maharaj was increasing with every passing day.

12

'Saath Jiyenge, Saath Marenge'

'I'm getting late, Arjun. Please take your injection right now, in front of me,' said Charu, caressing my head lovingly.

'Just go, please, Charu. I've had this hip and back pain for twenty-five years. I'll ask the nursing assistant to give me the injection later on,' I said wincing.

My ankylosing spondylitis was acting up again, it was an autoimmune disease I had suffered from for a long time. The pain was sudden and intense, always coming without warning. There was no permanent treatment except for TNF blockers. My doctor had asked me to continue sports in a mild manner to avoid stiffness in my joints, but I always overdid them. Two hours of rigorous tennis at my age was lung blasting anyway. My vanity would not let me accept that I was getting old and I was only making matters worse for myself.

'The nursing assistant is already here. I took the injection out of the ice box ten minutes ago. Now lie down and let the guy inject you,' Charu said, a very concerned. 'It has to be injected subcutaneous,' she said to the nursing assistant, giving him the vial.

I yelped as the needle pierced my skin.

'Does it hurt?' asked Charu, tears forming in her eyes.

'Come on now, sweetheart. It's just a prick,' I said and I have been taking these injections for so long now.

'It has side effects. Every injection reduces your immunity,' said Charu, sniffling.

'Nothing will happen to me,' I said.

'Promise me, *hum saath saath jiyenge, saath marenge*. We'll live together and die together,' Charu said, mopping her tears with a hanky.

'Nothing will happen to sir. Madam, *aap itna pyaar karte ho unko*, you love him so much,' said the nursing assistant.

I smiled at him. I was really fortunate to have such a loving wife.

'Okay, enough now, Charu. Go. Anu must be waiting for you. What's your plan today?' I asked.

'Anu and her NGO are doing a wonderful job. Every step they take is meaningful. That's why the NGO is called Sarthak. Today, I'm taking some boxes of my favourite peanut chikkis to distribute to the poor and homeless. We'll give them to jail inmates as well,' said Charu.

'Oh? Who got them for you? These chikkis are not available in Jalandhar,' I said, examining one of the boxes.

'I asked Papa to send me a few boxes from Jaipur,' said Charu, waving at me as she left.

Even as I wondered what I had done to deserve such a dedicated wife, Madhushree crept into my thoughts again.

13

Flirting with Danger

'Why don't you people do your work properly?' I said as I stared at my PA. 'I asked you to type a letter to the home secretary and instead you have addressed it to the home minister. And look at the spelling mistakes!'

The last few days had been stressful. There had been a spate of crime, and the opposition had come down heavily on the police. After all, it was an election year.

I was about to close my eyes to relax a bit when I saw a WhatsApp message on my phone. It was Madhushree.

'You didn't answer my question last time. But let me tell you what I think about you. You are very good looking. *Ekdam* hero!' read the message.

I smiled and waved off the PA. Surprised by my sudden change of mood, he scampered out.

'Thank you,' I replied to Madhushree.

'So you're happy to receive a compliment, but not willing to return it,' she said in another message.

'You are quite nice looking too,' I texted without thinking. Before I could delete my message, I saw the blue tick that confirmed that Madhushree had read it.

'I know,' came the reply. 'Rate me on a scale of one to ten.'

I took my time before answering.

'Should I lie or tell the truth?' I typed.

'The truth.'

'I'd say, 7, 7.5,' I replied, feeling bold enough to exchange messages. I was rather excited by this game and wanted it to continue.

'Okay, 8,' I texted.

There was quite a long delay from the other side. Had I offended her? Well, I had typed what I had thought. I would rate Charu 8.5 at the most.

'Shit! What the hell am I doing? Comparing my wife with an almost unknown entity. I'm really losing it,' I muttered aloud.

My cell phone buzzed again with a notification.

'Thank you for rating me so high. In fact, thanks for even thinking about me. I won't rate you. You are beyond ratings. You are priceless,' came the reply.

My PA entered the chamber again.

'What is it?' I frowned.

'Sir, the draft for the letter to be sent to the home secretary,' the PA replied, scared by my mood swings.

'Okay, now leave,' I said, taking the file from him.

I quickly deleted all the messages from my cell phone. What the hell was I doing? A happily married man flirting with a woman almost fifteen years younger than himself. A senior police officer supposed to be solving serious crimes was sending seductive messages to an attractive woman.

I left the office to go home for lunch. But I wasn't hungry. I just wanted to hear from Madhushree again.

***

That evening, I sat in front of the TV, waiting for a notification on my phone. Finally, the phone buzzed.

'Hi, thinking about you,' read the message from Madhushree.

I immediately got up to leave the room.

'Where are you going? The tiebreaker is about to start,' said Charu.

'Just going to the loo,' I said.

Ordinarily, I wouldn't have missed a moment of a match between Nadal and Djokovic. But the thought of Madhushree was more overpowering than the sight of two men grunting on a tennis court.

I locked the bathroom door and sat on the commode.

'What exactly are you thinking?' I texted.

'That I am in your arms and . . .'

My heart thumped. I had last felt like this when I'd met Charu all those years ago. Was it love? Of course not. I wasn't a teenager with raging hormones. I was the middle-aged father of two grown-up children. Was it lust? No. I had never been one of those sleazy men who thought of women as objects for their pleasure. This feeling was indescribable, somewhere between love and passion. I had started liking Madhushree, and I was physically attracted to her.

I exchanged a few messages with Madhushree and deleted them from my phone before flushing and stepping out of the bathroom.

'Oh, you just missed a wonderful rally. What took you so long?' asked Charu.

'Stomach upset,' I said sheepishly. 'But it's all good now.'

'I told you not to eat all that fried stuff, but you don't listen. *Aur khao pakode aur samose!* Anyway, the last set is on. Let's enjoy the game. Who do you think will win?'

'I really don't know,' I said, my mind not exactly on tennis.

The weather, which had been threatening rain the whole day, finally gave in to a torrential downpour. The storm interrupted the Tata Sky set top box's signal. 'Oh my God, we'll miss the end! Give me your phone. We'll watch it online,' said Charu, snatching my phone from my hands—she had left hers on charge—and searching for the live match.

Her excited face turned pale.

'Arjun, what is this?' said Charu slowly, showing me the phone. 'Have you been exchanging messages with Madhushree?'

'Sweet dreams,' read a message from Madhushree.

'Oh shit! How foolish of Madhushree,' I cursed silently to myself. Aloud, I said, 'I don't know. She must have typed this by mistake. You know she sends me a song every day.'

I clenched my fists, hoping Madhushree wouldn't send another message now. Fortunately, she didn't.

'Ohh, Djokovic lost,' said Charu, watching the match on the phone.

'Yeah, Rafa is the king of clay. Nobody can beat him at on this surface,' I answered, gulping in as much air as possible.

'Why is she texting you?' Charu asked again. 'And where is her good for nothing husband?'

'How do I know? You ask her husband,' I replied coolly, realizing the danger was not over yet. I began caressing Charu's hair lovingly.

'I think Madhushree has the hots for you,' said Charu, mollified.

'And I have the hots for *you*,' I said, snuggling into the quilt.

I found it very difficult to sleep though.

14

The Consignment

'The consignment will come tomorrow. Sukha's man in the village will show you the exact location,' said the voice on the phone.

The Ghost listened intently. His benefactor had finally called him.

'I'm forwarding the address to you,' said the authoritative voice on the other side.

The Ghost stared hard at the map. Thank God, he had been to the area earlier. There was no room for mistakes. The stakes were simply too high, for him and for his benefactor.

* * *

The Ghost looked around. The night was silent except for the sound of crickets. A few young men lay unconscious outside the temple.

'Bloody drug addicts,' he scoffed.

He walked down the village lanes and stopped at the gates of a large house. The owner is certainly prosperous, he thought.

He took out his cell phone and switched on its torch, checking once more to see if anyone was around. It was 1.30 a.m., an unearthly hour for villagers, unlike city folk. Still, he couldn't take a chance.

Finally, certain that nobody was watching, the Ghost pointed the mobile's torch towards a window on the first floor of the house. He switched off the torch and switched it on again a few times, flashing a message in Morse code.

After a few seconds, a silhouette appeared in the window and replied in a similar fashion with his own torch. The message was clear. It was safe for the meeting. The Ghost was inside the house in a few minutes.

'Good evening, janab. My name is Sartaj. I look after the operations of Sukha Saheb. It is a real privilege to meet you in person. I have heard so much about you,' said the man, extending his hand to the Ghost.

The Ghost ignored the drug dealer's invitation to a handshake. Even criminals call their shady business 'operations', he thought, amused.

But the term actually did fit. The narcotics trade was worth thousands of crores, and it had to be operated professionally. The Ghost had grown up reading stories about the notorious drug lord Pablo Escobar, the richest criminal in the history of the world, with a personal fortune of a few billion dollars. Though dealers like Sukha were not in the same league as the Escobars and El Chapos of the world, they certainly had the same ambitions. For people like Sukha to make it big, a lot of help was required. And Maharaj Saheb's sect was certainly big.

Cult organizations like those of Maharaj had a following that could be counted in the millions. These followers formed a ready market of consumers for the drugs supplied by Sukha. The cult organization also had a well-oiled distribution network, taking drugs across the state and into other parts of the country.

The ISI was game for expanding Sukha's operations in India. Not only did the ISI help Sukha smuggle drugs across the border, it also used the services of Sukha and other syndicates to smuggle arms and explosives to terrorists based in India. And, of course, terror groups such as the Germany-based Martyrs for Freedom backed this dangerous game of narcoterrorism. It was a win-win situation for all the parties concerned.

'Where is the delivery point? Is everything in order?' asked the Ghost.

'Absolutely, janab. We'll leave at 3 a.m. That's when the BSF jawans hand over their patrolling duty to the next guard. I'm keeping a watch on the BSF party from the terrace,' replied Sartaj.

'I'll join you,' said the Ghost.

They leaned against the terrace wall, watching for movement near the floodlit fence that had been erected by the BSF along the India–Pakistan border.

'The villages in Sri Ganganagar are quite close to the border. In fact, some of us even have farms across the fence. The BSF jawans open the gates for us and let us go through for our work, after checking us rigorously, of course. Over time, we have become well-versed with the BSF operations and protocols,' said Sartaj.

Of course, thought the Ghost.

'We'll wait a little longer to make our move. I've already confirmed that there is no special checking drive by the BSF tonight,' said Sartaj.

'What about the electric current in the fence? And the alarms and trip flares?' asked the Ghost.

'No need to bother about anything, janab,' smiled Sartaj confidently. 'We've taken care of everything.'

An hour or so later, Sartaj put his hand on the Ghost's arm. 'Now is the time, janab. Let's move quickly,' he said.

The Ghost followed Sartaj as quietly as possible. Once they were in the fields, hidden among the paddy crops, Sartaj took out his night vision device.

'The constables are moving towards their outpost now. And the next party is yet to come,' said Sartaj.

The Ghost took the device from Sartaj and looked towards the fence. He saw two jawans talking on a wireless set.

The BSF jawans must be dead tired, he thought. It's difficult to remain alert at such an unearthly hour and with little rest. Yet they were so sincere.

'See? I've been observing the BSF jawans from my house for months. While patrolling the area, some of them start moving towards their outpost about ten minutes before 3 a.m.,' said Sartaj with a wicked smile.

The Ghost checked his watch. It was 2.52 a.m. Sartaj was right. The BSF jawans had started moving.

There was a thud as a stone hit the ground close to them. The Ghost startled.

'Don't worry, it's a signal from our Pakistani handlers on the other side of the fence,' said Sartaj.

'Shouldn't we move to get the consignment then?' asked the Ghost a little impatiently.

'*Nahin*, janab, the consignment is coming to us,' said Sartaj, pointing at the sky.

The Ghost could see a faint UFO-like light in the sky. It was a drone.

15

'Why Do Happily Married Men
Have Affairs?'

'I'm going to call you on WhatsApp. Please see that no one is around,' I texted.

'Sure, sir,' came the reply. A heart emoji popped up on my phone screen.

I smiled and deleted the message.

After the last time, when my PA had popped into my chamber, I was being careful. I switched on the red light outside my office and instructed my orderly not to let anyone inside.

A red light outside a senior officer's chamber meant that she or he was busy with some serious official work or in a meeting and entering the chamber was strictly forbidden. When I switched on the red light now, however, my business was romance.

I called Madhushree.

'How foolish were you last night? Why did you send that "sweet dreams" message after our conversation had ended? Madam almost caught me. I'm very angry with you,' I fumed, though I was happy chatting with her.

'But, tell me, did you not dream about me?' asked Madhushree in a very naughty manner.

'Madhushree, I like you very much. But this flirting can't go on. I hope you understand,' I said, half unsure if I wanted these innuendos to stop.

'Sir, it might seem frivolous to you, but I'm actually falling in love with you. You're the first man in my life to treat me with respect and actually care for me,' Madhushree said emotionally.

I was taken aback.

'Okay, okay,' I said, flustered. 'But please delete all the conversations we have had. And call me on WhatsApp only and only during office hours.'

'Okay. I look forward to seeing you at tomorrow's party at Justice Madan's place,' she said.

'Great,' I replied, excited that I would see her soon. In fact, I waited for these parties now. And I recommended Shubham Orchestra to everyone who wanted live performances at their events. It was only a matter of time before Madhushree left for Canada. I wanted to see her as much as possible till then. 'And who knows she might cancel her plans for Canada?' I thought.

After I disconnected the call, I realized I didn't really want her to stop the chats. I was thoroughly enjoying our flirtatious messages. The romance of it was exciting. I knew that I was entering dangerous territory but the thrill of having the attention of a good looking woman was too overpowering for me. Anyway, I was just chatting with Madhushree, I had not had any physical relation with her. It's all harmless, I thought.

I looked at Charu's picture on my desk and felt a little guilty. 'Why can't I control myself?' I thought. So I picked up my cell phone and googled: 'Why do happily married men flirt?'

Looking at the results, I had a rush of dopamine and I changed my search to 'Why do happily married men have extramarital affairs?'

There were a number of reasons, I read. One of them was that men are basically jerks and do not understand the sanctity of a committed relationship. Another reason was that though their wives lose interest in the physical relationship with time, men still have raging hormones. Some married men may be promiscuous because they are unsatisfied or they do not have a happy marriage.

There were quite a few more stupid reasons but one in particular caught my attention. Middle-aged men know they are ageing, so they grab any opportunity that comes their way. 'Flames of desire flicker the brightest before they are extinguished', said the article.

I wasted the next hour scrolling various research articles and theories on infidelity but still couldn't find anything that truly justified my shenanigans.

* * *

'Doesn't she sing fabulously?' asked Justice Madan to the guests around him.

'Yes, sir, absolutely. She's quite pretty too!' said a brigadier who seemed to be enjoying the party thoroughly.

'I think we should pay more attention to her singing than her looks,' I said, overhearing the conversation. I was jealous. No man but me should be interested in how Madhushree looked.

'Ah, here you are, Arjun. Care for a drink?' said the judge.

'No, sir, I'm a teetotaller. But I'll get myself some juice,' I said.

Heading to the bar, I thought I heard the legendary singer Kishore Kumar's voice. It was not a song; it seemed like an interview. He appeared to be discussing classic songs with his son Amit. When that stopped, a few scratch recordings of Kishore da's songs played. I turned to look at the large screen placed on the lawn so guests outside could watch the band. The view of the stage just showed the band members milling about, though the music continued to play.

'This is amazing! Ravi, let's find the person playing this,' I said, pulling Ravi towards the stage where the music system had been arranged.

Ravi didn't protest. We were both crazy about Kishore Kumar. And I considered him the God of singing.

Just as I got to the stage, the sound stopped abruptly, and I saw Madhav pulling a pen drive out of the music system.

'Hey, Madhav, that was amazing. Where did you get it?' I asked excitedly.

'*Yeh toh maine galti se bajaa diya tha*, I played that by mistake,' said Madhav. 'Arre, sir, this is an original conversation between Kishore and his son Amit. I had gone to perform in Mumbai, and I sang so well that the chief guest of the event, Amit Kumar sir, became emotional and gave me this rare collection.'

'Can I buy it online? Where is it available?' I asked.

'This is not available in the market, not even on the internet,' said Madhav. 'This is a collector's item, a priceless treasure for fans like me, given to me by the legend's son Amit Kumar from his personal collection.'

Madhav sounded intoxicated. He examined the pen drive carefully and wiped it slowly with his handkerchief.

'Can you lend it to me? I'll make a copy and return it,' I requested.

'No, sir, no question of lending it to anyone. Sorry,' said Madhav.

'Come on, please, Madhav,' I pleaded.

'No, sir. I hope you understand because you are a true fan of Kishore da,' he said as he put the pen drive into a cover with an image of a bearded Kishore Kumar wearing a turban. It was a still from his movie *Badhti Ka Naam Dadhi*.

'Madhav, if Arjun Saheb is asking for it, why don't you give it? Or should we send a policeman to your house to take it?' said Ravi jokingly.

'Are you threatening me, sir? This is how you big officers behave with ordinary people like us,' said Madhav, not seeing the joke.

'Leave it, Ravi. He's drunk now,' I said.

'Yes, I'm drunk because nobody appreciates my singing. People are more bothered about Madhushree even though I sing better than her, just because she is an attractive woman. Now, she is going abroad. And I will remain here, singing in these goddamned parties where no one appreciates my talent,' said Madhav, on the verge of tears.

'*Kya hua*? What happened?' asked Charu as she joined us.

'Nothing, Charu. Madhav is getting unnecessarily emotional,' I said.

'Come, come. Cool down. Have another drink,' said Ravi gesturing to a waiter carrying a tray.

'And have some peanuts,' he added, giving Madhav a glass of whisky.

'*Marwaoge*, sir. You'll get me killed. Even a single peanut will kill me. I am allergic to them,' said Madhav.

'Really? Can a person really die just from eating peanuts? The good old *moongfali*?' asked Charu.

I shrugged. I had no idea.

'*Jhooth thodi bolunga* sir. I will die if I have peanuts,' Madhav repeated.

'Strange, isn't it? Charu, since you're so interested in crime thrillers, think up a murder mystery based on a peanut allergy,' said Ravi with a wink.

'Come, let's dance. I'm not interested in this inane conversation about death,' said Charu, holding my arm.

We danced to a beautiful number sung by Madhushree. Though Charu looked into my eyes, I turned every now and then to watch Madhushree on the stage.

'Why are you looking at the stage? Obviously, you're not interested in dancing with me,' snapped Charu, walking off the dance floor. I did not apologise to her and nor did I try to stop her.

'*Kya* sir? Can I not have a chance to dance with you?'

I turned around to see Madhushree walking towards me holding the cordless mic. She was smiling seductively at me and swaying slowly as she did so. I was tempted to hold her and dance all night to romantic songs, but I knew I could not do it publicly.

'Someday,' I said, smiling back at her.

* * *

From then on, Madhushree and I started talking more often, mostly on WhatsApp video calls. And though I worried about Charu catching me, I couldn't stop messaging her even when I was at home. The thrill of doing something taboo can be quite exciting.

I also started taking better care of myself than before. I was always well dressed and in a generally cheerful mood.

'*Kya baat hai*, what is the matter? You seem to be quite happy nowadays. And looking good too!' said Charu.

'Really? It's good to get a rare compliment from my wife,' I smiled.

'Na, na. I think Madhushree is flattering you. *Kuch zyada* interest *le rahe ho*. You're also showing quite a lot of interest in her. Stop watching her Instagram videos, please. You've been watching them every day,' said Charu, snatching my cell phone from me.

'Arre, it was you who said you loved her songs,' I complained.

'There are other things available for entertainment. Let's watch a movie,' said Charu, always game for a film.

'Okay. Let's watch *Pati, Patni Aur Woh*. It's an all-time classic about Sanjeev Kumar having an extramarital affair,' I said with an impish smile.

Charu was not amused.

* * *

'You did not come for the Rotary Club event. I had gone there just for you. And of all the places, you had to go and perform at that evil Maharaj's *satsang*!' I said, my tone a little gruff. Though I was upset with her, I kept adjusting my hair. Gosh, I was trying to impress Madhushree even during a video chat!

'Ravi Sir had asked me and Madhav to sing some bhajans at Maharaj Saheb's satsang. We couldn't say no to him. And Maharaj Saheb's satsang is a big platform for an artist like me,' said Madhushree.

'You should have told me at least,' I said, not bothering to hide my disappointment. I was upset with Ravi too. He should have consulted me before sending Madhushree there. But then again, why should he have asked? I didn't own Madhushree.

I had started becoming jealous, like a possessive boyfriend who thinks his girlfriend shouldn't talk to anyone else or go anywhere without him.

'I have some news,' said Madhushree.

'Good or bad?'

'Depends,' she said.

'Go on,' I said, irritated.

'I'm going to Canada in two days. I don't know when I'll come back,' maybe I'll try to settle there she said softly.

The news hit me hard. I felt a vacuum in my chest. There was silence from both sides.

Finally, Madhushree said, 'Sir, *meri ek ichcha puri kar dijiye*, please fulfil one wish for me.'

'What do you want?'

'I want to hug you. I want to feel your touch before I leave,' she said.

'All right. As you wish,' I replied with no hesitation. I was clearly more desperate than her. And I understood what a 'hug' could lead to. My faint smile soon turned into a wide grin.

'Where will we meet?' asked Madhushree.

'When is your flight and where are you leaving from?'

'Delhi on 5th May. At 4 a.m.'

'Then we will meet in Delhi.'

'How?'

My mind was working fast. My heart was racing.

'Come to the Hotel St. Tropez at Chanakyapuri. I will arrange for a room. Get there by 6 p.m. We'll spend the night together and you can go to the airport from there, early in the morning,' I said.

'Wonderful. Love you!' said Madhushree, sounding thrilled.

'Yeah. See you day after tomorrow,' I replied excitedly.

I was behaving like a teenager unable to control his raging hormones. I disconnected the call and deleted the WhatsApp call log and thought for a while. I picked up the phone again and called Ravi Bhushan.

'Hi Ravi, aren't you supposed to attend a meeting in Delhi sometime soon?' I asked.

'Yes, the IB has organized a meeting on 5 May to discuss the security arrangements for the PM's impending travels. Why are you asking?' said Ravi.

'Yaar, can I go instead of you? I have some important personal work in Delhi,' I said.

'Sure. I can attend Maharaj's satsang that day then. Good, you go instead of me.'

'Great. I will request the DGP to nominate me in your place,' I said happily as I hung up.

I searched my contacts and dialled another number.

'Hello, Ashutosh ji, how are you? It was so nice meeting you with Somveer. I had a wonderful stay at the St. Tropez last time. Do you have a suite available at your hotel on 4 May? I need it just for one night.'

16

The Rendezvous

I admired my reflection in the mirror.

Not bad for my age, I thought. My face was far more attractive than it had been when I was a gawky teenager. My achievements and societal recognitions had greatly elevated my confidence in the last few years and that was reflected in my posture and mannerisms. I had transformed from my IIT days.

Of course, there were shades of grey, particularly on the sideburns. And even on the chest. But I still had broad shoulders and well-defined arms because of years of sports and athletics.

I examined my body from every angle in the mirror. As a narcissist, I was very happy with it. And then I saw the love handles.

'Shucks, I can't do anything about them now. To hell with it, everyone must be having some fat on their waists. Even Akshay Kumar,' I muttered, gingerly touching the fat on my sides.

* * *

4 May 2021

'Charu, what are you doing? I have already packed my stuff,' I said, rushing to her, pulling her away from my suitcase.

'I was just packing your Glock. I'm surprised you'd forgotten it. Why are you holding my wrists?' said Charu, freeing her hands from my grip.

'I was just about to pack the gun. Also, Bhajan Singh will be with me, but thank you for your concern,' I said, hoping she had not spotted the contraceptives I had packed.

'Bhajan can't be with you all twenty-four hours. You keep reminding me that we have been threatened. Now I have to remind you,' said Charu with concern.

I just nodded.

'And why did you pack? I always pack for you. Chalo, never mind. Enjoy your stay in Delhi. You can meet your friends after the meeting,' said Charu, zipping up my suitcase.

I kissed her on the cheek and went to the car.

'Bhajan Singh, take care of sir,' Charu said.

I looked at her and felt a little guilty. She loved me so much and I was about to cheat on her.

* * *

The Ghost was surprised to see the number on his phone screen. The call had come sooner than he had expected.

'Come over. Be careful. Nobody should know that you are meeting me,' a hoarse voice said.

'Yes, of course,' replied the Ghost, even more surprised by the fact that he would soon meet his extremely secretive benefactor.

It was not for nothing that he was called the Ghost. He could disappear whenever he needed to. He had been trained by the best and that was why he was exceptional. As he waited at the isolated farmhouse, a large expanse of land with a few cottages in one corner, he blended right in.

These rich and powerful people must have many colourful nights here, spending time with girls half their age. While people like me put our lives at stake, sleeping in jungles or some roadside *dhaba*, he thought.

He abhorred these people. But now was not the time for sentiments.

He watched as a car entered the gates, leaving a trail of dust behind it. A tall figure stepped out of it when it stopped.

'Jai Hind, sir,' said the Ghost instinctively. Old habits die hard.

'Jai Hind,' replied the man as he pulled out his cell phone from his pocket. The Ghost looked at the colourful rings on the man's fingers. How can such powerful and important people be so superstitious, he wondered.

The man opened a folder on his phone, stepped closer to the Ghost and pressed play on a video. The Ghost was taken aback. The footage was damning. If the video was ever leaked, it would have disasterous consequences for the people involved.

'Find this person and extract the video. And then finish the person. This is the target's mobile number. You have less than twenty-four hours to do the job,' said the man.

'Yes, sir. Please remember your promise,' said the Ghost.

'Of course. This job is your passport to a new life,' said the man as he returned to the car.

Powerful people like this man were known to keep their word, the Ghost knew. And he had been yearning for action for quite some time.

* * *

'Bhajan Singh, put on some music,' I said, enjoying the drive to Delhi. Charu and I liked living in smaller cities, but had the best of both worlds—living in a sprawling bungalow in Jalandhar and enjoying the bustle of Delhi every fortnight or so.

Just as I enjoyed a lovely family life and would soon enjoy a one-night fling. The best of both worlds.

I did feel a bit guilty. A bit. But then I was a successful, powerful man who needed excitement in his life. My friends had had affairs and flings years ago. Now, it was my time to join the club. I smiled knowing that I would make any flimsy excuse to justify my dalliance.

My reverie was broken by my phone ringing. It was Charu.

'Yeah, sweetheart? I have just left and you're already missing me?' I chuckled.

'Why are there contraceptives in your shaving kit?' Charu asked tersely.

I was speechless for a moment. My heart almost stopped. Had I been caught? I needed to say something fast.

'There are? Oh yes! I'd put them in my bag for our last trip to Delhi, remember? We didn't use them, and I guess I forgot to take them out. Don't worry, we'll use them on our next holiday,' said as calmly as possible adding a few fake laughs.

'It's not funny! Don't get naughty ideas,' Charu replied. She didn't sound convinced.

'How did she know about the contraceptives? If she had seen the packet then, why didn't she ask me at home?' I thought.

Before she called, I had planned to enjoy a power nap in the car. Now I couldn't sleep a wink.

I let out a deep breath. 'I need to be careful,' I muttered. 'If Charu finds out, she'll kill me.'

* * *

'Welcome again to the St. Tropez, Mr Arjun. Your suite is ready for you. Can I please have your ID?' said the receptionist. She seemed to remember me from my last visit.

'Is an ID necessary?' I asked.

'Yes, sir, these are police orders, and we have to comply with them,' replied the receptionist with a smile.

The police! I frowned, cursing my department and showed her my PAN card. I never revealed my identity as a senior police officer at any hotel on principle so I avoided using my police ID card.

Up in my suite, I stretched my back and looked at the bed.

'Just one night and it will be over,' I thought. Despite the long drive, I was fighting fit and well prepared for the rendezvous. Though I had never needed one, I had even bought a few pills to improve my performance. Just in case.

'So, Arjun, this is what an extramarital affair feels like! This is what your friends do. Happy now?' I asked my reflection in the mirror.

I had sent my driver Pratap and bodyguard Bhajan Singh to the BSF campus to rest and now it was my turn to relax. But first, a shower, I thought.

Lying in bed, I waited impatiently for the phone to ring. Finally, Madhushree called on WhatsApp.

'Hi, I'm in the lobby,' she said.

'Wait there. I'll come for you,' I said, my voice barely hiding my excitement.

Since hotels insisted on the ID proof of their guests, there had been no question of booking the room in Madhushree's name as well as mine, as her presence would be recorded. And visitors cannot enter the suites at the upper levels unless they have the room card or the reception confirms with the guest to let the visitor come up. Even then, one of the hotel staff escorts the visitor to the room. Naturally, I wanted to avoid all these scenarios, so I had decided earlier to meet Madhushree in the lobby and bring her to the room myself.

I looked around in the lobby and saw her sitting in a corner, looking prettier than ever. Nice make-up, I thought, gesturing to her to join me in the lift.

* * *

Sitting in another corner of the lobby, a shadowy figure in a green NSG cap watched the numbers on the panel as the lift rose, noting the floor at which it stopped. The twelfth floor.

The person in the NSG cap stood and walked to the reception.

17

'I'll Be Ready for You'

Madhushree and I stayed quiet in the elevator, barely even making eye contact. I was as tense as I had been just before the UPSC interview. Madhushree smiled slightly, trying to make me comfortable.

I ushered her into the room and locked the door immediately.

'What a fantastic room, sir! It's beautiful,' she said, putting her luggage down.

'Yeah, I'm lucky to know the owner,' I said, rummaging through my own luggage, trying to avoid her eyes.

'Why are you so nervous? Please relax, sir,' said Madhushree.

I nodded, as I unpacked my suitcase. That was the best I could do at that moment as my mind had become numb with tension.

'Is that your gun?' she asked.

'Oh, yeah. I carry it for my personal safety.'

'Why? Are you under some threat?'

'Yes, a terrorist called Timur Ali has vowed to come after me.'

'You are such a brave man,' she said.

I smiled, happy to have impressed her. My ego was being massaged well and good.

'Can I see it? I have never held a gun in my life,' she said, picking up the Glock.

'Wait, it's not a toy. Be careful,' I shouted and grabbed her wrist.

A current ran down my spine when I touched her skin.

She looked at me and stepped into my arms. Sensations flashed through my body, as if I had reached a different realm.

We remained in each other's embrace for what felt like eternity. And then I woke up from my trance.

'I'm sorry, Madhushree. I can't do this,' I said, very embarrassed with myself.

'Why, what happened?' she asked, puzzled.

'*Main kya kar raha hoon*? What the hell am I doing? I have such a loving wife who puts me before everything in the entire world. And I'm going to break her trust,' I said, distraught. I had had no idea I could become so emotional.

'I know you and Charu Madam love each other,' said Madhushree, backing away. 'But I love you too. I am not a woman of loose character, I have genuine feelings for you. I will cherish the few moments I spend with you today for the rest of my life. *Uske baad aap apne ghar*, *main* Canada *mein*. After that you'll be at home and I'll be in Canada.'

I looked into her eyes and saw sincerity. She was going through emotional turmoil just as I was.

My phone rang. It was Ravi.

'Arjun, the meeting you had to attend regarding the PM's trip has been rescheduled. You must get to the IB HQ in an hour,' he said.

'Is it necessary to go right now? I'm quite busy. And I have dismissed the driver for the night,' I protested. I know it was a stupid question, but my mind was not working.

'Come on, Arjun, it's about security arrangements for the PM. That's serious stuff. How could you ever think of not going for the meeting? And it'll be a short meeting anyway,' said Ravi.

'Okay, I'm going,' I said, and hung up.

I turned to Madhushree. 'Listen, I have an urgent meeting. I'll return as soon as I can,' I said.

She pulled out a negligee from her bag and looked at me teasingly. 'I'll be ready when you're back,' she said.

I shivered. Was I really going to do this? I needed some quiet time to think. I shook my head and left the room immediately.

* * *

The elevator doors opened, and I stepped out. The silhouette had been waiting patiently in the lobby, from where the elevators were clearly visible.

'This is the time. It's now or never,' thought the person in the NSG cap as Arjun went out of the lobby to hail a cab.

* * *

'I was so unfocused at the meeting that I might as well have not attended it,' I thought as I stepped out of the IB HQ. This was not the season but suddenly it started raining, water splashed hard at my face, as if Charu was slapping me.

I stood there, lost in memories.

'Don't worry, Arjun. You'll be fine before the exams. There's still time,' Charu said, trying to smile.

'It's jaundice, Charu,' I said miserably. 'It will take its own course. And I am so weak. I don't know whether I will survive to take the exams.'

'Don't talk nonsense. You have to be strong. You have to do it. For me. For both of us,' said Charu. 'And if anything happens to you, I will die too,' she continued.

For the next month, Charu was by my side at the nursing home almost twenty-four hours a day. She went home only to bathe and bring back some food for me. She slept on the floor beside my bed, massaged my head, helped me change my clothes and took me to the bathroom.

I was discharged from the nursing home just a few days before the UPSC exams.

As I started recovering, she read my books to me. She went to the examination centre with me every day, waiting outside for hours until I returned.

Then the exam results arrived. I had cleared them on my first attempt. Charu stood in a corner near the bulletin board outside the UPSC office. She saw me and burst into tears.

'Why are you crying?' I asked, rushing to pull her into my arms.

'These are tears of joy, you fool,' she said, weeping even harder.

A flash of lightning lit up the night and I shivered, returning to the present. What would my children think of me if they learnt that I had cheated on their mother? They would never forgive me.

As thunder rumbled overhead, my head cleared. There was no longer any doubt. I would have to go to Madhushree and ask her to leave honourably.

18

All Police Are the Same

I rang the bell. There was no answer.

I rang again. Again, no answer. I knocked lightly, not wanting to disturb the other guests on the floor. There was still no response.

'She must be in the bathroom. Or maybe she fell asleep,' I thought as I opened the door with my key card.

There wasn't a sound as I entered the suite's drawing room. No sound of running water from the bathroom either. The room was eerily quiet.

'Madhushree?' I said, entering the large bedroom.

Dressed in a negligee, she was lying on the bed, her arms by her side. A pillow was over her face.

'She sleeps in quite a strange way,' I mused.

I saw my Glock in the corner of the bed.

What is the gun doing here? I should have rather taken it with me. I thought, angry with myself for forgetting the gun in the hotel room.

Reaching over Madhushree to pick up the gun, I stopped, startled. 'Wait. wait. She isn't breathing. Her chest is not moving at all.'

I moved close to her and lifted the pillow. Madhushree's eyes were open and staring blankly at the ceiling. I touched her face, and her head slid grotesquely to one side. She was dead.

I reared back, falling on the floor.

'Oh my God, oh my God. What the hell happened?' My head was spinning.

'She's dead. Did someone kill her? Did she commit suicide?'

I scrambled up to take another look. Had she been smothered with the pillow? My mind was too jumbled to make sense of things. Over the course of my long career, I had seen countless dead bodies, many people killed in the most macabre manner. But this was different. This was the body of someone I knew. This was a body in my own room.

'Oh my God, Madhushree is dead, and her body is in my room.'

I stumbled out of the bedroom and fell into an armchair in the drawing room, my imagination going wild. 'My entire world will crash.' I clutched my head. 'My reputation will be shredded. My family . . . they will never forgive me. I will be on the front pages of all newspapers, all TV channels. I will be all over the internet.'

'Woman found murdered in IPS officer's hotel room!'

'Front runner for CP post in an extramarital affair!'

I could see the headlines now. What was I to do? What?

I wanted to cry but even my tears failed me.

'I should call the police and tell them the truth,' I thought. I had years of hard work and proven integrity. They would believe I hadn't killed her.

'But what about my family, my reputation? How will I explain the dead body of a woman wearing a negligee in my room?'

I got up and paced the room, trying to pull myself together.

'No, the police will arrest me. I'm the prime suspect. Even if we saw the CCTV footage and found the killer entering the room, the police could not say for sure who was the killer, me or the intruder.' And anyway, the police won't let me go free. The media will go berserk and accuse Delhi Police of protecting me. No government wants such a controversy.

I looked around me, hoping against hope that the hotel had placed CCTV cameras at least in the drawing room. But the hope had been a flimsy one. No reputable hotel recorded their guests in their rooms.

Okay, calm down, I thought. Calm down. Sit.

The best-case scenario was that I told the police the truth and the police would let me go while they investigated the case. The worst case was that I'd go to jail. In either case, my dreams of becoming CP were over. My career would be finished. And my family would be ashamed of me. My friends and relatives would disown me. My children won't be able to go to their respective colleges out of humiliation. My world would shatter.

No matter which way I looked at it, I was royally screwed.

I got up and walked to the window, looking down at the city from the twelfth floor. The car park below was empty. Should I jump?

'Nah,' I muttered. I loved my life. I was scared to die. And what difference would it make anyway? Except for the fact that I would be dead and presumed guilty, the result would be the same. My family would still have to live with ignominy. And my death would mean a lot of questions would remain unanswered.

I stared at the traffic. The cars are moving like ants, I thought absently.

'Should I run away? Heck, then the body will be found by the police and I'll be declared an absconder, a criminal on the run. And where will I go anyway?'

I had run out of options. This was the end game. I stared out of the window, my mind blank.

Suddenly, my phone rang.

'Hey, hope you're all right. Did your meeting go well? Did you enjoy dinner with your friends?' asked Charu. Her voice sounded cold, totally unlike her normal, chirpy tone.

I wanted to cry and tell her the truth. But I wasn't ready to lose her. She would never forgive me if she knew about Madhushree.

'No, no. There's a major situation! Somveer was holidaying abroad. You know Somveer and his adulterous lifestyle? Seems he was with some girl in Monte Carlo and she happened to die in his room. He's shit scared. He doesn't want his wife to know about it nor does he want to tell the police. Since I'm in the police, he asked for my advice but I freaked out. I'm his friend but I can't get involved in his stupid business. I'll tell him to call the police. That's the only option,' I said all in one breath, marvelling at my ability to create a fictitious story instantly. It seemed that my analytical IIT brain had worked subconsciously to tackle Charu and solve my problem simultaneously.

There was a studied silence at the other end.

'He deserves to be kicked on his ass. He's been cheating for so many years, I have no sympathy for him,' Charu said finally.

'Yeah, yeah. Absolutely,' I replied, wondering how Charu would react if she found out my secret.

'But the best option would be to dispose of the dead body. The problem would be solved,' Charu continued.

'Good God, where do you get such macabre ideas from?' I asked incredulously.

'Oh, just watch any episode of *Crime Patrol* or read any murder mystery. You get so many ideas. You begin to think like a criminal,' she replied casually.

'But the Monte Carlo police are smart. They'll catch him,' I said.

'All the police in the world are the same. You can fool them easily. If there's no dead body, there's no crime. Why are *you* sounding so tense anyway? It's as though there's a dead body in *your* room,' she said, hanging up.

19

The Suitcase

I stepped back from the window, cursing myself.

'I'm such a dumbass! How did it not occur to me? I need to hide the body. No body, no crime.'

I shook my head, contemplating the brilliant yet diabolical mind of my wife, and went into the bedroom.

Madhushree lay still on the bed. I gazed at the mole below Madhushree's lip, her long eyelashes brushing her cheeks—she looked beautiful, even in death. I felt deep remorse for what had happened to her. But now was not the time to get emotional.

My policeman's mind started racing again.

'I need to take the body away,' I muttered. I looked at my bag. It was too small. So was Madhushree's bag, I realized when I opened the cupboard.

Should I cut up her body and then put the limbs and torso in the bags? I wondered.

To cut up her body, I would need a sharp butcher's knife or an axe. And a plastic sheet to place her body on. Even then a lot of blood would spill on the carpet and the bed sheets. I could wipe it away with chemicals, but traces of blood could easily be discovered by the forensic team of the police.

Fuck! How depraved have you become, Arjun! You're worse than an animal, I mentally shouted at myself for the macabre thought of chopping up Madhushree's body.

I looked at Madhushree again, not her face this time, but her body. She was around 5'2" without heels. A large bag or suitcase should do.

I opened the door slowly and peered out of the room. There was nobody in the corridor. I took the elevator and went to the Century Mall situated next to the hotel. It was already 7.45 p.m. and the mall would close soon.

'Bhaiya, is there a luggage shop here? VIP or Samsonite or anything?' I asked the security guard at the mall.

'Yes, Saheb, there is one at the end of this row of shops,' he said, pointing to a corridor. I ran, trying to avoid colliding with the shoppers.

'Samsonite' read the board outside a large shop. The staff inside were packing up for the day, switching off the lights one by one.

'Hello, please can I get the largest suitcase you have? I have an early international flight to catch,' I said, panting.

'We are closing now,' a salesgirl replied.

'Please, please, I beg of you. My suitcase is damaged, and I have a flight in the next four hours,' I said desperately.

'Okay. How about this,' she said, pointing at a suitcase on display.

'No, no, I need a bigger one. Almost double this size,' I said, looking frantically around me.

My eyes fell on another suitcase stacked with others on the floor.

'This one?' asked the salesgirl.

'Yes, this one,' I said, pointing to it.

'This is huge. Do you need to put a body in it or something?' she joked as she went to the register to bill me.

* * *

I wheeled the suitcase to my room and locked the door immediately.

In the bedroom, I laid the suitcase on the floor and opened it, measuring it against Madhushree's body on the bed.

Hmm, she should fit. Luckily she's not very tall, I thought.

I lifted her body and carefully put it in the suitcase. She mostly fit, but her legs and arms dangled out. I tried folding her limbs in various positions, before finally arranging her body in the foetal position.

'Yesssss!' I said triumphantly before zipping up the suitcase.

'Oh shit. My fingerprints! They'll be on her body! Shall I buy surgical gloves from a medicine shop? No, it's too late. And there's no time to lose anyway.'

I went to the bathroom, dampened a towel, unzipped the suitcase and gently wiped Madhushree's body with the towel. When I was done, I looked at her, feeling terrible. She had been a nice person whose life had been about to change for the better. She had deserved a good life, but instead, she had been murdered.

I took one last look at her and zipped up the suitcase again.

Standing and stretching, I surveyed the room, putting my police training to good use. Madhushree's luggage had to be taken care of too. There was nothing on the bed except for mussed sheets; the tables were clear of anything but the hotel's belongings and so was the bathroom. The towels were dry except for the one I had used after my shower and the one I had dampened to wipe Madhushree down.

I divided the rooms of the suite into imaginary grids and checked every inch. Some twenty-five minutes later, I was convinced that nothing revealed Madhushree's presence anywhere in the suite. Her luggage was packed, she had even neatly folded the clothes that she had been wearing earlier and put them in her suitcase. I wiped her suitcase with the damp towel and zipped it up, wiping the zip as well. The

AC was on at full blast and it was chilly, yet I could feel drops of sweat on my forehead and under my arms.

I surveyed the room one last time and called my friend Abhishek.

'Hi buddy, how are you? I'm in Delhi,' I said.

'Hey! When did you get in? But sorry bhai, I am out of town right now,' replied Abhishek.

'I just arrived today. Listen, can you send me your driver? I need to go to a friend's place.'

'Sure thing. Manoj will bring my new car. You can use it as long as you need.'

'Thanks, bhai. I'm at the St. Tropez. Please send the car there. I'll catch up with you later.'

'Sure. The driver will be there in twenty minutes,' said Abhishek.

20

The Burial

'Sir, I am Manoj, the driver. I am waiting in the parking lot,' said the voice at the other end of the line.

'Okay, I'll be down in five minutes,' I said, trying to pull the suitcase behind me. It was heavy, and I needed to drag it rather than lift it, but it moved. And then a wheel came off and the suitcase toppled.

I cursed. Would nothing go right today?

But I needed to stay calm. I picked up the wheel and shoved it in my bag. 'Shit, these guys put such small wheels on such a large bag. Don't they use their brains?' I thought angrily.

I dialled the reception.

'Good evening, Mr Arjun. How can we assist you?' said the receptionist in her impossibly sweet voice.

'Can you please send a bell boy with a luggage trolley to my room immediately?'

'Right away, sir,' said the receptionist.

I sat down and looked at the suitcases. One had Madhushree's stuff in it. And the other had Madhushree.

Finally, the bell rang. I opened the door to see a bell boy with a luggage trolley.

'Checking out, sir?' asked the porter with a smile.

'No, I just need to keep this stuff at a friend's place. I will return soon,' I said, pointing at the two suitcases.

'Oh, this one is large,' said the bell boy.

'Yeah, it's heavy too. I'll give you a hand with it,' I smiled nervously, though I was confident that the polycarbonate hard top of the suitcase would not give the porter any idea of what was inside.

We put the bags on the trolley and headed for the parking lot. When Manoj opened the boot, I helped the porter put the bags inside.

'Thank you,' I smiled, handing him a hefty tip.

* * *

'It's been a long time since I have driven you anywhere, sir. How are you?' asked Manoj.

'I am fine, Manoj. Just drive towards IIT, please,' I said, in no mood to exchange pleasantries.

'Where could I dispose of the suitcases?'

I could throw them in a canal or a pond, but what would I tell Manoj? He would certainly find it strange to see a senior IPS officer throwing a couple of bags in a body of water in the middle of the night. And anyway, the suitcases could rise to the surface soon and be discovered, leading to a police investigation.

'I could the take suitcases to the jungle and bury them there,' I thought, recalling the Sheena Bora case. Sheena Bora's mother, Indrani Mukerjea, had been arrested for allegedly killing her daughter and burying the body in a forest.

'But where are the jungles near Delhi? Are there any? And in any case, I have nothing to dig with,' I thought. I caught Manoj's eye in the rear-view mirror and shuddered. Indrani's driver had spilled the beans to the police. I could be caught the same way.

'Maybe I can burn Madhushree's body,' I pondered. To do that, I would need an isolated place and, of course, a bottle of petrol. Or . . . my mind cycled through all the cases of murder that I, a police officer, obviously knew about.

There was the infamous tandoor murder case in which Naina Sahni was killed by her husband Sushil Sharma, a politician. Sushil had shot Naina and put her body in the tandoor of a restaurant to burn. The flames emerging from the tandoor had alerted a police constable who had then discovered the body.

'Gosh, there is such a heavy price to pay for extramarital affairs. I should have known,' I cursed, recalling that both these cases had been the results of extramarital affairs. 'Think, Arjun, think.'

I should have had a plan before getting in the car. My normally cool brain was not working efficiently tonight. I needed a safe place to at least hide the body before figuring out how to dispose it. Looking out of the window, I suddenly remembered Somveer's farmhouse in Westend—only occupied by the caretaker and cook, Bhola.

'That's it! That's where I can hide the body, at least temporarily,' I thought feverishly. 'Yes! It's ideal! It's isolated and also a privately owned property and Somveer is rarely there!'

I pulled out my phone and dialled Bhola's number.

'*Haan* Bhola, hum *Arjun bol rahe hain*. This is Arjun, Somveer's friend,' I said.

'Yes, sir. *Pranam*. I remember you from your last visit with Somveer Sir and your other friends,' said Bhola excitedly.

'Listen, I need to stay at the farmhouse tonight. Is that okay?'

'Sure, sir. Somveer Sir is in London right now. Are you coming with some company? I'll make the arrangements,' said Bhola in a mischievous tone.

'No, I'm alone,' I said, irritated with Bhola's question. I understood what he meant by 'company'. I hung up.

'Manoj, let's go to Somveerji's farmhouse,' I said. 'Do you know the way?'

'Yes, sir. I know the location. It's in Westend,' he replied.

I sat back, thinking about the mess I was in. The drive to the farmhouse was long, at least an hour. Every time I saw a policeman on the road, I grew anxious. When we finally arrived, I leapt out, ready to grab the suitcases.

'Thanks, Manoj. You can come early tomorrow morning to pick me up,' I said, picking up the suitcases.

'Right, sir,' said Manoj and drove away.

'Here, give them to me. I'll put the suitcases in the guest room on the first floor,' said Bhola.

'No, no need. Make me something to eat first, I'm famished,' I replied.

The moment Bhola went into the kitchen, I stepped out to survey the grounds. Not very far from the residential area of the farmhouse, I found a patch of land that seemed suitable. It did not seem to be frequently used; scrubby-looking bushes and weeds had sprouted in the area and the soil also seemed quite loose. Happy with my discovery, I returned to the house, popping into the storeroom where I found some shovels, spades and other gardening materials.

I found Bhola in the kitchen, kneading dough for rotis. 'I will make some egg bhurji for you,' he smiled.

'But I think I'll enjoy the food more if I could have a drink,' I said with a wink.

'Sure, sir. The bar is in the drawing room,' he said.

'Yes, thank you. But I need some company. Come on, pour a drink for yourself as well,' I said.

'No, no, sir, what are you saying?' Bhola protested.

'Come on, don't act so innocent. You must be syphoning some away whenever the house is empty. You may as well have a drink tonight without actually stealing it,' I said.

Bhola looked at the glass full of the finest whisky that I held out to him. The bottle I had poured from must have cost double his monthly salary.

'Come on,' I said, raising my glass. Bhola hesitated for a moment and then picked up his glass.

I sipped my whisky slowly. As a teetotaller, it tasted bitter to me, like poison. I wondered how my friends enjoyed drinking such a lousy thing.

'Can you get me some ice?' I asked.

As Bhola moved towards the fridge, I quickly poured my drink into his glass.

'Come on, you're too slow. Bottoms up,' I said.

Encouraged by my gesture, Bhola immediately gulped down the whisky.

I played this game for the next hour.

'I can't believe my luck, sir. I'm drinking such an expensive whisky with a senior police officer from my home state, Bihar,' Bhola slurred. He was totally sozzled. One drink later, he passed out.

'Is he dead?' I wondered, a little tense. One dead body was enough for the night.

Fortunately, he began snoring, putting my anxiety to rest.

'Good,' I said, as I rushed towards the suitcases. With great effort, I managed to drag them to the corner of the farmhouse I had decided on, then rushed to the store for the shovels and spades.

Even with the loose soil, digging was no easy matter. As an inspector general of police, I had not done any manual labour for years! It was a humid night, and I was drenched in sweat. Wiping my sweat, I kept digging. I couldn't stop.

Who knew when Bhola would wake up. And I wanted Madhushree off my hands.

After half an hour, I had dug a pit big enough for the suitcase containing the body.

'Should I take out the body and bury it? And where will I hide the bag that contains Madhushree's belongings?' I wondered.

I dug harder, making the pit deep enough for both the suitcases. As Somveer employed gardeners and there was a problem with stray dogs in the area, I made the pit even deeper in case the area was accidentally dug up.

Finally, I put both the suitcases in the pit and buried them beneath the soil I had thrown up while digging. I spread the remaining soil over the area around the pit, then collected rocks and stones from here and there and planted them above the pit to give the ground a natural feel.

Then I walked back to the house, checking whether the suitcases I had dragged behind me had left a trail. It had rained earlier that evening, and the ground was soft. There were signs that something had been dragged across the ground, so I threw soil over the trail, trying to tamp it down.

Fortunately, the closer I got to the house, the thicker was the grass on the lawn, and I was confident that the grass would spring back and cover the trail by morning.

And then it started raining again. Phew! The rain would take care of any remaining footprints and other traces of activity.

I returned to the dining room to find Bhola still snoring deeply.

'So far, so good,' I thought, climbing the steps to the guest room.

I needed a shower. As the water fell on me, I finally began crying. My tears flowed without ending.

21

'Where Is the Phone?'

Bhola was still sleeping like a log by the time I crept out of the farmhouse.

'Good morning, sir,' said Manoj, as I stepped into the car.

My night had been terrible, and I had no idea how the day would unfold.

I was too tired to reply to Manoj, falling asleep the moment the car started.

'Hotel *aa gaye*, sir, we've reached the hotel,' said Manoj, waking me up. I entered my room, still feeling drowsy. It felt strange to be here after all that had happened the night before.

Madhushree was murdered in this room, I thought. But now was not the time for sentiment but survival. I checked every inch of the room again. There was nothing except my bag. Everything was as I had left it. Obviously, nobody had entered the room again.

I called the reception.

'Hello, please ask the housekeeping staff to clean my room,' I said.

Ten minutes later, the cleaning staff arrived.

'Sir, please sit comfortably while we clean the room,' said one of the men.

'I am obsessive about cleanliness. I hope you don't mind if I check while you clean,' I replied, following them as they worked. I needed to be certain I hadn't overlooked anything.

'Please wash the bathroom properly. And change the bed sheets and towels. And here are my clothes for laundry too,' I instructed the hotel personnel. The staff must have found my behaviour quite irritating.

'Here you are, sir. Your suite is squeaky clean,' said one of the men. By now I was quite confident that any trace of Madhushree had been wiped out. Feeling better, I dialled room service.

'Can you please send some breakfast?'

'Sure, sir, what can we get you?' asked the woman at the other end.

'Anything! I'll eat whatever you send,' I replied.

'Right, sir,' the woman chuckled.

When the doorbell rang, I saw a huge breakfast spread on the trolley. Within seconds, I was gorging on the food.

I never knew food could be so comforting, I thought, stuffing myself. I also wondered how humans could adapt so quickly to circumstances. I had been so distraught while burying Madhushree and now, here I was, enjoying delicious food. Had I become heartless? I focused on the situation I was in again, letting go of my emotions.

Was there anything else that could link Madhushree with St. Tropez?

'Of course. The hotel CCTV! How could I forget,' I cursed.

I left my breakfast half-eaten and picked up my phone.

* * *

'Ashutoshji, thanks once again for the suite. You're spoiling me with so much luxury,' I said.

'My pleasure, sir,' replied Ashutosh, beaming.

'I was wondering if I could see how your hotel security works, particularly the CCTV. It will be interesting to learn new security techniques,' I said, sounding as officious as possible.

'Always on duty! I've heard that about cops. Sure, I'll ask my CSO to take you around right away,' said Ashutosh.

* * *

'Hello, sir, I am Krishna Prakash, the chief security officer of the St. Tropez Hotel. Ashutosh Sir asked me to explain the way our security works. Shall we go?' said the tall, well-built man at my room door.

I nodded and we left.

'Shall we start with the fire fighting drill?' asked Krishna.

'No, I'm a little short of time, Krishna. Just tell me about the CCTV system,' I said.

'Sir, we have 360 cameras covering every entry and exit of the hotel. All the corridors are covered, obviously.'

'There are no cameras inside the rooms, right?' I asked.

He nodded, probably wondering why I had asked such a stupid question.

We entered the CCTV control room where two operators watched the multiple screens in front of them.

'Sir, the control room is manned twenty-four hours a day. The CCTV room is very important to us. No unauthorized person can enter it. Even the door is fireproof,' Krishna said proudly.

I was really not interested in any mumbo jumbo about the state-of-the-art CCTV room.

'I am curious to see some CCTV videos. Could I see the footage of the corridor where my suite is located? Particularly between 6.10 p.m. and 7.30 p.m.,' I said casually.

I remembered leaving at 6.07 p.m., so I deliberately gave him the time just after that.

'Sure, sir,' said Krishna.

As the CCTV operator rewound the video to that time, I waited with bated breath to see who had entered my suite.

In a few moments, I had a rear view of a person walking towards my room. Beyond the ill-fitting hoodie and jeans, there was nothing to identify this person. The camera angle was such that the exact proportions of the person could not be discerned.

'Can I see the footage from the camera on the other side of the corridor?' I asked, hoping I'd be able to see the face from that angle.

Even the fresh footage didn't help. The hoodie covered the person's face, a high-collar jacket concealed the mouth and sunglasses hid the eyes. The person was wearing a cap too. An NSG cap.

Where have I seen this cap before? I wondered. It seems familiar.

'Can you please zoom in?' I asked. Krishna gestured to the CCTV operator. I looked at the enlarged still from the video.

Of course! I thought. Charu has a similar cap!

Krishna looked at me inquiringly. 'You had a visitor in your room, sir?' he asked.

'Yeah, an old acquaintance,' I replied.

'Why is your friend all covered up?'

'Oh, unfortunately he suffers from a skin disease. He doesn't like to expose it,' I said.

'Oh, how unlucky. The way he's covered himself, I can't even tell whether it's a man or a woman,' said Krishna.

The person in the CCTV footage knocked on the door and entered the room a moment later.

'Either Madhushree knew someone was coming to meet her or she assumed it was me or some hotel staff,' I thought.

After exactly ten minutes, the hooded person exited the room.

'Stop, that's enough,' I said. I did not want to be seen entering my suite later on. Krishna might suspect that there had been someone in the suite in my absence.

The person in the hoodie was undoubtedly the killer. But I would never be able to identify him or her. In any case, it was more important to remove the entire day's footage. There was no way I could allow any evidence of Madhushree coming to my room to exist.

'Well, thanks, Krishna. How long before you delete the footage?' I asked, hoping he would say it was done every twenty-four hours. That would mean I'd be in the clear very soon.

'It can't be done from here,' he said. 'Our hotel is a part of an international chain called the Royal Manor, which has outsourced the CCTV work to a US-based company. Only the people of that company can delete the footage.'

'Can no footage be deleted from here?' I inquired, trying to behave as though his answer wasn't crucial.

'Well, sir, it can be done, but we'd need to use the admin passwords. There are a whole lot of checks and balances in our system,' he explained.

'Not even a small part of the footage?'

'No, sir. The only thing that happens is that the footage is automatically overwritten after thirty days,' said one of the CCTV operators.

'So it's not as easy as they show in the movies,' I said nonchalantly.

'Yes, sir. Not like the movies,' said Krishna.

* * *

'The arrangements were quite well done this time, sir. I had a comfortable stay in the BSF barracks,' said Bhajan Singh.

'Yes, sir, the BSF takes good care of us,' said my driver, Pratap.

I did not reply, staring out of the window and watching the traffic moving past us from the opposite side.

How is everything so normal so fast, I wondered. Just last night, I had been so emotionally overwrought that I had even contemplated suicide. I had been full of sadness about Madhushree, worried sick about Charu's reaction and terror-stricken by the thought of my children being ostracized if I was arrested. And here I was today, alive and breathing easy. Why, I had even polished off a hearty breakfast!

Once again, I considered the events that had taken place yesterday. I had taken extreme precautions in meeting Madhushree. And I had done my best to hide her body. People would think that she had flown off to Canada for two months and if she did not return, they would assume that she had settled there. By that time, the CCTV footage would have automatically been overwritten.

Now I wondered why Madhushree had been murdered in the first place.

Did someone hate her so much that they wanted her dead? Did she have an enemy of some sort? Or am I the target? Was she murdered because someone wanted to destroy my career, my life, by framing me for murder? I pondered.

I thought about how I might trace the killer, but knew I could do nothing to find him. In any case, even if I found him, I could be implicated too. Madhushree could have been killed for any reason. It would be best to let the murder remain a mystery. I should let sleeping dogs lie. It was in my best interest. And I had taken care of everything. There was nothing to show that Madhushree had been in my room.

And then it struck me like lightning. I hadn't seen Madhushree's phone in the room when I packed up her things. Where was it?

22

'I Know About You and Madhushree'

'Hi Charu! How are you doing?' I asked as I entered the bedroom.

'I'm all right,' said Charu, not looking particularly excited by my return.

Though I was in a sullen mood myself I was surprised that she had not leapt up to hug me. This was the first time in our more than two decades of marriage that she had not embraced me when I returned from an out-station trip.

'How was your trip? And how was your meeting?' asked Charu, her eyes on the TV screen as she surfed channels.

'It was a typical, boring trip and then there was a perfunctory meeting about the PM's visit to Punjab,' I said.

'And what about Somveer's problem?'

'What problem?' I asked, surprised.

'You explained in detail about the girl who had died in his bed,' said Charu.

I paled.

'Oh, yeah, yeah. He must have managed somehow. He's filthy rich. Rich enough to bribe people anywhere in the world. He didn't call me after that,' I said, opening my suitcase.

I laid my clothes on the bed and deliberately dropped the box of contraceptives in front of Charu to assure her that I had not had a fling or a one-night stand.

She just rolled over and went to sleep.

* * *

'So, how was the meeting in Delhi?' asked Ravi.

'It was all right. We discussed various issues regarding the PM's visit, nothing that we don't already know,' I replied grumpily.

'You're looking very dull. Usually you return from Delhi quite cheerful,' he observed.

'Yeah, yeah. A mood swing. I'm human,' I said.

'Or is it because you can't see Madhushree any more now that she has left?' said Ravi mischievously.

'Don't cross your limits, Ravi. This is not funny,' I said angrily, leaving Ravi's office and banging the door behind me.

* * *

I sat in my office in a particularly nasty mood. Negative thoughts clouded my mind. The office staff stayed away even though the light on the door was green.

What if someone digs up the body at Somveer's farmhouse? I will surely be found out, I thought. I should have gone to the police. Oh my God, I am definitely a criminal now! I didn't murder Madhushree, but I did try to destroy evidence. Maybe I should check with a lawyer about the implications of section 201 IPC.

I sat back and thought about the situation again.

Heck, that was the best possible option at the time. I made the choice for self preservation. Now I can only hope for the best. I've been lucky for a major part of my life. I need to be lucky just one more time.

* * *

'Sir, some Bagaria fellow has come to see you,' said my PA.

'Don't you know I'm busy? Can't you see the red light?' I said angrily. I was getting increasingly irritable and behaving totally unlike myself.

'I'm sorry, sir, but the light was green. I told him to come some other time, but he said it was urgent,' replied the PA.

'Send him in,' I said, trying to recall where I had heard the name before.

A short, balding man entered my chamber.

'Namaste, sir. Remember me? I met you at the party at the IPS mess,' said Bagaria.

I looked at him in shock. Holy shit! Madhushree's husband! What is he doing here? I thought.

He continued to stand. As was the usual protocol.

I gestured to him to sit down, wiping my face with a tissue. The AC was not strong enough to keep me from sweating.

'Yes?' I asked, fiddling with my pen nervously.

'Sir, I just came to thank you for helping with Madhushree's visa. You have helped her fulfil her dream,' said Bagaria.

'Oh, it was nothing!' I waved him off, relieved.

'Do you help every woman you meet? You like saving damsels in distress, don't you? Particularly beautiful women from their cruel husbands?'

The sarcasm in Bagaria's voice hit me hard.

'Mind your language. Do you know who you're talking to?' I thundered.

'Yes, I'm talking to a powerful man who fancies my wife. Madhushree hated me even more after she fell in love with you,' said Bagaria.

'I don't know what you're talking about, and I am not interested in your marital affairs,' I said.

'So you sent her away from me. And why has she not called anyone back home? It's been a week, her phone is continuously switched off,' said Bagaria.

'You imbecile. She has gone to Canada. She must have bought a new Canadian SIM card. How can you reach her on the phone if you don't know her number? And she certainly wouldn't want to remain in touch with a lousy husband like you anyway. That's probably why she hasn't called you.'

Bagaria stood and folded his hands.

'Namaste, sir,' he said and left.

* * *

It was impossible to sleep. My mind was full of Bagaria.

What can he do? He's an average, lower middle-class man. At the most he can lodge a missing complaint in a police station. And even if the officer in charge agrees to lodge his complaint, who will go looking for Madhushree? The police are too under-resourced and understaffed to look for some orchestra singer. And why would the police look for a woman who has travelled abroad to fulfil her dreams and escape an abusive husband? I thought.

I sat up and checked my cell phone. I had deleted all my WhatsApp chats and call logs with Madhushree. I had even hidden her body. Hopefully it wouldn't be found before it decomposed, and the CCTV footage at the St. Tropez would be overwritten by that time. Her visit to the St. Tropez had been a secret. Nobody had known she was coming to meet me.

Except her killer.

My phone buzzed. A WhatsApp message popped up on the screen.

'I know about you and Madhushree,' the message read.

23

Shubham Orchestra

I jumped out of bed, trying not to wake Charu. Even so, I tripped over my slippers and banged my knee on the wardrobe.

Whimpering in pain, I went out in the garden and read the message again and again.

'I know about you and Madhushree.'

The phone number was obviously not on my contact list.

I had thought the night of 4 May had been the darkest of my life. Now, I knew better. The nightmare had truly begun. I remained in the garden, waiting for morning to arrive.

* * *

Two days passed. I had lost my appetite and couldn't sleep. I had never been so stressed in my life.

There had been no other messages from that unknown number, but I knew it was not a prank. Somebody knew about us. But what did he know? Did he have the transcript of my messages to Madhushree? Did someone see me hiding her body?

The message was in English and Madhushree's name was spelt correctly. So naturally it could not have come from Bhola, Somveer's dumb cook, or Manoj, the driver. In any case, neither of them was stupid enough to mess with a senior police officer.

I had heard of 'honeytraps', but this was more sinister. Was the message the beginning of blackmail? I needed to find the person who sent it. Maybe I could shut his mouth by paying him a reasonable amount of money.

I called Vikram.

'Hi Vikram, I need a small favour. Please find me the name and other details of a number I have just messaged you,' I said.

'Yes, sir,' Vikram replied.

He called back within ten minutes.

'Sir, it's in the name of Murli Yadav of Samastipur, Bihar. But the tower location is here, in our district. Do you need any more details?' said Vikram.

'Just send me Murli Yadav's address. Thanks.'

Who is Murli Yadav? I wondered. I don't know anyone by that name. Why would someone from Bihar want to blackmail me?

The moment I got the address, I forwarded it to the SP of Samastipur and called him.

'Hi, Kundan, this is Arjun Kumar, '98 batch IPS.'

'Yes, yes, sir. I know you. You are a famous IPS officer, you are a hero for us,' said the SP enthusiastically.

I was embarrassed by the SP's lavish praise. Even worse, he had no idea that his hero was in deep trouble and had done the things only a 'villain' would do.

'Thanks! Listen, I need you to give me all the details about one Murli Yadav. I have sent you his address,' I said.

'Right away, sir. I'll tell the SHO of that area,' replied the SP.

* * *

'Jai Hind Sir, this is Kundan. Sir, this Murli Yadav has been working in Jalandhar since many years,' said the SP.

'Really? Do you have his address?'

'Sir, his parents are not sure of his address, but they told me he works as a drummer in an orchestra,' said the SP Samastipur.

'Name of the orchestra?'

'Shubham Orchestra, sir,' replied the SP.

***

Shubham Orchestra! The drummer from Shubham Orchestra knew about Madhushree and me! I was really worried now.

'How could Madhushree be so foolish? Did she talk about me? Did someone from the orchestra follow her to St. Tropez?' I wondered.

There was no time to waste. I needed to find the blackmailer and negotiate with him.

I got Murli Yadav's address through the manager of the orchestra and asked Pratap to drive me to his house immediately. I was at my wit's end. How would I deal with him? Should I threaten him? Or give in to his potential demand?

'Sir, such a senior officer has come to my house. I wanted to meet you at all those parties but never dared to. I am humbled that you are here. I am also from Bihar, just like you. *Hum bhi Bihar ke hai*,' said Yadav, seeming delighted to see me.

I was surprised. He didn't come across as a blackmailer. He even seemed happy to have me visit him at home.

'Murli, you sent me a WhatsApp message two days ago. Let's talk about it,' I said.

'Me? I sent you a message? Arre, sir, I wouldn't dare to do such a thing. I don't even have your number,' replied Murli, surprised.

It was clear that he was telling the truth.

'94**6897. Isn't this your number? And you sent me a message at 12.35 a.m.,' I said.

'Sir, the number is mine for sure. But I haven't sent you any message. Why would I? Anyway, I was playing the drums at a party at Hotel Atlanta at that time.'

He took his phone out of his pocket.

'And see, there is no message from my phone. See for yourself, sir,' said Yadav, showing me his phone.

'Did you give your phone to anyone?'

'No, sir. I kept it by the synthesizer when I played the drums.'

'Okay,' I said, realizing that Yadav was not the blackmailer.

Back in the car, I said, 'Pratap, Hotel Atlanta.'

Obviously, the blackmailer had used Yadav's phone and then deleted the message. I needed to find the sender of the message.

I'll give him whatever he wants. I just want to get on with my life, I thought, my brain almost exploding.

'Hello, Arjun Sir, how can I help you?' asked the receptionist.

I cursed myself for being so well-known.

'Ah, I am here for an investigation. I need to see the CCTV footage of the party you had in your hotel two days ago,' I said with authority.

In two minutes, I was in the CCTV room. It was very basic, nothing in comparison to the one at the St. Tropez. The operator quickly played the video of the party.

I watched the footage intently. It felt terrible to see another female singer in place of Madhushree on the stage. Life goes on, I thought. Nobody is irreplaceable. After a few moments, I saw Murli Yadav put his phone on the table near the synthesizer. And then I got what I wanted.

The female singer bowed to the audience after her performance, moved towards the synthesizer, and stopped to chat with the drummer. The male singer surreptitiously picked up the cell phone right then.

It was Madhav.

24

'Your Veg Pizza'

Madhav! Of course, it has to be someone who knew both Madhushree and me. Did Madhushree tell him about our meeting? Or did he see me hiding the body? I need to meet Madhav immediately.

I got Madhav's number from Murli and called him at once from my landline.

'Hello?' said a Kishore Kumar-like voice.

'Madhav, this is Arjun Kumar. I need to meet you.'

'Uh, why sir? What happened?' replied Madhav, sounding very worried.

'You know what's happened. Let's meet and discuss your terms,' I said.

My voice did not have its usual authoritative tone. In fact, I sounded rather weak.

'I don't know what you're talking about, sir,' said Madhav, his voice trembling too.

'The WhatsApp message. About Madhushree and me,' I said softly.

Madhav hung up.

* * *

'You were given one assignment and you failed. If you want your life back, don't mess up this time. I have sent the details on your cell phone,' said the rasping voice.

The Ghost remained silent, trembling with anger. It was true that he had not fully succeeded in his mission, though he had done his best.

The car sped away. This time the Ghost did not say 'Jai Hind'. The man in the car did not deserve it.

* * *

'Charu, I'm going to Praveen's farmhouse for a tennis match. It's just outside town. The mobile network is bad there, so don't worry if you can't reach me. I'll be back in a few hours,' I said, putting on my tracksuit.

Charu barely reacted.

I was getting increasingly uncomfortable with Charu's behaviour since my return from Delhi. We'd always been able to chat about anything, but now there was practically no conversation between us.

I placed my tennis racquet in the car and knowing that this was the perfect opportunity to drop in on Madhav. The man had thought he could escape me. He was no longer living at the address the orchestra manager had given me. But I had tracked him down.

'Bhajan, Pratap, why don't you two take a break? I'm going to a friend's place and will take some time. It's been years since I drove alone anyway,' I said, looking over at my trusted driver and bodyguard who were always with me like my shadow. I wanted to keep my meeting with Madhav a secret for obvious reasons.

'Sir, you are under threat and your security is my primary concern. I can't let you go alone, though you can drive if you want,' replied Bhajan.

I paused. The threat from Timur Ali was quite potent. I knew it was a bad idea not to take Bhajan with me. It would also make Charu suspicious if I went without him since I never travelled alone.

'Okay, you're right. Come on, let's go to Praveen's farmhouse,' I said.

I was not in my top form. My body was not all in sync with my mind, because I was thinking about Madhav rather than the ball in front of me. I checked my cell phone. It was 7.30 p.m. I needed to move.

'Thanks for the game, Praveen. See you soon,' I said, getting in the car.

'Bhajan, let's go to Satsang Colony. My Google Maps shows the area is just twelve minutes away,' I said.

'Satsang Colony? *Woh toh area theek nahin hai*, that area is not good,' replied Bhajan.

Pratap, my driver, nodded in agreement.

'Why?' I asked.

'A lot of antisocial elements live there. It's basically a colony of abandoned government houses. It's not a place for someone of your stature, sir', said Pratap.

'Drive. I have to meet someone there,' I said sternly.

Like all policemen, Pratap did not say a word. He simply followed my orders.

Satsang Colony was eerie. There was a line of abandoned apartment buildings, the remnants of a failed housing scheme, and very few people were around except for a couple of drunkards and junkies. Bhajan had been right about the area.

'House No. 26/B. Look for it,' I said.

'Yes, sir,' said Bhajan.

In five minutes, we were outside the apartment block.

'Wait here. I'll be back in about ten to fifteen minutes,' I said.

'Yes, sir,' saluted Bhajan Singh. This time he did not insist on coming with me.

I stepped out of the car, slowly walked a few steps and waited for Bhajan to look elsewhere. The moment he did, I ran to the back of the block.

'House No. 38/C. Yes, this is where he is hiding,' I thought.

It had not been easy to trace Madhav. But it had not been difficult either for a cop.

I had tried calling him again after he had hung up on me, but he hadn't answered. I had tried again from Bhajan's phone, a number Madhav would not have. But he still hadn't answered. Perhaps, he was smart enough to ignore calls from unknown numbers.

His home had been empty. His neighbours had said that he had packed up his stuff and left for some unknown place. But Madhav had made a mistake. He had kept his cell phone on.

I had simply sent Madhav's number to Vikram to place on the call observation service on priority. And then I had easily overheard Madhav's conversations on the phone I had bought with the secret service fund.

'Can you send me a veg pizza? Yes, and extra oregano. Thanks. The address is house No. 38/C, Satsang Colony. Please send it by 8 p.m.,' Madhav had told the guy at Domino's Pizza. So, I had received Madhav's location from the man himself. I smiled for the first time in days.

It was 7.55 p.m. now. I knocked on the door, certain that Madhav would be at home to receive his pizza.

He was. Seeing me on the other side of the door, his jaw dropped and he froze.

I shoved past him and entered the apartment.

'Hi, can we talk?'

'Sir! How the hell did you find me? I came here just today. It's my friend's place,' said Madhav.

'I'm a cop. It wasn't difficult to find you. But let's get down to business. What do you know about Madhushree? Do you have a video?' I said, wasting no time.

Madhav went absolutely pale.

'You know about the video?' he croaked.

'Oh my God! He actually had a video' I thought.!

Suddenly, there was a knock on the door.

'It must be the pizza guy,' said Madhav.

'Of course. Thirty minutes' delivery or the pizza is free,' I said, as Madhav opened the door.

A tall, well-built man was standing outside.

'Your pizza, sir,' he said, his face expressionless.

'Hey, this is not my pizza. I'm vegetarian,' Madhav protested, looking at the red sticker on the pizza box.

The pizza guy simply pushed him inside and entered the house.

'Arre, what are you doing? Get out,' shouted Madhav.

Then the pizza man saw me. His eyes opened wide. It seemed as though he knew me.

I looked at the pizza man again. Strong, muscular forearms, a solid torso and knuckles hard as steel. But his eyes looked lifeless, as if they had seen a lot of death.

You could be a villain in a Bollywood film, I thought of complimenting him. But before I could open my mouth, a punch landed on my face. It was the hardest I had ever been hit and I fell to the floor.

Then the man grabbed Madhav by the neck, glaring at him menacingly.

'Where is the video?' he snarled.

'Wha . . . What video?' Madhav stammered.

He screamed as the man twisted his fingers.

'Is it in your mobile? That's the most likely place. Where is your cell phone?' asked the man, continuing to twist Madhav's fingers. There was a cracking sound; at least one of the fingers had broken. Madhav screamed again.

'It's on the table,' he wept.

I got up slowly, still reeling from the impact of the punch. The 'pizza man', I realized, was a highly trained person, an expert. And he was very strong. There was no way I could beat him.

As he moved towards the table, bending to pick up the phone, I grabbed a lamp and hit him hard, aiming for his temple for maximum impact.

The man stumbled momentarily but was back on his feet just as quickly. Was he made of steel? He looked at me with bloodshot eyes and in one quick step, he was raining blows on my torso. It took less than a second for my own training to kick in. I blocked most of his blows instinctively, thanks to the hand-to-hand combat training I had taken at the National Police Academy and later with the National Security Guard.

It was clear that the man was surprised by my resistance, but he stepped up his attack and was moving for the final assault when suddenly he saw Madhav moving towards the table.

'Hey, wait!' he shouted, as Madhav picked up the phone and ran out. He dropped me like a hot potato and ran after Madhav. By then, I was up and jumped on him, hitting him hard with my elbow and pinning him down for a few seconds. But he kicked me away and was back on his feet in an instant.

'It's over. He's going to kill me,' I thought as the man loomed over me. But he simply stepped over me and ran out.

After a few moments, I got up slowly and limped back to my car. Bhajan opened the door for me. 'Sir, are you all right?' he asked.

'It's nothing, Bhajan. I think it's just a bout of ankylosing spondylitis. My back hurts a little. I shouldn't have played so much tennis.'

On the way home, I thought about what had happened. Madhav had a video for sure. It couldn't be an explicit video as nothing had happened between Madhushree and me.

The only illegal thing I had done was hide a dead body! That was a big deal, but Madhav could not have followed me all the way to Somveer's farmhouse.

And who the hell was that muscular guy? Why did he want the video? And how had he found Madhav's hideout?

* * *

From the terrace of a neighbouring building, Madhav watched as the Ghost lurked like a shadow in the alleys, looking for him, before finally giving up. From his position of safety, he watched the tall, devilish person fade away.

'There is only one place where I can be safe now,' he thought, still panting after the chase. 'I need to go to my childhood friend. Even the police can't find him.'

He pulled out his phone to call his friend and stopped. Arjun Kumar had probably traced him via his cell phone, he realized.

Madhav switched off his phone immediately.

* * *

Across the city, a tall, muscular man looked at himself in the mirror, gazing at his reflection with his one good eye. His face had become haggard, he had been hiding too long in this dark, depressing place. But now, he had everything he needed to execute his plans.

'I'll avenge the deaths of my family soon, it's just a matter of time.'

He turned around and tried to focus his squinting eye on the cowering girl in the corner. The girl shrieked as he pounced on her, his rage too overpowering for her to fight back. The partly deaf man paid no heed to her cries for help.

Her shrieks echoed off the walls of the soundproof room.

25

'Kya Mausam Hai'

29 May 2021
Jallandhar

'Doctor Saheb, the weather is lovely today. Let's go for a long drive,' said Surbhi. Her eyes glowed. Clearly, she was in a romantic mood.

Doctor Prashant looked at his wife and smiled. Life had been good to him. He had a lovely wife, a flourishing practice and a brand new, black BMW. The car had not received its registration as yet, but a short ride would not hurt anyone. Anyway, the picture of Bajrang Bali on the car's rear windshield would protect them, he thought.

Once in the car, the doctor played the evergreen '*Kya Mausam Hai*' song to set the mood. The two of them held hands as he took his new automatic car out on the street.

With no traffic on the roads, the drive was smooth. Just then, a fast-moving SUV overtook them and blocked their car. Two men in police uniform got down from the black Fortuner.

'Prashant, what is this? Have we broken a law?' asked Surbhi, worried.

One policeman approached Prashant with a pistol in his hand. The other, a younger man, stood by Surbhi's side of the car.

Sweat trickled down the doctor's forehead. Policemen do not travel in swanky SUVs, he knew. Something was wrong.

'Please take whatever you want but let us go. Take my watch, my cell phone. This is a brand-new car, take it too,' said Prashant, hands folded in supplication.

'Doctor, you are worth much more than this BMW,' said the man by his side. 'Both of you—out! Get in the back.'

'At least let my wife go,' pleaded Prashant.

'Let us go, please,' cried Surbhi.

'Don't make it difficult for yourselves,' said the man, pointing his pistol at the doctor. 'Get in the back.'

As the doctor and his wife were pushed into the back of the BMW, two other guys in civilian clothing alighted from the SUV and got in with the couple, flanking them in the car's spacious back seat.

'Put on these caps,' said one of them.

Silently, after exchanging a glance, the doctor and his wife put on the monkey caps and sunglasses handed to them by the man.

'And give me your cell phones.' The gang leader took their phones, switched them off and threw them away in the fields.

The man in charge sat in the driver's seat. Soon, they were cruising along the highway.

'Oh my God, have we been kidnapped?' Surbhi asked fearfully.

'Yes, you have been kidnapped. Be quiet now if you want to stay alive,' said the man at the wheel.

* * *

'Sir, there's been another kidnapping. This time it's the well-known Doctor Prashant Ahuja and his wife,' said the inspector.

'Oh! What happened?'

Vikram was worried. Only last month, a high-profile businessman had been kidnapped and the police had failed to recover him. Their credibility would be questioned again.

'The doctor's brother-in-law said he saw his new BMW going towards the city limits. He tried to call the doctor on his mobile phone, but it was switched off. And neither he nor his wife have been home since morning,' said the inspector.

'Did you say his wife has also been kidnapped?' asked Vikram. Vikram was quite surprised as he had never heard of a woman being kidnapped along with her husband.

If it was true, it was bad. Really bad.

* * *

'Please, let us go. I'll give you everything I have,' pleaded the doctor.

'Shut up,' said the driver.

'Oh God, what will happen to us? Please, please don't harm Surbhi,' shuddered the doctor. He had offered the kidnappers everything he had, trying to convince them to let Surbhi go at least, but to no avail. 'What can I do?' he thought frantically. 'What?'

'We're about to reach the toll plaza. See that their faces are properly covered,' said the driver to the men sitting at the back.

'This is my chance. It's now or never,' thought the doctor as the car slowed down at the toll plaza. Using all his strength, he punched the man next to him. The guy was startled for a moment, but this wasn't a movie. This was real life. By the time the doctor had scrambled for Surbhi's hand, intent on pulling her out of the car, the other guy had hit him hard on his temple with his pistol.

'Do you want to die? Do you want your wife to be killed in front of you?' snarled the guy, pointing his pistol at Surbhi.

'Please don't harm my wife. Please, please,' said the doctor, breaking down. Trembling, Surbhi burst into tears.

'We are not going to harm your wife in any way. If you think we're going to molest her, let me tell you we will treat her as our sister. Now just stay quiet,' said the man at the wheel.

The couple sank back disconsolately, somehow controlling their tears. Surbhi clutched the doctor's arm with one hand, caressing the bruise on his forehead with the other.

The SUV and the BMW passed through the toll plaza uneventfully.

* * *

'What is the progress? Any updates?' I asked.

This was a major incident, taking place after another kidnapping few months ago. As the IG of the range, I needed to be in control of the investigation. Already, I was grappling with serious personal issues. Now, there was this as well.

'Sir, we checked the footage of all the toll plazas in the district and found that the doctor's car crossed toll plaza number 28. Though we could not see the doctor and his wife in the car, we identified the car from the Bajrang Bali sticker on the rear window. The interesting part is that the BMW was following an SUV, a black Fortuner,' said the inspector.

'That means the kidnappers have taken the doctor and his wife out of our district. But they can't go far. We're checking all the exit points,' said Vikram.

'Yes, sir, that's what I think too. But the black Fortuner in front of the BMW reminds me of Chunnalal Shah's kidnapping,' said the inspector.

'Hmm,' I pondered. 'You're right. Chunnalal's car was blocked by a black Fortuner on the national highway just after he left his factory. It's unfortunate that we couldn't rescue Chunnalal in time. I still feel terrible that we failed.'

Chunnalal Shah had been a well-known industrialist in Jalandhar. A pious, God-fearing man, going by what we had learnt during our investigation. He was also very schedule-oriented and the fact that he visited his factory at the same time every day had made it easy for his kidnappers to get hold of him.

Though we worked tirelessly, we had been unable to make any headway in the case at all. The kidnappers had been smart. They had not used a cell phone to make their ransom call and, in fact, had not even made a call till a few days after the kidnapping, when the intensity of the police operations had somewhat reduced. Then, after they finally phoned Chunnalal's wife on the landline, she did not inform the police about it for reasons best known to her. Instead, she paid the ransom demanded by the kidnappers, hoping to have her husband with her soon. But the kidnappers had had other ideas. Chunnalal had been murdered even after the ransom had been paid.

I was determined that this tragedy would not happen again.

26

4 Crore Is a Huge Amount

'Please stop the car. I need to use the restroom,' said Surbhi.

'Restroom?' the man sitting next to her mocked. 'You are resting in the car. What is your problem?'

'She wants to go to the toilet,' explained the doctor.

'No, we can't stop the car,' said the driver.

'Are you crazy? I can't wait any longer,' said Surbhi, squirming in obvious discomfort.

'You have to stop. We've been travelling for hours now. We need a toilet break,' said Prashant.

'Okay. But don't try to be smart,' said the driver as he took the car down a *kutcha* lane towards the fields, stopping when they were far enough from the main road.

'Get down, madam,' said the man sitting next to Surbhi.

Surbhi hesitated and then got out of the car, stretching her back.

'Go on, madam. Choose any spot,' said the man, stepping out of the car himself.

'Are you out of mind? I'm not going in the fields. And how dare you try and come with me,' shouted Surbhi.

'Oye, madam, control yourself. You think I am a fool to let you go to a restaurant or hotel for your bathroom break?' said the kidnapper.

'Please, I beg of you. I can't control it anymore,' pleaded Surbhi.

'Even I need to relieve myself,' said Dr Prashant.

'Okay, okay,' said the driver, irritated.

He gestured to one of his men to go to the SUV. The man returned in a few moments with a pair of handcuffs.

'Give me your hands,' the man said to Surbhi.

'What nonsense is this? You cannot tie me up like this and expect me to go with you to the fields,' Surbhi said angrily.

The man did not reply. He simply locked Surbhi's wrist into one end of the handcuffs and locked the other end on Prashant's wrist.

Prashant heaved a sigh of relief.

'This is a much better idea,' said Surbhi.

'Shut up and go. We'll keep an eye on you from here. And remember, don't try anything *filmi*,' said the driver.

As they walked deeper into the fields, Surbhi nudged Prashant. 'Prashant, this is our best chance. Let's run to the other side of the field and shout for help when we reach the road,' she said softly.

'Surbhi, please. Don't make these escape plans. We will be in bad trouble if they catch us,' said Prashant nervously.

'Come on, don't be scared. On my count, 1 . . . 2 . . . 3,'

Prashant and Surbhi ran for their lives, but the handcuffs made it impossible for them to coordinate their steps. Within seconds, Prashant had tripped and fallen down, taking Surbhi with him.

'Are you all right, Surbhi?' he asked, resigned to his fate.

'Yeah, I'm fine. You?' asked Surbhi, similarly subdued.

'*Bahut pyaar karte ho*, you love each other very much. But it seems you don't want to live long,' snarled a voice.

Surbhi and Prashant looked up to see themselves surrounded by the kidnappers.

'Please *humme mat maaro*, don't hit us,' pleaded Prashant.

The kidnappers took them to the SUV, shoved them in the back, covering their faces with monkey caps. The rest of the journey was uneventful. There were no more attempts to escape.

***

'Any other inputs?' I asked.

'Sir, I'm convinced that a person called Sarju Prakash is behind this kidnapping. The modus operandi of all his kidnappings is the same. An SUV blocks the victim's car, then the vehicles are taken out of the state,' said the inspector.

'But the problem is Prakash does not use mobile phones. He is so careful that he does not even make WhatsApp calls, it's impossible to track him. And we don't have any police records of him, not even a photograph,' Vikram lamented.

'I think you're right. I have the same feeling. But he has to ask for ransom. After all, that is the purpose of a kidnapping. He will make a call to demand money,' I said.

'Yes sir, but what do we do now?' asked Vikram.

'Put the phone numbers of all their relatives and close friends on call observation. Also include the doctor's staff, like his compounder and nursing assistant. The kidnappers will make a call in a few days,' I said.

'Right, sir,' said the inspector, even as Vikram worried out loud about the kidnappers' cunning.

'They've evaded us for so long, sir,' Vikram said. 'We know who they are, but we've never found proof. I hope they don't come up with some other way to demand the ransom.'

I thought hard about the various ways in which the ransom could be demanded. We couldn't have another failure on our hands.

***

Surbhi and Prashant were pulled out of the SUV and pushed towards the elevator. They were stiff after hours of sitting in the cramped rear of the SUV, but the kidnappers were in no mood to pander to them now.

Looking around, the doctor and his wife were taken aback to find themselves in an apartment building. They had imagined they'd be taken to some isolated place, maybe an abandoned house. Several cars were parked in the basement. It was late at night and no resident was in sight. When the elevator reached level nine, Surbhi and Prashant were ushered into an apartment and shown to a room.

'This will be your room for the next few days. I'll get some food for you,' said a man who seemed to be the caretaker of the apartment.

When the caretaker returned with a tray, the doctor and his wife were sound asleep on the floor. They had been too exhausted to even think about food.

'It's time to ask for the ransom. We can't wait for long this time,' said the boss when he saw the couple asleep. His accomplices nodded. They knew the police would soon be hot on their trail.

* * *

Every morning for the last twenty years, Balraj Saxena had taken his morning walk in Central Park, no matter the weather. This morning was cool and breezy, perfect for a bit of people watching. Normally, he would be delighted, but today he was low-spirited. His best friend Prashant and his wife Surbhi had both been kidnapped.

Prashant has a roaring practice. The kidnappers will ask for a huge ransom but I'm sure he'll earn all that money back quite fast. I just hope they're safe. Money does not matter, thought Balraj, increasing the pace of his walk.

A jogger suddenly came out of nowhere and banged hard into Balraj.

'*Bhaiyya, dekh ke chalo*. Look where you're going,' Balraj said, annoyed.

'Do you want your friend Prashant safe? If yes, listen to me very carefully,' said the jogger.

Perplexed, Balraj looked at the lean, athletic figure. The jogger's face was covered by a hood and his eyes were shielded by sunglasses.

'Don't stare at me. You don't know me so you won't recognize me anyway. If you want your friend and his wife back, arrange for Rs 4 crore in cash and take it to the Secretariat bus stand this Friday. From there, board the bus to King's Club at 10.30 a.m. Then leave the bag under your seat and get off at the next stop. If you tell the police or anyone else, you will be responsible for the deaths of your friends,' said the man.

'But . . . but . . . Rs 4 crore is a huge amount. How can I arrange it?' protested Balraj.

'Oh come on, you're a wealthy man. Take the money from Prashant on his return,' said the man, turning and jogging off before Balraj could say anything more.

* * *

Balraj looked around, feeling harried. He knew he could pay the ransom. The kidnapper also knew this fact. If he did not pay, Prashant and Surbhi would surely be killed. Was it worth losing his friends for Rs 4 crore?

He picked up his phone and called his CA.

'Subhashji, this is Balraj. Yeah, I'm fine. I have an emergency. I require a large amount of money in cash,' said Balraj.

'Balrajji, I sent you a decent amount last month. It is very difficult to adjust your books when it comes to cash.

The IT department keeps an eye on all transactions,' replied Subhash.

'I know, but this is important. Please help me one last time,' pleaded Balraj.

'Okay, how much do you want?' asked Subhash.

'Exactly four crores,' sighed Balraj.

The CA was shocked. 'What are you talking about? You know things have been tight since the pandemic,' he said.

'I know, but I had sent you a bigger amount earlier. And you promised you would help me convert it into white for a hefty commission. Please give me four crores in cash or the entire amount I gave you,' said Balraj.

'I gave your money to a realtor and I can't get it back easily. It's locked in for another six months. I'll arrange your money in a week's time,' said Subhash.

'No, no, Subhashji, I need it in twenty-four hours. Arrange it somehow, please,' said Balraj.

* * *

Surbhi looked out of the window. Children were playing in the compound, their mothers watched them and gossiped with each other.

'Are you thinking of shouting for help?' scoffed the man by her side.

'Of course! Who wouldn't?' snapped Surbhi. But she knew it wasn't possible. The kidnappers had been sitting in their room the whole day, turn by turn, never taking their eyes off them. Moreover, they were on the ninth floor. There was no way Surbhi would be heard by the people in the compound.

'Anything you want to eat?' asked the man.

'Yes, can we have pizza?' said Surbhi.

'And could we please watch some TV? We're bored to death. You've taken away our cell phones, so there's nothing to do,' said Prashant sheepishly.

The man was silent. But he got up, switched on the TV and slipped a pen drive into it.

'Enjoy,' he said, and went back to his chair.

'Thanks,' said Prashant and Surbhi in unison.

As the movie began, the couple discovered to their horror that it was *Radhe*. They were already stressed and feeling tortured. Now this!

'Can't you put on anything else?' asked Prashant.

'This is the only movie we have. We do not have cable or an internet connection in this apartment. Watch it or not, your choice,' said the man.

'At least get us some pizza,' said Surbhi.

27

The GPS Tracker

Balraj could not bear the tension any more. Would paying the ransom really mean the safe return of Prashant and Surbhi? He remembered what had happened to Chunnalal Shah and came to a decision. He had to inform the police. If he didn't, he would forever blame himself if something went wrong.

Within an hour, he was at the police headquarters.

* * *

'Sir, what should I do?' said Balraj, wiping the sweat from his forehead. He had just given Vikram and me a detailed description of his meeting with the man in the park.

'Hmm, this is clever of the kidnappers. Nevertheless, we are back in the game. So, Rakesh, what do you suggest?' I asked the city SP.

Rakesh was a young IPS officer known for thinking out of the box. He was a maverick in the police department, a risk-taker, but I knew that his adventures were all based on experience and common sense. He had been away for the last two weeks for his wedding and honeymoon but was back in the office today.

'Sir, why don't we let technology help us?' said Rakesh.

'Hmm, yes. Let's put a GPS tracker in the bag. It should hopefully lead us straight to the kidnappers,' I said.

'That's a very good idea! Let's do it,' said Vikram, excited.

We ordered a GPS tracker and Vikram and Rakesh uploaded its software on their laptop and cell phone respectively.

Then, I turned my attention to Balraj.

'Balrajji, this is the bag you will use for the money. We will stitch the tracker into the lower side of the bag so that it stays concealed. The batteries are fully charged and it should work for at least forty-eight hours,' I said.

'Yes, sir. This is quite a good GPS tracker. It's the size of a car key, so it can be easily hidden. It is also very effective and should give us a location that is accurate to five metres,' added Rakesh. 'Now, here's the plan.'

Balraj listened intently.

'We will follow the bus in an unmarked private vehicle. Two of my men will board the bus before you do,' said Rakesh.

'We'll keep an eye on you,' I interjected. 'Please remain calm.'

'And don't worry. We will not try to catch the kidnapper, we will just follow him,' added Vikram. 'That way, the doctor and his wife will remain safe and so will you.'

Vikram's soothing words did not instil much confidence in Balraj. He was very nervous and understandably so. But he had to play this game now, even if it was by someone else's rules.

***

7 June 2021
Jalandhar

Nervously looking at his watch, Balraj waited for the bus to arrive.

I hope I have not missed it, he thought, his palpitations increasing every moment.

After a few moments that felt like infinity, the bus arrived and Balraj boarded it, clutching his bag firmly. He found a seat and sat down, his eyes darting back and forth as he tried to spot someone who looked like a member of a gang. But all the passengers appeared to be normal, middle-class people. No one seemed suspicious. There was definitely no sign of the guy who had accosted him in the park; nor could he see anyone who looked like a policeman.

He cursed himself for overthinking. 'Why am I worried? Maybe the policemen are in civilian clothing. I just need to put the bag under my seat and leave, that's all. It's the job of the policemen to track the kidnappers,' he thought.

The next stop came rather abruptly. Balraj looked at the bag. It was still under the seat. He sighed and got down. There was nothing else he could do.

* * *

'Sir, *bahut gadbad ho gaya hai.* A disaster has happened. The two constables I had detailed to follow Balraj boarded the wrong bus by mistake,' said Rakesh, crestfallen.

'Oh no, this is bad. But the GPS tracker must still be working. We still have a chance,' I said, regaining my composure. I knew I should have fired the two inept constables when I had the time.

'Yes, sir. I'm following the tracker on my cell phone,' said Rakesh.

* * *

Rakesh asked his driver to catch up with the bus as fast as possible. Soon, his SUV was about fifty metres behind it.

According to the tracker, the bag was still on the bus. In such a crowded bus, there seemed no question of someone taking out the money and putting it in another bag without being seen, Rakesh thought.

'Driver, keep the car close to the bus,' he said.

The vehicles drove on without incident until they reached a traffic signal. The bus sped past the intersection just as the light turned red and Rakesh's car was left behind.

Without a police siren, there was no way for the unmarked SUV to move forward. Not wasting any time, Rakesh jumped out of the car and started running towards the bus, his bodyguard following him closely. Weaving through traffic and ignoring curses from drivers who had to abruptly brake or veer to the side to avoid hitting them, the two policemen soon made it within a 100 metres of the bus, which was slowing down for the next stop.

Even as the bus continued to move, Rakesh saw a man get down, holding the bag containing the money. He sprinted towards the man at full speed but collided with someone on the footpath and lost his balance, falling and hurting his shin badly. His bodyguard was quick to get him up, but they were too late. The man carrying the bag was lost in the crowd of commuters.

'Shit, shit, where the hell has he gone?' cursed Rakesh, grimacing with pain. He pulled out his cell phone and tracked the bag. It was about 200 metres away.

Rakesh tried to run, but his ankle simply could not support him and he had to walk towards the bag at a brisk pace. The bag's location had been static for the last few seconds, so if they moved fast, they could catch up with the man.

Fifty metres. Thirty metres. Fifteen metres. The bag was still in the same place.

'Oh God, I hope it does not turn out to be what I'm thinking,' muttered Rakesh. He looked inside a garbage bin and found the bag in the filth. Ignoring the stench, he quickly unzipped the bag. The money was gone.

28

Seek and Find

'Shit! What a terrible day this is turning out to be!' Rakesh cursed.

His bodyguard felt bad for his boss.

Saheb has been working so hard. We were so close and now so far, he thought, looking at Rakesh's sweat-soaked shirt. This is the problem with police work. You either have 100 per cent success or 100 per cent failure. You can't achieve even 90 per cent of the target and call yourself a winner.

* * *

'Sir, we lost the man. He vanished in the crowd. And he left the bag in a garbage bin, so we are back to square one,' Rakesh said to me over the phone. The man was clearly disappointed.

'No, not at all. The guy must have transferred the money to another bag somewhere close by. Grab footage from all the CCTVs in the area and look for him. We'll definitely find a lead,' I said.

'Yes, sir, I'll call my team and do it right away,' Rakesh said, sounding enthused again.

* * *

Within fifteen minutes, the entire area was swarming with police teams in plain clothes. They entered shops and other establishments and scanned the CCTV footage of the last hour. Finally, an officer phoned Rakesh.

'Sir, please come to the Woodlands store. I have a video of the man you're looking for,' said the officer.

Rakesh set off immediately.

The Woodlands store had a camera overlooking the street in front of it. As Rakesh played the video, he could clearly see the man he had been following, still carrying the bag with the concealed GPS tracker. As he moved, he was intercepted by another man, who tapped him on the shoulder. The second man looked annoyed. He snatched the bag from the first man, unzipped another and dumped the money into it by simply turning the original bag upside down. He then threw the original bag into the garbage bin.

The two men then left, walking towards C Street till they were out of the camera's range.

'So far, so good,' Rakesh thought. 'There are bound to be CCTV cameras on C Street, so we should know where they're headed.'

But C Street shops were simply holes in the wall, selling nothing of much value. None of them had CCTV cameras.

Rakesh kicked a lamp post in anger, only to hurt his foot again. He yelped in pain but refused to give up, gesturing to his bodyguard to join him as he walked further down C Street.

Slowly, the street opened up to a number of apartment blocks.

'The two guys must have gone into one of these buildings. If they had to go far away, they would have used a vehicle,' said Rakesh, trusting his instincts.

He summoned his team and issued orders.

'Form pairs and go to all the buildings on this street. Ask the watchmen if there has been any suspicious activity in the premises. Also look for a black Fortuner and a black BMW in the parking lot; the BMW has an image of Bajrang Bali on the rear windshield. A watchman could definitely tell you if the two cars arrived together a few days ago. Now come on, move!' said Rakesh.

His men saluted and dispersed immediately. The young city SP leaned against a wall and waited. His gut told him he was very close to the kidnappers' den.

29

The Policeman's Son

Surbhi looked down from the bathroom window. Once again, she was tempted to shout, but she knew it would be useless. She came out of the bathroom, resigned to her fate.

Bored, she began a conversation with the man on guard. He was the same man who had driven the car when they'd been abducted. She was certain he was the boss.

'You seem to be a decent person. Even when you were driving us, you behaved quite well with me. What made you turn to crime?' asked Surbhi.

The man ignored her.

'Come on, you can talk to me. It won't make any difference if you talk. You're in charge here and you know it,' continued Surbhi.

'Surbhi, leave it. He does not want to speak. Why are you pestering him?' said Prashant, scared that the man might get angry. He looked at the man and apologized. 'Bhaiya, please ignore her. She is a little talkative.'

The man maintained a studied silence. Prashant and Surbhi shifted their attention to the TV screen to watch *Radhe* for the sixth time in two days.

'My father was a police officer. He was a DSP in the state police,' said the man.

Prashant and Surbhi were startled. The man had spoken!

'My father had great expectations of me. He wanted me to join the police too. I was a bright student but inspite of my best efforts, I did not succeed. I could not fulfil my father's dreams. I failed,' the man continued.

He paused for a minute.

'I started a few businesses, but they failed too. In just a few years, I was burdened with big debts. I had no other alternative but to consider crime,' continued the man, his voice full of emotion. 'Kidnapping brings in a lot of money, so that's what I did. Initially, I thought I would stop after I had paid my dues, but then I got used to the easy money. I have a good life; I won't deny it. Kidnapping is a low-risk business with very high returns.'

'Your father was in the police! No wonder, you know how to hoodwink them,' said Surbhi, sounding as though it all finally made sense. Prashant remained quiet.

The man smiled slyly.

'Yes, madam, you are right. I could not become a policeman, but I wear a police uniform. It gives me a high and, of course, helps me get away after a kidnapping. I know how the police track criminals. That's why I do not use cell phones or even have an internet connection in this house,' said the man, pride written all over his face. He had kidnapped five businessmen so far, and now the doctor and his wife. The police had failed to catch him every time because he had taken every precaution. He had even had different sets of people involved in every kidnapping and he often switched things up. This time, he had brought the couple back to the city after a long drive outside the district limits, throwing the police off their track. He smiled again, marvelling at his own ingenuity.

The doorbell rang.

The man got up and stepped out, locking Surbhi and Prashant in the room. He looked through the peephole. It was a member of his team, accompanied by Madhav, his childhood friend.

'Sir, I told you not to give this rookie the task of collecting the ransom money. He did not dump the original bag for a long time,' said the man with Madhav.

The boss frowned.

'Sarju, I did exactly as you told me. You know I have never done this kind of work before,' said Madhav, seeking forgiveness.

'Were you followed? Did you see any policemen on your trail?' asked Sarju.

'No, boss, I'm pretty sure about that. I managed to mingle with the crowd, even while being accompanied by this imbecile,' said the gang member looking derisively at Madhav.

'Okay, go rest,' said Sarju, taking the bag and dismissing them.

He didn't say so, but the kidnapping mastermind was worried.

* * *

Madhav went to the balcony of the room he was sharing with two of the kidnappers.

What have I landed myself in! I'm a simple person and my only passion is music. My greed has made me a criminal. My life is in danger too. Oh God, please get me out of this mess, he thought frantically.

After the encounter with the pizza delivery guy and IG Arjun, Madhav had been terrified. The only person he'd feel safe with, he'd thought, was his childhood friend, Sarju. Over the last few years he had grown quite envious of Sarju's luxe lifestyle, even though it was sponsored by criminal activities. Madhav had always looked up to Sarju. He had never been surprised by the way his friend evaded the police. After all, as the son of a police officer, Sarju knew all the tricks of the trade.

He took out his wallet and looked at the picture of his girlfriend, Rohini. She was his life. He wanted to marry her, but he needed money to give her a comfortable life. Rohini's father had clearly told Madhav that he'd get her married to someone else soon if Madhav did not have at least twenty lakh in his bank account within fifteen days.

He considered phoning Rohini but stopped himself in time. His mobile phone had led not one, but two people to his hideout. Arjun Kumar and the muscular attacker. He remembered his assailant's cold, steely eyes and a chill ran down his spine.

* * *

'Sir, sir, I have found the apartment,' said Subinspector Shivinder. He was brimming with excitement.

'Tell me,' asked Rakesh, trying to control his thrill. The job was still unfinished; it would be unwise to make any assumptions at this stage.

'Sir, I checked Atlanta apartments. The parking lot had a black Fortuner and a black BMW, though the two cars were parked on different levels,' Shivinder began.

'There are hundreds of BMWs and Fortuners in Jalandhar,' said Rakesh.

'Sir, I checked with the watchman. He said that the Fortuner had entered the building first, followed by the BMW, on the night of 30 May. He had never seen the BMW in the apartment complex before, though the Fortuner belongs to a resident.'

'That's a great lead! Let's go to the apartment,' said Rakesh.

Within ten minutes, Rakesh, his bodyguard and Shivinder were at Atlanta apartments. While Shivinder and Rakesh's bodyguard indulged in idle talk with the watchman, Rakesh went to the basement parking lot.

When he saw the BMW parked in a corner, he checked the number plate. There was no registration number.

He stepped towards the back of the car. There it was. A picture of Bajrang Bali on the rear windshield. Just like Prashant's car.

'Jai Bajrang Bali ki!' smiled Rakesh.

He immediately returned to the building's main level to meet the watchman.

'Who is the owner of the Fortuner?' asked Rakesh.

'Sir, I don't know. He does not look like a local. He rented the apartment only a few days ago.'

'How many people are in the apartment?' asked Rakesh.

'There must be seven or eight people at least, sir,' said the watchman. 'The caretaker takes up quite a number of milk packets every day. Even the groceries are in greater quantities than an average household.'

'This has to be the place,' said Rakesh, turning to Shivinder.

'Should we go in for the kill now?' asked Shivinder.

'No, no, Shivinder. We have to first check if the doctor and his wife are here. And we have to ascertain the situation inside. But call all the teams here immediately. Ask them to take position at all the exits and entries of this building,' said Rakesh.

'Shall we wait here for everyone to gather or meet them elsewhere?' asked Rakesh's bodyguard.

'Here, I have a plan,' said Rakesh.

* * *

The watchman rang the doorbell of the apartment on level nine, Shivinder by his side.

One of the kidnappers peeped through and saw the two of them. He opened the door reluctantly, but he had no option. He had to appear as normal as possible.

'Yes, what is it?' he asked gruffly.

'Sir, this is Shivinder sir from the RWA,' said the watchman.

'RWA?' asked the man.

'Residents Welfare Association. I have received a complaint about leakage from your house. The residents in the flat below yours are very upset about water dripping from their ceiling,' said Shivinder, entering the flat.

'Hey, where are you going?' protested the kidnapper. A few of his associates emerged from a room when they heard the commotion.

'I have to check all your bathrooms to find the exact location of the leakage,' said Shivinder as coolly as possible.

An experienced policeman, Shivinder did not miss the tension in the eyes of all the men standing in front of him. As he stepped forward, his path was blocked by another man.

'There is no leakage in any of our bathrooms. Please leave immediately,' said Sarju with conviction.

Shivinder looked at Sarju for a few moments.

'Okay, I will ask the building plumber to check the pipes again,' he said, and left with the watchman.

Five minutes later, Shivinder was with Rakesh.

'Sir, there are seven or eight people in the house. And their boss seems to be there too. At least, all the men looked at him to take the lead,' said Shivinder.

'What about the doctor couple?'

'Sir, I am absolutely sure that they are there. One room was latched from the outside and I saw two plates on the floor outside that door,' said Shivinder confidently.

'Okay, we're good to go. Let me call Arjun Sir. We will need our best men to extract the doctor and his wife,' said Rakesh.

* * *

Sarju did not have a good feeling. The RWA secretary Shivinder had looked too much in control of himself. He had had a clear air of authority about him as though he was used to a certain level of power. Sarju's DSP father had been like that.

The kidnapper looked out of the window of his apartment. There was a lot of activity in the compound. Somehow, the police have found us. I need to hide fast, he thought.

He quietly left the apartment. His men were dispensable. Even if they were arrested, they knew nothing real about him and could not tell the police anything useful. The police would never be able to catch him.

* * *

Madhav got up from his bed and lazily stepped on to the balcony. Still half asleep, he mopped his face with his handkerchief and casually glanced down.

What he saw totally shook him up. There was a crowd of security forces carrying assault rifles, dressed all in black. It was a scene straight from a Hollywood action flick.

Oh shit, they look like commandos. I'm going to be killed, Madhav thought, panic-stricken.

His mind was in a flux. How could he get out of this situation?

* * *

Watching the special task force prepare for the assault, I was startled when my phone rang suddenly.

'Unknown number,' said the message on the screen. If this is from the call centre of some credit card company, I'll kill them, I thought, answering the phone nevertheless. Before I could say a word, I heard a frightened voice at the other end.

'Sir, this is Madhav. I'm about to be arrested by the police in connection with the kidnapping of the doctor. Please ask the police to let me go,' Madhav blurted in almost one breath.

'How the hell are you involved in the kidnapping? And what makes you think I can help you? If you are arrested for the kidnapping, you'll go straight to the police station like all the others,' I said, stunned.

I was astounded. There I was in the middle of a major police operation and the one person who had already screwed up my happiness was about to jeopardize a rescue mission.

'Sir, you need to get me out. I can't go to jail. My girlfriend's father will marry her off to someone else. Use your authority to get me out. Do anything but get me out. Or else you'll be in trouble. I'll spill the beans about you and Madhushree,' said Madhav.

His voice shook.

'The police are about to enter the apartment. They will take away my phone. This might be the last call I make,' said Madhav.

* * *

Madhav inched towards the door, but before he could even open it, it burst open and three STF commandos entered the flat, their Heckler & Koch guns pointing straight at Madhav.

'I'm innocent! I was just a conduit. I was not involved in the kidnapping in any way,' Madhav shouted hysterically, raising his arms in surrender.

One of the commandos gestured him to stay quiet, raising his eyebrows to ask the location of the other people in the house.

Madhav rolled his eyes towards his left.

The commandos moved forward, covering each other as five more policemen entered the apartment. They stopped abruptly. They had heard a sound. The unmistakable sound of a pistol cocking.

The team leader gestured to his men to take position. They nodded in unison. While they appeared cool, they were tense. Not only were they in danger themselves, they could not afford to let any harm come to the doctor and his wife during a police operation.

The first commando pulled out a mirror from his pocket, moving it from side to side, tied to look into a room through its partly open door.

'Yes,' he murmured, catching a glimpse of the doctor couple sitting on the floor, their hands tied and their faces tense. The doctor was gazing at the door. Someone must be behind it, the commando thought. He put on his mask, the other commandos following suit, pulled out a smoke grenade from his explosives vest and pulled off its safety pin.

'One, two, three,' he signalled with his fingers and threw the grenade into the hall. As dense smoke billowed around them, the commandos rushed inside. The first man in the room fired at the door, bringing down a gun-weilding man. Another man standing next to the doctor and his wife was easily overpowered by the policemen while the commandos untied the couple and whisked them out.

A second team of commandos had already checked and cleared the other rooms. They gave each other a thumbs up and escorted the rescued couple down the stairs.

* * *

'Doctor Prashant, I am Arjun Kumar, the IGP, and this is SSP Vikram. I hope you are all right. And you, madam, all good?' I said.

'Yes, yes. Thank you, sir, thank you so much,' said Surbhi. The doctor was still too shocked to speak.

'Sir, one guy was killed in the gun battle. And these are the guys from the apartment. And this fellow keeps saying that he's not a kidnapper,' said the commando team leader pushing Madhav towards the SSP.

I looked at Madhav from a distance as I deliberately mingled with the crowd of policemen. I did not want him to see me and create a scene. As it was, I had been flabbergasted by his presence at the scene since he had phoned me. What was Madhav doing with these criminals? I had been trying to trace him through his cell phone but had failed since it had been continuously switched off.

'Are these the guys who were involved in the kidnapping?' Vikram asked Dr Prashant.

'Sir, I don't know. Really, I can't recall anything,' said the doctor, still a little dizzy.

'Sir, I will tell you. I know the main guy. Please let me go,' shouted Madhav.

'Where is he?' asked Vikram.

Madhav looked around, puzzled.

'He doesn't seem to be here,' he said. 'He seems to have vanished.'

* * *

'That bastard, Madhav! It's because of him that the kidnapping failed. And now I bet he's ratting me out,' fumed Sarju in his hiding place on the terrace.

He looked down at the melee of policemen and onlookers in the compound.

'I will find him and kill him with my bare hands.'

30

'A Powerful Man'

I was tense when I came back home.

'Why are you looking so lost? You've just rescued the kidnapped couple. You're the man of the hour!' said Charu.

'I'm just worried about Somveer. It's not a big problem, though,' I replied, happy to see that Charu still cared about me. She had been quite aloof for the last few days. But then I had been quiet too. I was worried that Madhav would blackmail me from the confines of a police lock-up!

'What's the problem? Tell me,' she said.

'Remember I'd told you about that dead girl in Somveer's hotel room? I don't know what he did, but he somehow managed to wriggle out of that disastrous situation at the time,' I said.

'What happened now?' asked Charu.

'All of a sudden, he got a call from a blackmailer,' I said tensely.

'I know he's your friend, but you're fretting too much,' said Charu disdainfully.

'Of course! I feel bad for him,' I said. 'Even though he's often stupid and reckless, he's very dear to me.'

'Somveer is such a wealthy guy. Why doesn't he just meet the blackmailer and pay up? After all, what good is all that money and power if you don't use it?' said Charu.

'Yes, perhaps,' I nodded.

'Though he's your friend and you care for him, if you ask me, a cheat like Somveer deserves to be punished,' said Charu switching on the TV. It was time for the next episode of *Crime Patrol*.

* * *

'Shit, Charu is absolutely right. What's the point of being in such a senior position in the police if I can't save my own neck?' I thought as I got in the car.

'Pratap, take me to Sector 26 police station,' I said.

The guard at the police station was surprised when a car with a flag and two stars drew up. He saluted smartly as the officer in charge rushed out to receive me. The IG of Jalandhar range did not often visit the smaller police stations and the entire police force in the room stood at attention.

'Jai Hind, sir. I am Inspector Kunwar Pratap,' said the station house officer nervously.

'Jai Hind, inspector. Congratulations on the successful recovery of the doctor couple. I just wanted to pat your men on their backs myself,' I said.

'Thank you so much, sir. It was all due to your guidance,' said the beaming SHO.

'The kidnapping has been making headlines for the last three or four days. It's you people who deserve the credit,' I said, smiling at the SHO's flattery.

'Yes, sir. It was a wonderful operation, and we recovered the couple safely,' said Kunwar proudly.

'Excellent work! Now tell me about the criminals involved. I'd like to know how these modern-day criminals plan their crimes, you know with all these technologies like WhatsApp and so on.'

'Why not speak to them yourself, sir? They are in the lock-up,' replied the inspector.

He escorted me to the lock-up where I saw a few men sitting on the floor staring aimlessly at the wall. But I was not interested in these people.

'Are these the only people who were arrested?' I inquired.

'There is one more. Some Madhav fellow. We have put him in a separate room. He is giving us vital clues about the mastermind behind this sensational kidnapping. He is going to turn an approver and his testimony will help us. Do you want to meet him?'

When I nodded, the inspector ushered me to the ante room of his chamber. Madhav was sitting in a corner, eating his lunch.

'Kunwar, I would like to speak to him in private to find out more about the kidnapping. Maybe he will be more open if I question him,' I said.

'Sure, sir,' said Kunwar, saluting me before he left the room.

Madhav stopped eating and looked me in the eye. He was no longer afraid of me. He knew he had the upper hand.

'Come on, sir. Get me out. If I don't get out now, my girlfriend will marry someone else in a few days. I have to go to her. It's a matter of life or death for me,' said Madhav.

'Don't be silly. I can't just order the inspector to release you,' I snapped.

'Then I will tell your secret,' threatened Madhav.

'What secret? What do you think you know?' I challenged him.

'I know about you and Madhushree,' he taunted. '*Aap logo ka lafda chal raha hai*, you are having an affair.'

My skin turned ashen.

'Even you can't hide an affair, sir,' Madhav said, coughing.

I remained speechless. My mind whirled with self-recrimination.

What have I done with my life! I've reduced myself to such a low that an orchestra singer is able to threaten an IG of police, I thought, cursing myself. I wanted to bang my head against the wall.

'*Koi nahi*, no problem, sir. *Ishq ki umar thodi hoti hai.* There is no particular age for romance,' Madhav continued to taunt me. He clearly enjoyed humiliating me.

I pulled myself together. I had come to the police station for one reason only: to extricate myself from the quagmire I was in. I could still take charge of my life.

'What about that message you sent from Murli Yadav's cell phone?' I asked.

'Arre, that night I was quite drunk. I drank to overcome my frustration. I was always the better singer, far better than Madhushree. But nobody noticed me, nobody cared for me. She got all the attention, all the applause just because she was good looking,' said Madhav, disgust in his eyes. He coughed again, harder this time. It seemed he was finding it difficult to breathe.

'And then you officers started coming to our orchestra parties and started swooning over Madhushree. But she was attracted to you. She made it so obvious. That woman dressed to please you, she sang looking at you. And I knew you were attracted to her too. It was in your eyes. I knew something was going on between the two of you. You had so much chemistry with her. No wonder you helped her get so many events and concerts.'

'So? So what could I do about it? I am a nobody compared to you. The only thing I could do was rob you of your mental peace. So I sent you that message. And I know it rattled you,' said Madhav.

The man was coughing badly now, clearly unwell.

'Why did you use Murli Yadav's phone to send the message?'

'I was drunk, but I still had the sense not to use my phone. Why would I want you to know that I sent the message? That's why I was so scared when you called me. I thought you would thrash me. You could finish me, you know. You're a powerful man,' said Madhav.

Powerful man? I have probably been the most powerless man on earth since 4 May, I thought bitterly. I wanted to hit Madhav hard, beat him to pulp. He had robbed me of my mental peace and scared the living daylights out of me.

'Okay, Madhav. Tell me what evidence you have,' I said as calmly as possible, controlling my anger.

'Ah sir, I have all the lovey-dovey chats you had with that lousy singer. And of course, I have a few of your mushy-mushy pictures and videos,' said Madhav, his eyes gleaming with derision.

He snorted. 'Your chats were quite romantic but I was expecting some X-rated stuff too,' he said.

I realized how easily Madhav could have accessed Madhushree's phone. After all, he was the one who shot her videos. I cursed Madhushree for not deleting our chats from her phone.

I could not take it any more. I sprang at him and grabbed his throat.

'I will kill you, you lowly, good-for-nothing singer,' I hissed, looking straight into Madhav's eyes.

'Sir, *haath hataiye*, remove your hands. You are suffocating me,' gasped Madhav, squirming in my grasp. But I was too livid to stop.

'Tell me about the video,' I snarled, tightening my grip on his throat.

'How do you know about the video?' asked Madhav. His skin was pale now, fear written large on his face. He coughed again, very badly.

'Tell me,' I said through gritted teeth. It took an effort not to shout, but I didn't want the SHO or any other person to hear what was going on. I was desperate to find the video and put an end to my ordeal.

'Sir, I should not have made the video . . . It was the biggest mistake of my life,' choked Madhav.

Suddenly, I had vomit all over my hands. I stepped back in horror as Madhav puked furiously. He was wheezing, thrashing about on the floor.

'Look for Ki . . . Ki . . . Kishore Kumar.' Madhav coughed furiously and passed out.

'Help, someone help,' I shouted at the top of my lungs. Oh my God, what have I done? I am an ass. Please, please God. Save him. I don't want another death on my hands, I thought, panic-stricken.

I tried to revive Madhav by patting his face and pressing his chest. His eyes had swollen, his skin was red. And then he slumped.

Madhav was dead.

I sat back, shocked. For the second time in ten days, I had a dead body in my arms.

The inspector and a number of constables slammed the door of the ante room open, stopping with shock when they saw Madhav's lifeless body soiled with his own vomit.

31

'What Is She Hiding from Me?'

'Sir, I am shocked. I was conducting raids to nab the remaining kidnappers when I heard about this incident in the police station and rushed here,' said the SSP.

'It's sheer bad luck, Vikram. I knew you were busy so I thought I would personally interrogate the criminals to get to the mastermind and close the investigation,' I said, barely able to look Vikram in the eye.

'It's quite intriguing, sir. That singer Madhushree is missing. And now another member of the same orchestra, this Madhav guy, is dead,' Vikram said pensively.

I was taken aback by the mention of Madhushree.

'What are you talking about? Who's Madhushree?' I asked, feigning ignorance.

'You don't know, sir? I thought you knew her. A few days ago, a person called Bagaria came to my office to lodge a missing person report for his wife, Madhushree. He told me you had helped Madhushree get a visa for Canada,' said Vikram.

'I don't recall any Madhushree, but maybe I helped her if somebody asked me to. Arre, you know that as senior police officers we meet so many people. And if one phone call can make a difference to someone's life, why not help? Gosh, we get so many requests and references every day,' I said, trying desperately to conceal my nervousness.

'Please don't worry, sir. I just mentioned her name in passing,' said Vikram, anxious that he might have upset me. When I realized this, I decided to take advantage of being Vikram's boss.

'So, what headway have you made in finding this Madhushree? Any leads?' I asked.

'No, sir. You know how busy we are, particularly with the impending elections. I told the cyber cell to track her phone, but it has been switched off since 4 May. Her last location was Chanakyapuri, Delhi.'

'We have so many other pressing issues right now. Maybe she's gone to Canada,' I said.

'Yes, sir, we will investigate Madhushree's disappearance later on,' said Vikram.

'Yeah, after the elections,' I said and paused before speaking again.

'Vikram, I'd be glad if you'd keep me out of the inquiry of Mahadv's death. For all practical purposes, I was not here, okay? You know I'm in the race for a very important post,' I said, a little embarrassed.

'Yes, sir. I know you are the front runner for the post of the CP. Don't worry. We will not show you in any records. I will ask the inspector not to mention your visit in the station diary too. I will ensure that nothing is leaked to the media,' Vikram said.

'Thanks so much, partner,' I replied. I knew Vikram would keep his word. After all, he owed me so much. I had saved his life.

'I need to catch the mastermind of this kidnapping. I'm sure he was involved in the abduction of the other businessmen too. With Madhav gone, we have lost a very important lead,' said Vikram.

'How did this Madhav fellow get so sick so suddenly? He was quite all right when I first saw him,' I said curiously.

'Yes, sir, we are also surprised. I have asked for a medical report. Let's see what it says,' replied Vikram.

'Okay, then I'll leave. It has been a bad night. Very unfortunate that an inmate died in front of me,' I said as I got into the car, mopping the sweat off my face.

* * *

To say that I was in shock was a huge understatement. Within a few days, a beautiful woman had died in my bed and a perfectly fine man had dropped dead in front of me. The same man had been attacked earlier and almost been killed at that time. Someone had wanted Madhav dead.

I mentally went through the conversation I had had with Madhav but could not remember anything worthwhile. Were the deaths of Madhushree and Madhav related? I was sure that Madhushree had been smothered to death. But Madhav had died right in front of me, without any apparent cause. No gunshot, no asphyxiation, no injury. What if someone wanted to kill him to frame me?

The only silver lining in this entire episode was that with Madhav's death, the blackmail was hopefully over.

'I have become quite heartless,' I thought. But my survival was the most important thing at this time. And I wasn't responsible for the deaths of either Madhav or Madhushree. Or was I?

I looked out of the window as Pratap drove me back home, my thoughts going wild. Is it not possible that somebody wants to harm me or end my chances of becoming the CP by creating a controversy just a few days before the meeting of the high-level committee?' I wondered. Or is this the work of some criminal who hates me enough to finish me off?'

Madhav had talked about a video. Even though the chance of blackmail had ended with his death, I could not rest till I learnt what the video was about.

*　*　*

Back home, I rushed inside, desperate for a hot shower to soothe my nerves. The last few days had been tumultuous in the extreme.

'How come you're home so early? And you could have knocked at least,' said Charu, disconnecting the phone. She had seemed quite surprised when I burst into the room.

'What do you mean? Do I need your permission before entering the bedroom?' I asked, annoyed.

The abrupt way she had disconnected the call had shown me that she had not wanted me to hear what she was saying. I wanted to ask her what that was about, but with so many dark secrets of my own, I simply did not have the courage to ask her anything.

What is she hiding from me? I wondered as I rummaged through the cupboard for fresh clothes. As I opened a drawer, my eyes fell on Charu's favourite cap. The one with the smart NSG monogram.

Huh! I thought, picking it up. I remembered the footage of the CCTV video I had seen at the St. Tropez Hotel. Madhushree's killer had worn a similar cap. What a coincidence!

*　*　*

I was in the middle of a meeting with Ravi when Vikram called.

'Sir, would you like to know how Madhav died? You will be very surprised. I have the postmortem report,' he said.

'Yeah, I'll come to the office immediately,' I said. I had to get to the bottom of the mystery of Madhav's death.

'Where are you going? We have a meeting with the IB in an hour, about the PM's visit,' complained Ravi.

'Some important work, Ravi. Please make an excuse for me,' I said.

'What can be more important than the PM's visit?' Ravi asked angrily. I did not reply, merely closing my briefcase and leaving.

* * *

Ravi was not amused. He had been in a bad mood for days now. His wife had created even more trouble for him, and he was certain that he had already lost the race for the post of CP.

'If only I had Arjun's life,' Ravi sighed, staring out of his glass cubicle. He had never felt more trapped.

32

Peanut Chikki

'Can you believe it? The cause of death is anaphylaxis, a severe reaction to nuts. Madhav died of an allergy that was triggered by eating peanuts,' said Vikram, showing me the postmortem report.

'According to the doctors, it is one of the most common causes of food-related death. I never knew eating peanuts could kill somebody,' he continued.

I read the PM report closely.

'Why would he eat peanuts if he was allergic to them?' I asked.

'We had given him food while he was in our custody, which contained peanuts in some form. Madhav ate it unknowingly,' surmised Vikram.

'Vikram could be right,' I thought. 'Or maybe someone killed him. It would be the easiest way to murder Madhav without raising suspicion. Maybe it was the mastermind of the kidnapping ring. His plan for ransom went for a toss because of Madhav.'

But then darker thoughts intruded. 'Could be someone wanting to frame me for the deaths of Madhushree and Madhav. Could it be the person who attacked Madhav and me that day? The pizza delivery man?'

I recalled the man's vampire-like eyes and shuddered.

'Trace the origin of the food, Vikram,' I said. 'Where did it come from?'

'Yes, sir, I've already done that,' he smiled. 'An NGO provides food to the jail and our police stations at a subsidized rate. That night the food came from the same NGO.'

'Then you must send a team there immediately,' I said.

'I've already sent a team to the NGO's office. The NGO is called Sarthak and its management seems quite clean,' said Vikram.

Where have I heard the name Sarthak before? I mused. It sounds so familiar.

'So there are no leads?' I said aloud.

'Not exactly, sir. The food was quite simple and had no traces of peanuts. It had been prepared in the kitchen of the NGO. But the sweet dish had been procured from outside. Rather, it was sent to the NGO as a donation,' said Vikram.

'Tell me more,' I said.

'The sweet dish was chikkis; they had peanuts finely grounded in it and looked like protein bars. This is not commonly found in our state so we weren't aware of what was in it,' Vikram replied.

'Who gave them to the NGO?' I asked.

'Sir, they were gifted by Charu Ma'am. Your wife.'

***

Perplexed by the strange coincidence of Charu's favourite chikkis finding their way to Madhav, I tried vainly to concentrate on my work. The meeting for the selection of the CP was to happen in just about a few days from now. I prayed that Madhushree's body would not be found till after the meeting. Or ever.

My PA entered the chamber and stood at attention.

'Sir, since you are about to be transferred out, we have organized your personal files. Madam's files too,' he said.

'Where am I being transferred, Gahlot?' I asked, irritated.

'Sir, it is on the grapevine that you'll be the next commissioner of police. You're the most deserving officer anyway, considering your impeccable reputation and spotless integrity,' Gahlot said ingratiatingly.

I scoffed.

'Enough of this flattery. Nobody knows who will become the CP. There are many factors in the selection. Sometimes, the selection is like the elimination round of a quiz, with the government getting rid of officers they don't want in that post. Anyway, since you've done the work, show me the files,' I replied.

'Here, sir. These are your IT returns. And these are Madam's returns. And here is some correspondence related to the reimbursement of expenses like travel, hotel stays and so on,' said Gahlot, showing me the files.

I glanced through the IT returns. There was nothing special to see as I had no source of income other than my salary. In fact, I had lost some money in the stock market and my CA had taken that into account.

Now I went through the travel files. I had claimed reimbursement for all my official tours except for the last one on the fateful day of 4 May. Though I had travelled to Delhi for a meeting, I had not claimed reimbursement for my expenses.

As if I have done a big service to the nation by this sacrifice or my conscience will clear because I forgo a few thousand rupees. Shame on me, I cursed myself silently.

I was about to close the file when I saw a printout of a flight ticket.

It was a ticket from Jalandhar to Delhi on 4 May. And it was in the name of Charu Kumar.

33

Chain of Evidence

'Oh, my God. Charu! Charu killed Madhushree!'

I couldn't believe what I was thinking, but that ticket . . . It was unarguable. Charu. Charu, my beloved wife, had killed Madhushree in revenge for my affair with the singer and was punishing me by making me the prime suspect if the murder was ever discovered. Tears filled my eyes, and I slipped on my sunglasses so Bhajan Singh and Pratap could not see me cry.

I spent the drive back home assembling the chain of evidence against Charu.

Charu had already been suspicious, thanks to the late-night WhatsApp messages I had received from Madhushree. She had found contraceptives in my shaving kit the day I had left for Delhi, which further corroborated her doubts. She must have taken the flight and arrived in Delhi at almost the same time as me. She had known, of course, where I would be staying, and she had also known that the owner of the St. Tropez would give me nothing less than the presidential suite. After all, she had stayed there with me just a few weeks earlier.

She must have waited for me to leave for my meeting and then gone to the suite. She must have confronted Madhushree about our affair and killed her in the heat of the moment. Given her mental condition because of her family's medical history, she must have been baying for Madhushree's blood.

My Glock had been lying on the bed. But Charu was too intelligent to have even thought about using it. To shoot a moving target at close quarters would mean having a steady hand, and she would have known that she could not have been precise when she was so angry. And she knew my gun didn't have a silencer. If she had used it, the sound of the shot would certainly have brought people running to the suite. Also, no shooting meant no stains anywhere and no danger of a bullet ricocheting. Charu was a fit, strong woman. She must have smothered Madhushree with a pillow.

And she was the one who had told me how to hide the body! I recalled how cold she had been about the whole thing. She loved reading and watching murder mysteries and suspense thrillers. What if she had turned fiction into reality with these murders? She had always been fascinated with the macabre.

After that, Charu sent the peanut chikki to the NGO that supplied the police station so that Madhav, who was in custody, would eat it. Thinking back, I recalled that Charu had known Madhav was allergic to peanuts. Getting Madhav to die in front of me could potentially finish my career and reputation.

It was all very clear now. Charu's family's violent history had finally taken over.

'Do not let your wife be emotionally disturbed. It can trigger a chemical imbalance in her brain and make her violent,' I remembered the doctor's warning.

My beautiful, loving wife was the cold-blooded killer of two people.

As my world fell apart, I could no longer hide my tears.

* * *

I burst into the room, utterly distraught.

'Charu, I know I have done, rather I was about to do something that would forever change our relationship. You had every right to be angry with me. But I simply can't believe that you could do something as drastic as this. Oh my love, what have you done!!' I said, weeping again.

Charu stopped playing her game of solitaire and looked at me quizzically.

'What the hell is wrong with you? What are you talking about?' she asked, surprised at my crying.

'If you had told me, or even scolded me for my mistake, things would have been totally different. I wish we had consulted a doctor. I shouldn't have taken that violent family history of yours lightly. At least you would not have killed two people,' I said.

'Are you out of your mind? What are you saying and why are you crying like a baby?' Charu snapped.

'How can you be so cold-blooded? You have killed two people and you are asking me to be normal,' I said, unable to control my emotions. 'I know you knew about my one-night stand with Madhushree. But this vengeance was beyond my imagination.'

My tears had almost stopped now. Even tear ducts have their limits.

'Yes, I knew about your dalliance with Madhushree but that doesn't mean I'd kill people,' Charu hissed. 'I really don't know what you are talking about.'

'Don't act smart, Charu. Did you not kill Madhushree?'

Charu got off the bed angrily. 'You've gone mad. I can't believe you think I actually killed someone. Is Madhushree dead?'

I looked into her eyes hesitatingly and instantly realized that Charu was telling the truth. I had been plain stupid to doubt my wife of over twenty years.

'Yes, Madhushree is dead. She was murdered,' I said, looking away. My eyes welled again. I was overcome with emotion. I had cheated on my wife who was totally devoted to me. While another promising life had ended in my bed.

Charu looked at me in utter shock. There was a deafening silence. After a few moments that felt like eternity, she finally spoke.

'Tell me what happened,' she said. Her voice was steady.

I stammered, trying to speak. But my throat had gone dry. I was totally at a loss for words. Where could I even begin the story of that night!

'Tell me, Arjun! Keeping quiet will not absolve you of your misdeeds,' said Charu.

I recalled that fateful night with great remorse and blurted out the whole story from my exchange of WhatsApp messages with Madhushree to burying her in Somveer's farmhouse to the attack on Madhav and to his death in police custody.

Charu listened carefully. When I finally ended the sordid story, she did not say a word.

I looked at her tearfully. She stood up, walked to me and raised her hand to slap me. I did not react. I deserved all her hatred. But at the last minute, she stopped.

'You are such a lousy person, Arjun, that you don't even deserve to be touched by me,' she said, her voice choked with rage.

I felt terrible but could say nothing. She returned to the bed, sat down and stared at the wall. Unable to take this silence any more, I drummed up my courage and asked, 'Who told you about my meeting with Madhushree? And what about this ticket for Delhi?' I said, pushing the printout of the ticket towards Charu.

When Charu spoke, it was in a tone of disgust, as though she could not believe that I still had the guts to talk to her, and about the Madhushree affair at that.

'Though I sensed Madhushree's infatuation with you, I didn't know about your meeting with her. Someone called me on WhatsApp and cautioned me to keep an eye on you. He told me you were having an affair with Madhushree,' she said. Her voice broke and her eyes welled with tears.

'When I saw the contraceptives in your shaving kit, I was really angry and I wanted to catch you red-handed. I asked your PA to get my ticket the moment you left, but then I cancelled my plans.'

'Why?' I asked sheepishly.

'Because I did not want to confirm my worst fear. I loved you and I love my children. I did not want my dream life to shatter.'

'And your suggestions to dump the body and talk to the blackmailer about the video?'

'I can't believe you're so dumb. I gave you all those ideas casually because I watch mystery movies and read crime books. How would I have known that you were actually with a dead body and that you were being blackmailed?'

'The NSG cap? The killer had the same one.'

'Come on, Arjun. That isn't the only NSG cap in the world. There must be a thousand of them at least. But the killer must certainly have some connection with the NSG.'

'Madhav died when he ate peanut chikkis supplied by an NGO to the police station. You had donated those peanut chikkis to the NGO,' I said, unable to muster up the courage to ask Charu a direct question.

She looked at me as if I was being stupid.

'Pure coincidence. No killer in the world could ensure that the victim ate the chikkis at exactly the time you entered the police station.'

She paused and drew a deep breath.

'If you thought I had murdered Madhushree, the best thing you could have done was check if I had actually boarded the flight. You're the IGP. The airline would have given you the details without an argument,' said Charu.

'Of course,' I thought, mentally slapping myself for my idiocy.

'God, your IQ must be zero. You believed so easily that your wife is capable of murdering people. You don't deserve to be the CP,' Charu said with utter contempt.

'Yes,' I nodded, ashamed.

'And you don't deserve to be my husband.'

She broke down finally, weeping inconsolably.

'How could you do it, Arjun? How could you even think of cheating on me? And then accusing me of being a murderer?'

'No. Believe me,' I said frantically. 'I strayed, I am not denying it. But I did not get physical with Madhushree. In fact, I was very upset with myself. That's why I stayed away from the hotel for so long after the meeting.'

'Oh, thank you. You did me a wonderful favour. My children and I are so grateful to you,' she said sarcastically, crying bitter tears.

I couldn't bear it. I couldn't bear to see my strong, bright Charu cry. I stepped forward to embrace her, but she flung herself away from me.

'Don't touch me. Don't even come close to me. I don't want to see you ever again. Please leave.'

'I know you're angry, Charu. In fact, that's an understatement. I can well imagine what must be going on in your mind . . .' I began, but Charu wouldn't let me continue.

'Arjun Kumar, you will never know what is going on in my heart because you are incapable of understanding anyone's feelings. You are the most selfish person I have ever come across,' she sobbed. 'Why did you do it? Why did you cheat on me?'

'I told you, I didn't do anything. I swear on you and the children,' I pleaded.

'Don't mention my children again, Arjun. You invited Madhushree to your hotel,' Charu snarled.

'It was a momentary lapse of judgement. I'm human. I'm sorry, so sorry. I made a mistake and I'll take any punishment,' I said in a low voice.

She stood up, glaring at me, and stormed out of the room.

'Thank God I didn't try to justify myself by saying that men are programmed to seek multiple partners,' I thought, shaken by the emotional storms of the day.

34

Criminal in Uniform

The Ghost examined his reflection in the mirror. He had always looked good in the uniform. It had been nine years since he had last worn it.

His life flashed before him.

He had been the best probationer in his batch of subinspectors, fighting fit, strong, agile and passionate about policing. He had grown up watching his father wear his uniform before going to the police station for his duty. By the time his father came home every day, he was usually asleep, and when he woke up, his father was either gone or asleep. His father had seldom been present at family functions and had never been around for festivals. Like almost every policeman in the country, he had been on duty for Holi, Eid, Diwali, Christmas, New Year. He had never known how his family really lived or how his son had grown up in his absence.

He had been tired of his father's honesty too, for his family had lived a very frugal life. There had been no toys, no new clothes, nothing to make his life exciting in any way. Though the Ghost had hated his father for this, he had also been enamoured with the police uniform and the power it brought with it. But when his ambition of becoming a policeman had finally come true, he had promised himself that he would always be by the side of his family, his children, whenever they needed him. He wouldn't be like his father.

The Ghost had been selected as a subinspector in the Punjab police force at a young age. He had started off as a typical rookie, but due to his expert sharpshooting skills and exceptional bravado, his seniors had soon picked him for a special team called the Tiger Squad.

The Tiger Squad's job had been to hunt down criminals. Within days of the squad's formation, it had become the nemesis of the underworld. Dons had found themselves losing men faster than the Indian team would lose wickets for the 36 they would make in Australia in 2020.

The Tiger Squad became too powerful. Like most 'encounter specialists', the members of the squad became corrupt. Soon, they were bypassing their direct bosses, the senior police officers, and taking orders from politicians and a few unscrupulous police officers. Some of them even started taking on contracts from businessmen to bump off their rivals. It was all easy money.

The Ghost had resisted the temptation to take contracts for quite a while, for he still followed his father's ideals, but destiny had had other plans for him. One day, while training at the NSG, he had coughed up some blood. At first, he had thought it must have been the result of the extreme physical stress of the training, but when the blood in his sputum became regular, he had gone to a doctor.

The doctor at the NSG had referred him to AIIMS, where the Ghost had been diagnosed with lung cancer.

'If you go for chemotherapy and take the best medical treatment available, you might live for a few years longer,' the doctor had told him.

The Ghost had been shattered.

He had had a very difficult childhood. Now, he was working with the utmost honesty and dedication. Yet the

Gods were punishing him. His entire world had come crashing down.

For a few days, he had been filled with self pity. He had not told his family about the cancer, because he had not wanted to worry them. But he had wanted to provide for their future, so that they would not be impoverished without him. His meagre government salary was already insufficient for the mortgage of their house and other expenses. His pension wouldn't make things better either.

If the Gods are so cruel to me, then why should I care? he had thought, glaring at the green NSG cap that he had been awarded due to his outstanding performance during the training. I cannot let my family suffer the way I suffered because of my father's indifference.

Within days, he became just like the other members of the Tiger Squad. Even as he had continued to work for the police, he had also started working as a hitman, selling his services to politicians, corporations and other desperate or evil people. As a mercenary, he had carried out a number of assassinations and been paid very well for them. He had learnt to murder without remorse. He had become a criminal in uniform, the very antithesis of what he had aspired to be when he had joined the police.

While amassing money for his family's future, he had continued his treatment for cancer. And to his and his doctor's great surprise, the treatment had worked. The Ghost no longer faced a death sentence. His cancer had gone into remission.

'Your prognosis is quite good. Your health is improving,' the doctor had said, looking at his report. The Ghost had been delighted. Finally safe, he could break the news to his family. He had run home, excited. And then, once again, his world had come crashing down.

As he had entered the house, calling for his wife, she had emerged from the bedroom, holding a wad of notes.

'What is this? Where did you get this money from?' she had asked angrily.

'Where did you find this?' a shell-shocked Ghost had asked.

'It was hidden under the sink. The plumber gave me this bag when he came to repair the sink,' his wife had replied.

'Rachna, let me explain,' he had said.

'Don't you explain anything. I'm sure this is bribe money or your "hafta" from bars and hotels. I know your mates in the police indulge in illegal activities.'

'No, Rachna, it is not that. It is money I earned for my skills, my expertise. I have earned it, I deserve this money,' the Ghost had pleaded.

'Skills? What skills? You are not a scientist to have invented something or a software engineer with a new computer programme. This is illegal money,' Rachna had said.

'I did it for you, for our son. We deserve a good life. I do not want my family to suffer the way I did as a child.'

Rachna had dragged their three-year-old son in front of him.

'Beta, tell me, did you ask Papa for money?' she had asked the boy affectionately. The bewildered child had just clutched his mother's *pallu*, not saying a word.

'See, he doesn't even understand the meaning of money. Don't justify your sins by saying you are doing it for us. You are doing it for yourself,' Rachna had said, breaking down.

The Ghost had quietly stepped out of the house, numb with pain. She will forgive me soon. She knows I love her and our son more than my life. They mean everything to me. Things will be all right soon, he had thought, trying to rally his spirits.

But the next few days had been even worse.

* * *

The entire mohalla had gathered outside his house as the CID team searched the premises, digging into every nook and cranny.

'Sir, these are the bundles of notes we found near the sink. And this is a pistol from behind the fridge,' a policeman had said.

'Good, send the pistol to the forensic lab. The ballistics expert will tell us if it had been used to shoot the industrialist Rajan Parekh, though I am quite sure of it,' the leader of the team, a DSP, had replied.

After a thorough search of the house and scrutiny of his accounts, the CID team had little doubt about the course of action.

'You are arrested for killing Rajan Parekh. You also have to explain the money found in your house and why your bank passbooks show more money than could come from your known source of income,' the DSP had said, handcuffing the Ghost.

Rachna had been horrified, both by the raid on her house and the fact that her husband had been accused of murder. With one swift step, she had snatched the pistol from the policeman and shot at her son, missing him by inches. Then she had put the gun to her head but had been overpowered by the policemen in the nick of time.

As the policemen had restrained Rachna, she had looked at her husband with hatred in her eyes, watching as he was marched out of his house to the waiting police vehicle. Turning for a last look at his formerly happy home, he had vowed never to touch a pistol again because guns had been the root cause of the destruction of his life.

The Ghost had been suspended from service the same day. His name had been splashed everywhere, on the front pages of newspapers, on TV channels and on social media.

'Encounter Specialist Turned Contract Killer Arrested for Industrialist Murder,' the headlines had screamed.

When he had returned home a few months later, released on parole, Rachna had refused to see him or let him anywhere near his son. And he had become a pariah in his department. His colleagues and bosses had deserted him. The politicians he had protected with his life had refused to even meet him.

'Oh God, I wish the cancer had not been cured,' he had cursed, feeling like an outcast. He had cried bitterly on returning to jail.

'Show your face here only when you are absolved of all the charges. Redeem our honour!'

Rachna's last words to him as she had thrown him out of their house had stuck in his mind.

35

The Mystery Policeman

I went for a run in the park near the secretariat tennis courts but gave up after just half a round. My mind refused to focus on anything but my crumbling life.

'Come on, don't be a quitter. You've been a mentally and emotionally strong person throughout your life,' I tried to boost my spirits.

Walking back to the office, I thought through everything that had happened in the last few days, trying to weigh the positives and the negatives.

Madhushree's body is hidden and should remain so for the next few days at least, I began. Maybe I'll shift it somewhere else and burn it. But I'll have to wait for the right opportunity. Somveer won't be coming back to India for the next six months, thanks to his love for London. Nobody will go to the farmhouse in Somveer's absence. And Bhola must be too piss-drunk, finishing all those bottles of premium whisky, to dig up anything.'

So that was a positive.

'The CCTV footage will be overwritten soon. Then there will be no records of Madhushree meeting me. Madhav the blackmailer is dead.'

Another two positives.

'Over time, Charu will forgive me. She has no option. She loves me and the children too much. Yes, she will also hate me for my mistake for the rest of our lives, but I guess

I can live with that,' I analysed, the way I was trained to as a cop.

Yet another positive. I was safe.

'Oh no, I'm not!' I realized, crossing the road and entering the building, nodding to the constables who saluted me. 'No. There's a killer out there somewhere. Someone who killed Madhushree and someone who tried to kill Madhav.'

I sank into my seat in my chamber and switched on the red light. I needed to work this out properly.

Then I thought about Madhushree and Madhav's cell phones. I wasn't sure if Madhushree had deleted all my messages from her phone. I didn't find Madhushree's phone in the hotel room. Did the killer take her phone? And why did the attacker want Madhav's phone? What was the video Madhav was talking about?

'There's a link between their cell phones and their murders,' I concluded. 'And I am somehow linked to them. Someone was desperate to get their cell phones, so I need to find them too and retrieve the video. Before anyone else.'

I sat back and picked up my phone.

* * *

'Hello, Kunwar? This is Arjun.'

'Jai Hind, sir!' replied Inspector Kunwar.

'I wanted to congratulate you again on your stellar success. What an operation it was! Officers like you make the police department very proud.'

'Sir, it's all thanks to your guidance. I am very happy that such a senior and distinguished officer as you has called me,' Kunwar flattered.

'I thought I might come over and have a cup of tea with you.'

'Sure, sir, it will be my privilege.'

The inspector could not believe he was about to have tea with the future commissioner of police. Here he was, at the bottom of the food chain, and yet he was about to have a private session with the man at the very top.

* * *

'Jai Hind, sir, welcome,' said Inspector Kunwar, receiving me at the entrance of the police station.

'I'm sorry I could not talk to you properly that day,' I said.

'Yes, sir, that was quite unfortunate. A custodial death is a policeman's worst nightmare.'

'How are things now?'

'The report should be in our favour, sir. The magistrate noted that there were no external injuries on the man's body and the postmortem report also clearly stated that he died due to anaphylaxis.'

'How is the police station so deserted?' I asked, perplexed. On my way to the inspector's cabin, I had seen just three or four policemen around.

'Oh, sir, most of my men are on duty for an election rally,' replied Kunwar.

'Yeah, yeah, the elections are around the corner. Even the PM is scheduled to visit. We have to ensure the safety and security of all the candidates,' I nodded.

'Yes, sir, we will be on our toes for quite some time,' said the inspector.

'Yes, inspector, that is the life of the policeman. By the way, since I'm here, I'd like to see Madhav's cell phone,' I said.

'Sir, Madahav's cell phone?' asked Inspector Kunwar.

'Yes, to check for clues. Maybe we can learn more about the kidnapping mastermind through Madhav's phone,' I said.

'Oh, yes! But it's a very normal, ordinary smartphone. No encryption, no security. We asked our mobile experts to unlock it to check for clues, but there was nothing useful,' said the inspector.

'Nevertheless, I'd like to see it,' I said authoritatively.

The inspector ceased to argue and called for the phone to be brought from the *malkhana*, repository. When I asked him to leave me alone with it for some time, he looked confused and reluctant to move but eventually stepped out.

As I turned the cell phone over, examining it, I felt my heart beat faster. Perhaps it had the video that the attacker had been after. There was also a 1 per cent chance that it had a video related to Madhushree and me.

I switched on the phone and began checking the albums.

* * *

'Jai Hind, sir,' saluted the guard at the entrance of the police station.

'Jai Hind,' replied the well-built police officer, striding into the station and looking for the room of the officer in charge. As a former policeman, the Ghost knew that was where police officers usually kept important evidence or gadgets like cell phones. With very few policemen on the premises, the Ghost found it easy to move around.

'Inspector Kunwar', read the nameplate on the door.

The Ghost peered inside and saw Arjun Kumar in the SHO's chair. He paled and seethed with rage, but then he saw the inspector walking towards his cabin. This is no time to do anything reckless, he thought, moving away before the inspector could see an unknown policeman in the station and grow suspicious.

* * *

I checked the albums. Nothing.

I checked all the other folders and media storage files. Nothing again. 'Why is there nothing on the cell phone,' I wondered, perplexed. Should I take it with me on some pretext? Maybe I'll ask an expert if there are some hidden videos in thephone.

I examined the albums again, glancing up when the door opened. A giant of an officer stuck his head inside the room and instantly withdrew.

'Must be looking for Kunwar,' I thought absently. 'But why does he seem familiar?'

I set the cell phone down for a second, wondering if I had really seen those dead, emotionless eyes before, then returned to the problem at hand.

I could pull rank on Kunwar and take the phone with me. But he would certainly tell Vikram about it, and that I could not afford. I had persuaded Vikram to keep my name out of the inquiry in relation to the custodial death, but if I took away the cell phone, he would definitely be suspicious. Could I smuggle it out after replacing it with a similar cell phone?

There was a knock at the door. 'Excuse me, sir, some tea for you,' the inspector said with a smile.

I did not return his smile. Kunwar looked at the cell phone in my hands.

'Sir, what is so special about this phone?' he burst out. 'Even other senior officers have been interested in its contents.'

'Really? Who?' I asked.

'Our cadre senior, IPS Ravi Bhushan Sir. He called twice to find out if we had found any video or picture in the phone that could help with the investigation,' replied Kunwar.

I was surprised. 'Why is Ravi interested in Madhav's cell phone? Is he also investigating the kidnapping case? Or is he interested in the mysterious death of Madhav?' I wondered.

I drank my tea and made some desultory conversation with the inspector before returning to my car.

As the driver took Bhajan Singh and me back to the office, I stared out of the window pensively. I was very disappointed that I had not found anything on the phone.

At the same time, I was relieved that no one in the police had discovered any video or chat that incriminated me. But a video did exist. Madhav had hinted about it. And I needed to find it.

Who was that man? I thought again, remembering the dead eyes of the policeman who had been looking for the inspector.

Suddenly it struck me! He was the same man who had attacked Madhav and me just a few days earlier. And here he was again. Of course! He had gone to the police station for Madhav's cell phone.

'Pratap, take me to the office of Ravi Bhushan Saheb,' I said.

***

Entering Ravi's office building, I saw his back to the glass walls of his chamber as he talked to someone on his cell phone. The red light outside his door was on.

'He's busy. Okay, I'll wait,' I thought. And then suddenly I realized why there had been no video on Madhav's cell phone.

'What a fool I am! This must have been a new phone! Madhav must have understood that he was being traced via his cell phone so he must have bought a new phone and SIM card. And he must have either switched off his old phone or destroyed it and transferred the video to a pen drive or a laptop or something!'

I looked up to see if Ravi was free just as he turned around. He waved to me to come in and disconnected his call.

As I entered his chamber, my phone buzzed. It was Charu.

I gestured to Ravi to wait and went to a corner to talk.

'Yes, Charu,' I said.

I was quite surprised as it was after a long time that she had called me.

'My secret informant called again. He told me that you had had a fling with Madhushree and I should not trust you,' she said.

'Did you recognize his voice, by any chance?' I asked.

'No, it was a little muffed. But it was strangely familiar,' Charu replied. 'I called you the moment he disconnected.'

'Okay, Charu, I've got to go. We'll talk when I come home,' I said.

'The second I hang up, you get a call,' laughed Ravi. 'Long time, buddy, long time! Why were you waiting outside? You could have come in.'

'I saw the red light so I thought you needed some privacy. How are things?' I asked.

'The same as always. You do the same kind of work as a police officer whether you are an ASP or a DGP,' he said, fiddling with his phone.

'Is that a new phone? It looks quite ordinary. In fact, it doesn't even seem like a smartphone,' I said.

'Oh, this piece of crap? This is a basic smartphone I use for secret phone calls to my sources. I can buy only these cheap Chinese phones with my secret service fund. I tell you, our SS fund is quite a pittance nowadays,' Ravi said sheepishly, putting the phone in his drawer. 'So, what brings you here?' he asked.

'Nothing, I was just wondering how Madhav died. He was quite a young fellow with a promising career,' I said.

'Yes, it was so unfortunate, dying by peanut allergy of all things! Everybody is not as lucky as Madhushree. She found a benefactor in you and today she is in a different world,' said Ravi with a smile.

I was not amused but controlled my emotions and carried on some small talk with Ravi, deliberately avoiding more questions about Madhav and his phone in case he fired a salvo of questions at me too. There was no way I could tell Ravi that I was desperate to get Madhav's phone so I could prevent being implicated in Madhushree's murder.

36

'Is He Really Happy for Me?'

Could Ravi have been behind all these events of the last few days? I wondered on my way home. 'But he's been a friend for years! We've been best buddies since we began preparing for the civil services exams!'

Ravi and I had trained together at the NPA as well. Then, due to our different postings, we had been in touch less frequently, but we had revived our friendship over the last few years when we were posted together at Punjab HQ. He was one of my most trustworthy friends, who had always encouraged me to do my best. He had supported me when I was down in the dumps while preparing for the UPSC exams, and now, he was happy that I had a strong chance of becoming the CP.

But was he really happy for me?

It is impossible to decipher the human mind. People can become greedy for even the smallest things. During the course of my career, I had seen quite a few of my colleagues conspiring against officers who were in line to become DGPs. These men would pull out skeletons from closets at inopportune moments, leaving many candidates certain of an appointment cruelly stranded at their last post. All because of well-hidden jealousy.

What am I thinking! Just yesterday I thought Charu was framing me for Madhushree's murder, now I'm imagining Ravi is out to get me! Nah, I'm the only one hiding a secret. The secret of a dead body, I thought.

Disappointed with not finding the video, I returned home to be even more irked when Charu ignored me as she sat in the bedroom playing solitaire.

I missed the smile she would have on the days I returned from work earlier than usual. I knew I deserved every possible punishment because I had been a cheat, I had broken the trust of a woman who had given up everything for our marriage. I wished there was something I could do to have her forgive me.

I sat quietly at the edge of the bed.

After a few minutes, Charu finally spoke.

'Why are you looking so sad?'

I perked up. She still loved me. Still cared for me. She was the only one who knew what I was thinking just by looking in my eyes.

'I went to the police station today to see if I could find a video on Madhav's phone, but there was nothing,' I said, explaining why it was important. 'Obviously Madhav switched off or destroyed his original phone so he could not be traced any more,' I concluded, explaining the nuances of mobile tracking to Charu.

'Don't mansplain,' she snapped. 'I hate it. I know all about these things.'

She was right. She understood all the technicalities and had also helped me in my investigations in the past with just her common sense.

'He was probably too scared to keep that old cell phone knowing that both you and the attacker had tracked him with it, so he must have destroyed both the phone and the SIM card. That's what I would have done, at least. You see this kind of thing in any suspense movie,' she said casually.

She was absolutely right. I would have done the same thing too.

'Would he have destroyed that video too?' I asked.

'Don't be silly. Why destroy the video? It was his passport to money and freedom. He must certainly have kept a copy of the video somewhere,' said Charu, pausing to shuffle her cards.

She looked up. 'Destroying the video would not make any difference to the threat on his life. Keeping it would be his only guarantee of safety.'

She is so damn intelligent. How did I think I could fool her by lying about my affair, I admitted to myself.

'Madhav was an ordinary person, who would not be very capable with modern technology. So it's unlikely that he uploaded the video to the cloud or anything like that. What could he have done with it? Where could it be?' I asked.

'You're right. He must have copied the video on his laptop, but even that isn't for certain. Think about how he recorded the video in the first place. Or did he get it from someone else?' said Charu.

'No, I don't think he got the video from someone else. If that was the case, someone else would have been attacked, not Madhav. And he would have told me something when I met him in the lock-up,' I said.

'What did he say?' asked Charu.

'Nothing in particular, but it was obvious from his conversation that he had made a video for sure. And then he started vomiting. His voice slurred, so there was nothing coherent,' I said, recalling how Madhav had died right in front of me.

'I think you should look in his house. There is a small chance that his laptop is still there. Maybe he has hidden the video on his laptop.'

'Okay, that makes sense. But how will I log into his laptop? Obviously. I don't know his password.'

'First, just get the laptop. You can try opening it later,' said Charu.

'You're right. Yes. I can get a professional hacker to open the laptop and extract the files from it later,' I said.

I stood up, re-energized after my talk with Charu. Her sharp intellect and common sense were spot on, every time.

'How did you not know about my fling with Madhushree, that I had some juvenile WhatsApp chats with her?' I asked, embarrassed with myself.

'Don't be foolish. I knew. But I had faith.'

'In me?'

'No, not in you. I had faith in myself,' replied Charu.

37

'I Need to Absolve Myself'

I needed to go to Madhav's house.

I dialled Yadav, the drummer.

'Yadav, this is Arjun Kumar. Yes, *pranam*. Can I have Madhav's address please?' I seem to have misplaced it.' I said, cursing myself for being so casual.

'Yes, sir, right away. Though his house is vacant now, I think. A few of his relatives might come in a few days to collect his things. It was unfortunate to lose such a talented member of our orchestra,' said Yadav.

Within seconds, I had Madhav's address on my mobile phone.

* * *

'Bhajan, you stay here. I have to meet someone privately,' I said, getting out of the car.

I was a bit worried about my safety having been attacked the last time I met Madhav, but I couldn't take Bhajan with me. Not when I was about to break into Madhav's house. I saw the nameplate on the door—Madhav Charan—and a big lock.

Should I really break in? I wondered. It's absolutely illegal. But . . . come on. I've buried the dead body of a woman with whom I was about to have a one-night stand! I can hardly talk about legal and illegal. I don't have an option. I have to find the video and unearth the reason for Madhushree's murder. She needs justice and I need to absolve myself.'

I looked around me. There was nobody. Quickly, I opened the lock with a standard pin trick that I had learnt during my IIT days. Thank heavens lower middle-class people still had simple locks, unlike the complicated ones in high-end apartments. And of course, there was no CCTV around Madhav's modest house.

Stale air filled my nostrils as I entered the flat. I exhaled from my mouth and looked around me, deciding where I should begin my search for Madhav's cell phone and laptop.

This small two-BHK apartment shouldn't take long to search. Thankfully, there wasn't much furniture either, I suppose Madhav couldn't afford much.

I began with his cupboard, rummaging through the clothes. Then I went from room to room, opening cabinets and examining everything big enough to hold a pen drive, cell phone or laptop, including the kitchen utensils, the harmonium and even the dustbin.

No pen drive. No mobile phone. No laptop.

Mopping the sweat on my forehead, I opened the bathroom door. The smell that emerged was exceedingly foul and pungent, enough to make me gag but I checked under the washbasin and the cistern, even going so far as to lift the dirty soap case. Disappointed, I emerged into the sitting room only to glimpse a tall silhouette from the corner of my eye.

It was the same man who had attacked me and Madhav. The man who had been at the police station. Was this man some kind of a ghost? He was everywhere yet vanished into nothing in an instant.

This time I was in real danger. He had obviously come for the video, and he knew I was here for it too. I was the only one standing between him and the video now.

He threw a punch and I ducked instinctively, blocking the punch with my elbow.

Unsurprised by my resistance this time, he grabbed my throat and pushed me hard against the wall, choking me.

But I pushed against the wall with my feet, hitting my head against his nose. No matter how strong or muscular a man may be, his eyes, nose and groin are always vulnerable.

The intruder reeled back, pulling me along with him, as he crashed on to a glass table causing it to shatter to pieces. Before I could get up, he was at my throat again.

My vision blurring, I flailed my arms frantically, seeking a piece of glass. As my fingers closed over a sharp shard, I gathered my remaining strength and stabbed him with it in the eye.

He let go of me with a shriek, clutching his face. Without wasting a moment, I took out my phone and called my bodyguard.

'Bhajan, Bhajan, come quickly,' I shouted into the cell phone even before the call connected.

The intruder had already got up to attack me again— my God, even a bleeding eye was not enough to stop him— but the moment he heard Bhajan's voice answering me over the phone, he ran out of the house and vanished.

'You called, sir? This is Bhajan,' said Bhajan Singh.

'It's all right. There's nothing. I called you by mistake. Wait for me near the car,' I said, cutting the call as I slowly got up. I took a deep breath and surveyed the mess around me. Much of Madhav's paltry furniture was broken in bits and scattered everywhere.

I picked up the guitar lying on the floor. It was almost broken in two while I had scuffled with the intruder. I patted it as though it had been a live creature and was about to put it down when I heard a sound from inside its cavity.

Removing the strings, I broke open the cavity. There was a small case taped to the side of the interior. On the cover was a picture of the Kishore Kumar film *Badhti Ka Naam Dadhi*. Hadn't Madhav mentioned Kishore Kumar while taking his last breath? I scrambled to open the case, a feeling of elation coursing through me when I saw what was inside—the Kishore Kumar pen drive that Madhav had cherished more than anything.

Did he transfer the video to this pen drive? Is that why he hid it? My mind was racing. I picked it up and left the house, the lock clicking as I pulled the door.

I got into the car quietly as Bhajan stood by the door.

'This is the third time in the last few days that I have seen this man. On two occasions he even attacked me,' I thought about the huge guy, looking at the pen drive in my hand.

When we stopped at a signal on the main road, Bhajan spoke.

'Sir, I was surprised to see Atulkar Sir today. It's been years since anyone saw him!'

I made an un-interested sound, hoping the conversation would die down but Bhajan continued.

'I waved to him but he ignored me and disappeared.'

'Bhajan, why are you telling me about some Atulkar fellow? I'm not interested,' I said, irritated now.

'Sorry, sir. But Atulkar Sir was one of the most daring police officers in the city before he was sent to jail. After he came out, he vanished without a trace. Today, I suddenly saw him out of the blue. He was bleeding profusely from his head, as if somebody had cut him with a knife,' said Bhajan.

'What did you say?' I said, putting down the pen drive and leaning forward, my heart beating fast at the possibility of finally identifying my mysterious attacker. 'Can you describe him? His height? His build?'

'He is a giant, sir! He is 6'2" tall and has biceps the size of a man's thighs,' replied Bhajan.

I had no doubt that I had found my man.

'How can I find out more about him? This Atulkar fellow seems quite interesting,' I said casually.

'Sir, you can ask Ravi Bhushan Sir. He was the one who recruited Atulkar for the crack anti-crime unit called Tiger Squad,' said Bhajan.

37

Maharaj Saheb

When I got home, I went straight to the bedroom, shut the door and put the pen drive into my laptop.

Clicking on the first visible file, my heart pounding furiously as the screen lit up with rare footage of Kishore Kumar singing in a studio. On any ordinary day, I would have been ecstatic. The personal collection of my favourite singer, the legendary Kishore Kumar, was in my hands!

How I had envied Madhav at the club that day. But right now, Kishore Kumar was not on my mind. I watched the videos for a good half an hour but found nothing but songs. My heart sank. I had no hope now. I had done everything I could to find the mysterious video, but I had failed.

I sat back and resigned myself to my fate.

'Chalo, at least I'll see and hear more of Kishore's rare songs.'

I took a sip of water and continued to watch the video as I looked through the files on the pen drive. Suddenly, the great Kishore Kumar vanished from the screen, replaced by another figure. It was Madhushree, as beautiful as always. She was on a large terrace, singing Lata songs and dancing happily. Then, another voice joined hers. It was Madhav's. It was obvious Madhav was making a video of Madhushree at some kind of a farmhouse.

After a few minutes of singing, Madhushree stood by the parapet, the light falling on her face, making it even more radiant. I smiled, lovely memories of my chats with her filling my head.

After a few seconds of focusing on Madhushree, Madhav moved the camera to a panoramic view. There were a few rooms, a large terrace and a garden. On one corner of the terrace a name was embossed in large letters. Mehta Farms. The video ended abruptly.

Huh? What happened? What was so special about this ordinary video that Madhav would store it along with rare and priceless footage of Kishore Kumar?

I played the clip again. That was when I saw it. The camera had caught some movement behind Madhushree. I paused the video and zoomed in. Now I saw some people carrying a figure in their arms. Over the next few stills, I could see the figure being taken down some stairs to an underground chamber next to a swimming pool. The pictures were very hazy. Madhav's video camera must not have had a very high resolution.

'When did Madhushree and Madhav go to Mehta Farms?' I wondered. I cast my mind back and then remembered Madhushree telling me she had gone there one evening to perform satsang for the Maharaj.

'And Ravi Bhushan had invited her on behalf of the Maharaj.'

* * *

There was a loud knock on the door.

'Why did you shut the door?' asked Charu as she entered.

'I needed some privacy to watch the video I found on Madhav's pen drive. I think it's related to Madhushree's murder somehow,' I said excitedly, explaining the turn of events and the attack on me.

'Were you attacked again? Are you hurt?' asked a worried Charu, caressing my face.

Though I had narrowly missed being killed, I thanked my attacker for the love I got from Charu.

'No, no. I'm fine. Thank you,' I said happily.

She dropped her hand. 'Show me the clip.' She had become cold again.

I played the video for Charu, watching as she looked on intently.

'Of course this is the video your attacker was looking for,' said Charu.

'How are you so sure?' I asked.

'Common sense. Why would he spoil his priceless Kishore Kumar pen drive by adding this clip unless it was something even more valuable? And you can clearly see suspicious movement in the background. Maybe Madhav saw something that caught his eye, but the recording was blurred because of poor lighting and a cheap camera.'

She watched the video again.

'Do you remember when Madhushree and Madhav went for the satsang?' asked Charu.

'It won't be difficult to find out. I'll just ask Ravi. He had asked Madhushree to perform at Maharaj's satsang,' I replied.

'Okay, do it,' said Charu.

'On second thought, I shouldn't call him. He is a suspect now,' I said, sitting down. 'The guy who attacked me today had once been a key member of a squad headed by Ravi himself. And Ravi also called Vikram a number of times to find out the developments in the investigation of Madhav's death. These events can't be purely coincidental. Ravi is a devout follower of Maharaj. He won't listen to anything against the God-man. It'll be pointless to ask him anything related to Maharaj.'

'Hmm. Yes, you're right,' said Charu.

'I know someone else who will help us.'

I picked up my phone and called Yadav, the drummer.

'Yadav, this is IG Arjun. Do you remember when Madhushree and Madhav went to Maharaj's satsang?' I asked.

'Sir, it was 1 May. Our orchestra had to cancel the event at the Rotary Club because neither of our lead singers was available,' said Yadav.

I disconnected the call and thought for a few moments.

'Arjun, do you remember the news around April end?' asked Charu.

'What news?' I asked.

'Arre, a couple from Ludhiana had sent their daughter to Maharaj for some ceremony. The girl never came back. Though her parents accused Maharaj of foul play, no action was taken against him,' said Charu.

'I really don't remember this,' I said.

'It didn't make it to any newspaper or TV channel, just an obscure YouTube channel that I stumbled upon. Even that channel had no updates. Maharaj is too powerful for simple people like that Ludhiana couple,' said Charu.

'What are you trying to say? What connection does that have with the video?'

'I have a feeling that the girl was murdered in the ashram. And it is her being carried in the video.'

I hadn't thought of this. 'You might be right. The ashram doesn't have a good reputation. All kinds of illicit activities take place there. I have often heard complaints of Maharaj's insatiable appetite for young women. He was even accused of trafficking them. And of course, it is an open secret that Maharaj's cult is involved in drug smuggling.'

'Let's see what we can find about the girl who went missing from the ashram,' said Charu, switching to the browser on the laptop.

Less than an instant later, only two links related to the missing girl appeared on the screen.

'Gosh, though this Google thing is better than the newspapers. There is such little information here,' I said, looking at pictures of a sweet-looking teenage girl. Her name was Sunidhi Khirwar.

'Why don't you speak to Sunidhi's father?' asked
Charu after we went through the links on the screen and
discovered that there really wasn't much about the girl.

'Good idea. Her father will throw some more light on
the mysterious disappearance of his daughter,' I said.

'Why don't you call the police station where the father
lodged the complaint? The SHO will be able to give you
the father's contact details,' suggested Charu.

'No, Charu, it's best not to. Maharaj is too powerful. He
has ministers and senior officers as devotees. Why, even Ravi
is a staunch follower. If I call the police station inquiring
about the missing girl, Maharaj will certainly be alerted. And
knowing his clout, I'm sure the police must have just lodged
the missing complaint and done nothing else. I bet they
haven't even started an investigation,' I said.

'I can't believe you've become such a cynic, Arjun,' said
Charu, all fired up. 'There are a lot of good men in the police
who do their jobs without fear. If that wasn't the case, none
of the fraud God-men in our country would ever have been
arrested.'

I winced at the scolding. 'Yes, you're right. I have become
too negative over the last few days. I also thought that I wanted
the same police to be inefficient in finding Madhushree!'

'If you won't call the police station, how will you contact
Sunidhi's father?' she asked.

'It shouldn't be a problem in today's social-media
world,' I quipped, opening Facebook on my phone and
searching for Sunidhi Khirwar.

A number of Sunidhis popped up on my screen. I scrolled
down for a few seconds and finally got the Sunidhi I was
looking for, her picture matching the one we had found on
Google. Luckily, she had not locked her profile.

I found out her father's name from her posts and then
moved to his profile. Obviously new to social media and
unaware of its perils, her father, like most people of the

older generation, had uploaded all his information. I noted down his details and dialled his number.

'Mr Jaywant? I am Arjun Kumar, IGP. Are you free to talk for a minute?'

'What do you want to talk about? You people have not done anything to find my Sunidhi,' Jaywant replied, anger dripping from his words.

'Jaywantji, I apologize for the inaction. I will take her case personally. Please tell me all you can about Sunidhi's disappearance. When was the last time you saw her?' I asked sincerely.

There was a weighted silence on the other side.

Finally, the cell phone crackled again.

'Sir, my Sunidhi is a lovely girl. She is very hardworking and has great ambitions. She wants to be a choreographer,' said Jaywant, his voice breaking with emotion.

'Go on,' I urged him.

'My wife and I regularly visited Maharaj Saheb's ashram. Sunidhi used to accompany us sometimes to perform classical dances during the satsangs. Maharaj was very impressed and began calling her regularly. We were so happy that our revered Maharaj was so fond of our daughter,' continued Jaywant.

'On the night of 1 May, Maharaj specifically asked Sunidhi to come alone to his friend's farmhouse. It is owned by Chandan Mehta, a wealthy industrialist and a staunch devotee of Maharaj. He said that a special satsang was being organized for some VIPs. We were thrilled by the invitation but had no idea that that would be the last time we'd see our beloved daughter,' said Jaywant. He was weeping now.

'Did you not look for her? What did Maharaj say?' I asked.

'She didn't turn up at home that night. When we got to the ashram, Maharaj's security did not let us enter. They also refused to acknowledge that Sunidhi had gone to Mehta Farms that night,' Jaywant choked.

'What about the police?'

'The police asked for evidence. We had none. The ashram does not have CCTV and nor does Mehta Farms. Mr Mehta just said that the farm was private property, and he did not want technology to intrude on his personal space. When we went to the media, and even they refused to listen, except for one or two local channels. We were helpless,' said Jaywant.

'I'm very sorry, Jaywantji. I'll try my best to find your daughter. Keep this conversation between you and me, please,' I said.

My heart sank as I put the phone down. I had a bad feeling about Sunidhi.

'Charu, I think that girl in the video is Sunidhi. She could be dead. And her body must have been buried in the farmhouse.'

'What makes you think so?' asked Charu.

'Just a gut feeling. You know, a policeman's intuition.'

I put the pen drive back in the laptop. 'Let's see if there's anything more,' I said. 'We didn't watch it to the end.'

After the blurred video of Madhushree, there were some more interviews with Kishore Kumar. Though they were treasures for a music buff like me, I didn't care. All I hoped for was another video of the night of the satsang.

I was about to give up when I heard Charu squeal.

'Again, see. There's another video! This time it's clear,' she said.

Madhushree appeared on the screen again, but this time she wasn't the focus, though we could clearly hear her singing in the background. Instead, the camera panned the gardens of the farmhouse. Three disciples of Maharaj's cult were carrying an unconscious girl. Her face was clearly visible in this video. She was Sunidhi Khirwar. Then, suddenly, the camera focused on a man wearing long ochre robes and a huge turban.

It was Maharaj. The god-man himself.

38

The Hypothesis

Charu and I sat there, shocked.

'That poor girl is dead,' Charu said tearfully.

I remained quiet.

I had never had a good opinion of Maharaj, but I had never imagined that he could be a murderer.

My heart broke for Madhushree and Sunidhi. I was desperate to bring Maharaj to justice but what could I do?

'Okay, I can visualize the entire chain of events and now I know why Madhushree was killed,' I said, looking at Charu.

Charu wiped her tears. 'God, why do you think I can't understand something so obvious,' she said angrily. 'You don't need to explain anything to me. I will tell you what happened.'

'Gosh, you are such a strong-headed woman,' I muttered.

'Ever since Maharaj saw Sunidhi, he must have lusted for her. He called her to the farmhouse on the pretext of performing in the satsang. He must have tried to molest her the first opportunity he got and Sunidhi must have resisted. Whether he succeeded in his evil designs, I don't know, but it seems quite clear that he killed Sunidhi either intentionally or accidentally during a scuffle they had,' said Charu.

'Yes, that's logical. But what makes you think it was Maharaj who killed Sunidhi?' I asked.

'He must have, or why would he personally supervise the men taking away her body? He looks tense in the video,' replied Charu.

'Yes, I saw that. He looked very nervous. And hiding Sunidhi in his own backyard was the best thing to do at that time. He just made the body vanish. No body, no murder,' I mused.

'Yes, that's right. You should know,' said Charu, looking at me with disgust.

I was hurt by her snide comment, but she was right. I had done the exact same thing just a few days ago.

'Anyway, to continue my hypothesis. Madhushree and Madhav were invited to the same satsang to perform for the VIPs. As we have seen, Madhushree was very fond of making videos for Instagram and all that nonsense,' Charu said, the disdain clear in her voice.

'Charu, Instagram and other social media are very powerful tools to publicize work. You simply cannot survive without these applications today,' I interjected.

'Of course, you'll defend these things since you are so addicted to the cell phone yourself. Your own dear Kishore Kumar did not have social media in his time, yet he is still famous. Why? Because he was talented, not because he made silly videos,' retorted Charu.

'Okay, okay. Point conceded. Continue with your hypothesis,' I said.

'While looking for a suitable location to shoot her video, Madhushree must have ventured on the terrace for a view of the sprawling farmhouse. She must have then asked Madhav to shoot her video. When he started recording, he must have realized that something fishy was happening in the background,' Charu continued.

'He must have been curious and got closer to the scene to record the video clearly. But he was smart enough to keep Madhushree in the foreground still,' said Charu, picking up a bottle for a sip of water.

I filled in the remaining parts of the story.

'Madhav must have been careful to keep a suitable distance from the burial site, so he used the camera zoom to record. You can see that Madhushree is quite prominent in the first video, but in the second, she is not in focus. She is not the primary subject.

'Madhav deliberately continued to record, with Madhushree in front of him, to avoid any suspicion. If the farmhouse guys had caught them, he would have tried to get away with it by saying that they were making a video,' I said.

'*Sahi hai*. Correct,' said Charu.

I was delighted that my wife agreed with me, though it wouldn't make any difference to her feelings for me. We had crossed that bridge. Forever.

I cut short my emotional digression and returned to the crime scene.

'The moment Madhav saw the girl with Maharaj and his accolytes, he must have sensed that he had stumbled upon something valuable. He could blackmail Maharaj with the video and extort a huge sum. He must have sent that video to Maharaj through an email or WhatsApp message or even a pen drive. I don't know how, but that's irrelevant,' I said.

'Go on,' commanded Charu.

'Since the videos clearly show Madhushree in the foreground, Maharaj must have inferred that Madhushree was the blackmailer, and her phone must have the incriminating videos. So, he sent a hitman, an assassin, who would retrieve the video and eliminate Madhushree.'

'Who was the assassin?' asked Charu.

I knew now.

'Rajesh Atulkar, also known as "The Ghost". He's an ex-cop, a highly trained and lethal one. He's the guy who attacked me twice,' I said.

'And you think Ravi Bhushan asked him to carry out the murder,' Charu stated. It was not a question. She knew the way my mind worked.

'Yes, there's a very high probability that it was Ravi. Ravi is an extremely devoted follower of that rascal of a God-man; he was the one who recruited Atulkar to the Tiger Squad and also sent Madhushree to the farmhouse,' I said.

'So, the Ghost goes to the hotel where you and Madhushree are about to have a . . . colourful night,' said Charu, her voice choked.

I nodded, shame creeping up on me on hearing my wife say these words.

Charu looked at me with hatred in her eyes. I mustered up my courage and continued to speak, my eyes looking everywhere but into hers.

'He kills Madhushree and checks her cell phone, or the other way around. Either way, he does not find the video on her cell phone because it was never there in the first place. So he simply takes away the phone as proof or a souvenir for Maharaj.'

I took a deep breath, remembering that fateful night.

'I checked if Madhushree's phone had a new SIM card or if any calls were made from it. But it has been switched off since the murder,' I said, before continuing the story as I saw it.

'Maharaj must have received, blackmail calls even after Madhushree's murder messages. So the Ghost and Maharaj shift their attention to the second suspect, Madhav. He had been at the farmhouse with Madhushree to perform in the satsang. His voice is clearly audible in the video. The Ghost tracks Madhav easily using mobile surveillance and attacks him. Fortunately for us, he still has not been able to get the original video,' I said, ending my hypothesis.

'Arjun, this Maharaj is pure evil. He has to pay for his sins. I cannot live with the fact that he is still treated as a God while he is the devil incarnate,' said Charu, her eyes brimming with fire.

39

'Be Serious, Charu'

'You were given one simple task, and you couldn't do it even though you had so many chances. I can't believe you were the famous sharpshooter of the Tiger Squad. You want to get back in the police service, but I don't think you deserve to,' his boss thundered.

'I'm really sorry, sir,' the Ghost muttered feebly, the humiliation clear in his tone.

'Sorry? Forget about getting reinstated into the service. Forget redeeming your honour. Forget your family, your son,' replied his boss, tapping his ring-laden fingers on the car's bonnet.

'Sir, please don't say that. You are my only hope to get my family back,' the Ghost said, almost in tears.

'You know, Atulkar, if that video is leaked, I'll never reach the position I have coveted throughout my life. I will never have the power and prestige that I wanted all my life. If I don't get what I want, neither will you,' said the man, his voice trembling with rage.

* * *

'You should confront Ravi immediately. I want to give him one tight slap. How could he murder someone? I can't believe he could stoop so low,' said Charu.

'You're right, it's a big betrayal. But I can't confront Ravi. I have no evidence against him. And if I tell him anything about the video, he will alert Maharaj. And the worst part is that I am so deeply involved in Madhushree's murder. After all, I'm the one who hid her body,' I said, absolutely frustrated with the quandary I was in.

The room was silent, barring the sound of Charu shuffling her cards as she thought to herself. She finally packed the cards in their box and looked at me.

'It's because of Maharaj that Madhushree is dead. And you had to hide her body because you thought you had no way to prove your innocence,' she said, looking at me intently.

'So, this is what we'll do now. We'll dig up Madhushree's body from Somveer's farmhouse and bury it at Mehta Farm.'

The idea was so bizarre that I couldn't help laughing.

'You're joking!' I said.

'You think it's funny?' she said, her face expressionless.

'Yes! It's an absolutely preposterous idea,' I said.

'I'm very serious. This is your best option,' she said.

'Charu, you know it's a weird idea. It's something that's only done in movies. And how would I shift the body anyway?'

'No, it's not a filmi idea. It's practical and it's the only option. You bury the body in the Mehta farmhouse the same way you did in Somveer's farmhouse. We will plant the evidence right where the crime originated.'

'You're crazy. Watching all these cheesy web series and crime dramas has given you macabre fantasies,' I said, angry now. 'Charu, be serious. This is not a joke.'

'It can be done, Arjun. You know it. You have seen it in real life too. Think about what will happen if Madhushree's body is discovered at Somveer's farmhouse someday or if Vikram somehow finds out that Madhushree was last seen with you. You will be the prime suspect.'

I took a deep breath. As always, Charu was right. In my present circumstances, this was the best idea.

'Okay. How do we do it?' I asked.

* * *

'Hi Ravi, how are you? I need a small favour. I hope you won't disappoint me,' I said in a melancholic voice.

'Arjun! What happened? You sound so low! This is so unlike you,' replied Ravi.

'Charu and I are having some issues. Nothing big, just like any other marriage. Could you get us a private appointment with Maharaj Saheb?' I asked, looking at Charu and hoping for some reaction from her.

Her face remained expressionless.

'You want an appointment with Maharaj? I'm surprised. I thought you hated gurus like Maharaj.'

'Well, we're desperate to work on our problems and there must be something in Maharaj that appeals to an educated person like you. Maybe he can guide us too.'

'You're in luck. Maharaj Saheb is having a satsang this Friday for a select few VIPs at his ashram located at Mehta Farm. You can come with me,' said Ravi.

'That's great news! Charu and I will be there,' I said excitedly.

* * *

Ravi swiveled around in his office chair, his gaze sweeping over the glass walls of his swanky office.

Disconnecting the call, a sadistic smile graced his face. Finally, he thought, the perfect couple has issues in their marriage.

* * *

'Hello, Arjun Sir, it's a pleasure to welcome you to the ashram. I'm sure you'll be enthralled by Maharaj Saheb's sermons,' said Chandan Mehta ebulliently.

Mehta was a wealthy businessman who networked on behalf of Maharaj. Nobody knew the exact nature of his business, but the grapevine indicated that it acted as a front for the ashram's illegal activities.

'Yes, that's why we are here,' I said, smiling at Ravi, who was a regular at these satsangs.

'Yes, Arjun, I'm so happy that Charu and you have finally decided to become devotees of Maharaj Saheb,' said Ravi.

Charu and I nodded in unison.

'Mr Mehta, why don't you give us a tour of your property until Maharaj Saheb arrives?' asked Charu, smiling radiantly.

'Of course, madam. It will be a pleasure,' said Mehta gleefully. 'Though it is my farmhouse, I treat it as an ashram for VIP devotees like you. In any case, all these things are due to the benevolence of Maharaj Saheb.'

The charm of a beautiful woman always works! I thought, following Mehta as he led us deeper into the property.

The farmhouse was huge, with a large garden and a few villas scattered over the main area.

'I'm sure there must be some more beautiful areas in this majestic property,' said Charu. 'You haven't shown us the swimming pool.'

'Madam, the swimming pool area is out of bounds because it is Maharaj Saheb's private residence when he visits the farm. Only his staff is allowed there,' said Mehta.

'Oh, come on, Chandanji. Let me enjoy the splendour of this beautiful farmhouse. Don't you want me to visit again?'

Looking a tad uneasy, Mehta caved, 'Okay, madam, since Maharaj Saheb is not in residence at this time, I will show you that side of the building. *Chaliye*, follow me please.'

As we walked to the other side of the farmhouse, Mehta pointed to a vast tract of barren land.

'That is where we will do a tree plantation drive tomorrow. Maharaj's devotees will do a voluntary work, *shramdaan*, after the satsang as part of a special course,' said Mehta.

'Oh, how lovely! We'd love to register for that course,' said Charu excitedly.

'Of course, madam. You can also contribute to saving our planet by joining us in our humble effort,' said Mehta.

Fortunately, he was looking at Charu, so he did not see the contempt on my face.

Finally, we had a look at the god-man's private quarters at the rear of the farmhouse. Charu deliberately did not ask to go inside to avoid raising Mehta's suspicions.

As we walked around, exploring the area, the two of us suddenly stopped in our tracks at a spot near the swimming pool. The neon lit 'Mehta Farm' sign was right in front of us, shining from the top floor of the main building.

So that's where Madhushree was standing when Madhav filmed her. And Sunidhi's body must have been dumped somewhere close by, I thought, replaying the video in my mind.

Charu and I looked at each other. We were determined to punish Maharaj for his sins.

'How come the grass is so overgrown? This garden seems a little shabby for such a beautiful property,' I said.

'Arre, sir, I come here only once in a few weeks and only when Maharaj Saheb is here. I don't keep a lot of staff because Maharaj Saheb doesn't want his meditation and *kriyas* disturbed. That's why the lawns are a bit poorly maintained,' said Mehta sheepishly.

'Meditation and kriyas. What kind of kriyas does Maharaj do? Tormenting young girls?' I wondered.

'Mehtaji, I don't see CCTV cameras anywhere. Are they concealed?' asked Charu.

'No, madam. We don't have CCTVs in this farmhouse. Maharaj Saheb does not like technology to intrude on his private sessions with his followers,' replied Mehta.

Private sessions, my foot! I could well imagine the kind of misdeeds the God-man carries out in his private sessions.

'And is there a basement? An underground room?' asked Charu casually.

'It's time to go, madam. Maharaj Saheb is about to arrive for the satsang,' said Mehta, ignoring Charu's question. He was clearly uncomfortable with the conversation about the private quarters of the god-man. His smile had given way to a deep frown.

'Yes, let's go, Charu,' I said, hoping that Mehta did not become suspicious of her queries.

We returned to the front of the farmhouse and mingled with the select crowd invited for the private satsang. I recognized some rich businessmen and socialites who featured regularly in the newspapers. I could not believe that such rich and supposedly educated people could have so much faith in a God-man like Maharaj.

Suddenly, a hush fell over the room. There was a pin drop silence as Maharaj entered the hall.

'An ordinary man with a paunch, exuding no aura, yet so powerful. So this is what the scoundrel looks like in flesh and blood,' I thought, disgusted that I had to be here among his devotees.

Maharaj adjusted his turban and sat on a throne, just like an emperor in the olden days. He started his sermon, continuously caressing his flowing beard. Every one of his fingers bore a ring, similar to my friend Ravi Bhushan's.

After a few inane statements pandering largely to the hypocrisies of the elite, Maharaj changed the topic of his discourse.

'Our sect has to assert its supremacy. We have to reclaim our lost glory. If we do not get what is our right, we have to grab it forcefully,' thundered the God-man, tapping his fingers on the armrest of his throne.

'The laws of the land are not beneficial to us at all, they exist to appease a few communities that are far inferior to us.

'We need a new order, where *our* sect rules this country,' continued Maharaj.

His devotees listened with rapt attention, as if hypnotized. After a while I could not bear it any longer.

'Ravi, Maharaj sounds like a megalomaniac. He is talking such rubbish about the democratic framework of our country. As government officers, we should not be here,' I told Ravi.

Ravi did not reply. He simply smiled and gestured towards the entrance. A posse of commandos dressed in black entered the hall, followed by the home minister of the state. Minister Ajit Sood climbed the stage and sprawled at the feet of the God-man in obeisance.

* * *

'We have done a sufficient recce of the Mehta farmhouse. There are just a few men on the campus, mostly volunteers, two guards, a cook and a gardener as staff. I think we should get Madhushree's body tomorrow and bury it there,' said Charu.

I was amazed at how casual Charu was about the whole idea. Perhaps my befuddlement was visible on my face.

'Don't look at me like that. I'm confident that this will work. That Mehta was like any other man. I just gave him the slightest bit of attention and he was more than eager to answer all my questions. That's why I know the number of staff and other details about the farm,' continued Charu.

I had no option but to go with Charu's plan. It was the best bet to get me out of the quagmire I was in.

'Okay then, I'll leave tomorrow afternoon for Somveer's farm,' I said. 'I will take a day's leave from the DGP and go alone in our personal car. Naturally, I can't take Bhajan with me.'

'I'm coming with you,' said Charu, pulling out a suitcase.

'No, you can't come with me. It's too risky. It can potentially send both of us to jail. If at all somebody needs to pay for my misdeeds, it is me. You don't have to be part of this,' I said.

Charu continued to pack, not even looking at me.

'Charu, please. I am begging you. Please don't come with me.'

She stopped packing and looked at me.

'I don't know how you feel, but I have loved you with all my heart and soul for all these years. I vowed to you when we decided to marry that I would always be by your side, through thick and thin. I can't leave you and I won't. And anyway, you won't be able to do this without me,' said Charu.

I was overwhelmed. I had never been an expressive person, but now I just couldn't control myself. I pulled Charu into my arms and hugged her tightly. She stood within my embrace as stiff as a board, but she didn't push me away and that was a good sign. I tried to look into her eyes, seeking forgiveness. She stepped away without a word and packed one last thing in the bag.

The Glock pistol.

40

A Rotting Corpse

'Hello Bhola, how are you?' I smiled.

Bhola was surprised to see me, naturally. 'Sir, *aap yahan kaise*, how come you are here?' he asked.

Then, when Charu entered the house a minute later, his expression changed to something like mischief. 'Oh, *this* is the matter,' he said.

'No, no, Bhola. It's not what you think. This is my wife,' I said, squeezing his shoulders.

'Oh, sorry, sir, please pardon me. I have become so accustomed to Somveer Sir coming to the farmhouse with a different girl every time, you know,' he said with a wink.

Charu was quite offended. She marched upstairs to the guest room, carrying her own bag.

'So this is what your friends do. And this is what you learn from them,' she said, putting her luggage in the cupboard.

I did not answer because I had no answer.

* * *

When night fell, Charu and I took the spade from the storehouse and walked towards the outer area of the farmhouse.

I looked with relief at the pots and stones that I had arranged at the burial site. They were still exactly as I had left them.

'Are you sure this is the spot?' asked Charu as she put on her gloves. I did not know how to look her in the eye, so I just nodded and started digging. She stepped up to help me.

'Charu, you are too delicate. You won't be able to lift the spade, it's very heavy. Please let me do it alone. You will hurt yourself,' I said.

'Stop talking and wasting time. We don't know how long Bhola will sleep under the influence of alcohol. Hurry. We don't have all night,' she said.

She was right. We began digging furiously.

After about half an hour, my spade hit the bag. A stench rose from the ground and hit our noses. We turned our faces and moved away while the gases escaped.

A rotting corpse is a complex ecosystem. Our bodies start decomposing several minutes after death through a process called autolysis or self-digestion. After the heart stops, cells become deprived of oxygen and start breaking down. Once self-digestion is underway and bacteria have started to escape from the gastrointestinal tract, decay sets in. The process of decomposition produces gases such as methane and hydrogen sulphide.

The stench remained unbearable even after a few minutes, but I ignored it, leaning into the pit and pulling out the suitcase. Then I steeled my nerves and unzipped it, looking at the corpse within. Madhushree's beautiful face had turned into a grotesque skull. Her body's soft tissues had decayed, exposing the skeleton. The summer heat had helped the body decompose faster, turning it into a skeleton in a few weeks.

So far, so good, I just need to remove some lingering flesh from the bones, I mused and then mentally cursed myself. Sure, self-preservation was the most important thing on my mind, but I really didn't need to lose my humanity like this.

I was about to extract the disarticulated bones of the skeleton when Charu gestured to me to stop.

'Bhola, what are you doing here?' she said.

I whipped around to see Bhola standing in front of us.

* * *

'Bhola, *tum yahaan kaise? Soye nahin*? How come you're here, didn't you sleep?' I asked.

'Na, sir, *thoda bathroom jaana tha*. I needed to go to the bathroom,' he replied, still reeling from the effect of the alcohol.

He coughed. 'What is this foul odour?' he asked, barely able to keep his eyes open.

'Probably some dead rats. Go back and sleep,' I said, hiding the shovel behind me.

'Come, let me help you. You need a few more drinks too,' said Charu, walking Bhola back to the residence.

I wanted to protest. Which man would want to see his wife escort a drunken man to a bar? But Charu gestured for me to continue with my work.

I took the skeleton out of the suitcase and put it in a bag. Then I pulled Madhushree's suitcase away and started refilling the pit. In twenty minutes, I was done.

I arranged the soil and the pots around the pit to make it look natural and checked everything again. The shovels, spades, pots and rocks. Everything was in order.

I put the bag and the suitcase in the boot of my car and went inside to call Charu, hoping that Bhola had dozed off.

'Madamji, *bas karo*. Please stop. I can't drink any more,' I heard Bhola say. He was still awake but absolutely inebriated. I gestured to Charu and without saying a word, we boarded the car and sped away.

The drive back was smooth, with absolutely no traffic. It was almost surreal.

I played my favourite Kishore Kumar songs to enliven the mood, but Charu kept looking out of the window. I wished we had been together in better circumstances.

When we finally saw people on the road, who else could they have been but the police!

A subinspector waved and asked us to stop. My heart almost stopped beating. What if he wanted to check the boot?

'Arre, you know there is an agitation at the Delhi border. Why are you roaming around? Go back,' he said imperiously.

I looked at the SI's nameplate.

'Vishwas, I am Arjun Kumar. My wife and I had come to Delhi for a medical emergency. We need to go back to Jallandhar now,' I said to the policeman.

Vishwas's back instinctinvely straightened and he snapped into a salute. He knew without a doubt that I was a senior IPS officer. A common man can never speak to a policeman with such authority.

'Sir, you can take the diversion two kilometres from here. The road goes through the villages. Have a safe journey. Jai Hind!' said Vishwas as he guided us.

40

'Maharaj ki Jai!'

'Welcome, sir, can we please take your luggage?' said a volunteer.

I was about to protest, but Charu gestured me to stop.

'Yes, please. We need some rest because we have a lot to do this evening,' said Charu, letting the volunteer pick up our suitcases.

Though he seemed unfazed by the weight of the larger case, I remained nervous till we were ushered into our plush suite and he put the suitcases down.

'Thank you so much,' I said, relieved that the volunteer had not seemed suspicious of us.

'The satsang will start at 5 p.m. After that you can rest and then go to the back of the farmhouse for the shramdaan. A lot of cleaning and plantation has to be done,' said the volunteer.

'I think Maharaj plans to plant about ten thousand trees in the ashram,' Charu remarked.

'That's right. Maharaj Saheb is very conscientious. He wants our future generations to inherit a green planet. *Maharaj ki jai!*' said the volunteer.

'Maharaj ki jai,' I replied, closing the door.

I immediately put the bigger suitcase on the bed and opened it, checking that the black bag within was still secure.

'Where will the skeleton go? Will it run on its own? Stop being so paranoid,' said Charu, sipping the tea she had made in the pantry.

'I'm just a bit nervous,' I admitted.

'We're here for a three-day course. We'll look for an appropriate location in the evening. I'm sure our plan will work out well.'

'Hmm. Well, yes. If you are with me, I can do anything in the world. *Tum jo pakad lo haath mera, duniya badal sakta hoon main*,' I replied, crooning the evergreen song of love.

The second I closed my mouth, I cringed knowing that I had said something really cheesy, and in such uncomfortable circumstances at that.

Charu tried to hide it, but there was a slight smile on her face.

***

Sitting on the *gaddas* (mattresses) along with about fifty other people, I squirmed uncomfortably.

'Why can't he have chairs for his satsang? My back hurts when I sit cross legged and my ankylosing spondylitis might even be aggravated,' I complained.

'So much for your fitness, Mr Sportsman. You have a weak core. That's why you aren't able to sit on the floor,' replied Charu.

I knew very well what she meant by "a weak core". But I couldn't settle down.

'Look at these hypocrites,' I said contemptuously glancing at the throng of rich and wealthy devotees. 'I don't know why they need a scoundrel like Maharaj to guide them.'

'Well, these high-class people, these elite, have got almost everything anyone desires, money, power and fame. Now they need something else to give meaning to their lives. To each his own,' said Charu nonchalantly.

Of course, Charu was right. But Maharaj was not only a charlatan, he was an actual threat to the country, at least if judged by last week's sermon. Though I did not have any evidence of it, I knew the Maharaj's ashrams were dens of drug smuggling and worse. He probably supported anti-national activities as well. He had a lot of support from not only the rich and powerful in India but also the diaspora. A source in the IB had recently informed me that fronts for terror organizations based in countries like Germany and the Netherlands were suspected of regularly funding his activities. Maharaj was smart enough to use some of his ill-gotten wealth to help the millions of his poor and socially backward followers. In fact, he had become a messiah for the downtrodden, supported by the very people who had trampled upon them. At the same time, he had carefully cultivated an image of a powerful mystic, which brought him followers from among the country's high and mighty. With ministers and bureaucrats surrendering to him, it was as if he was beyond the law.

The buzz of conversation in the room hushed as Maharaj entered the hall, looking from side to side and surveying the people who had come for his three-day course.

He nodded and smiled at everyone, stopping for a moment when he saw us. As Mehta whispered something in his ear, the Maharaj smiled broadly at us. Obviously, he was quite pleased to see the IG of the range among his audience.

I could barely tolerate him and his nonsensical, egotistical talks. Some of his so-called sermons were positively seditious, but what could I do when the powers that be were among his followers? The state home minister had sprawled at Maharaj's feet in front of my eyes just a day earlier.

More determined than ever, I decided that whenever I got the opportunity to carry out our plan, I would grab on to it with both hands.

* * *

'The satsang is now over. All those who have volunteered for shramdaan can join us in the backyard in half an hour,' announced Mehta, the coordinator of our camp.

Charu and I looked at each other, raring to rush off and begin work on the plan. We absolutely could not wait for even half an hour! But we had no choice. If we wandered out to the backyard on our own, we would just attract attention, and that was the last thing we needed.

Finally, the bell tolled for the devotees to assemble again.

'Now that your break is over, we can start our community work,' said Mehta. 'This ashram and all the other premises of our sect are maintained by voluntary work done by devotees like you. So today, all those who want to tend to the sick and old can go to the infirmary. Those of you who would like to help with the preparation of dinner, go to the langar. The rest of you can move to the ground at the back to plant trees.'

Charu and I picked up our shovels and moved with a motley group of people towards the ground designated for the trees. Once there, the men spread out and started digging while the women brought the saplings that were to be planted.

After some time, I gestured to Charu to come and talk to me.

'This should be a good site. What do you say?' I asked, putting my shovel down.

'Yes, it seems perfect,' she replied.

I picked up the shovel again to dig pits for the saplings. Looking around after a while, I noticed that the other volunteers were busy with their work. Immediately, I began digging a pit bigger and deeper than the other ones.

'This should do,' I thought, gesturing to Charu to join me again.

'Isn't it a bit small for a body?' she asked.

'No, we have to just bury a skeleton, not a body. And I can't dig a pit too big, or it'll arouse the suspicions of the ashram staff.'

'Okay. You know better than me how to bury bodies,' said Charu, her sarcasm hitting me straight in my face.

She took the shovel from me and started pushing loose soil back into the pit.

'What are you doing?' I protested.

'Just making the pit look smaller. We can easily remove the loose soil when we return with the skeleton.'

* * *

I somehow managed to survive the ordeal that was the next day. All the participants had to do yoga in the morning and sing in a bhajan session. Then, we attended some more boring monologues by Maharaj.

'What a self-obsessed man this Maharaj is,' I grumbled.

'Just be patient till the evening,' Charu hissed.

When the satsang ended, we went to our room immediately.

I opened the suitcase, took out the skeleton and put the bones and Madhushree's belongings into two backpacks. Thankfully, we had taken the precaution of locking the suitcase in the closet, so the putrid smell had not spread through the room.

'Come, let's go,' I said, handing one of the bags to Charu.

On our way to the ground, we bumped into Mehta.

'What do you have in those bags?' he asked curiously.

I went quiet, but as always, Charu came to my rescue.

'Oh, Mehtaji, we are just carrying some snacks and beverages. It's exhausting to plant trees in such hot weather,' she said.

'Oh, yes, of course, madam. Please take care. Shall I send you something else?' replied Mehta.

'You're so sweet. I'll let you know. Thanks,' Charu said with a smile.

Men! We're all the same, I thought bitterly, watching Mehta simper back at Charu.

When we got to the site, we put down the backpacks and began planting the saplings like all the other volunteers.

'Now this is the right time,' Charu said softly about half an hour later, 'it's getting dark and everyone is busy.'

I quickly removed the loose soil from the pit I had dug the day before while Charu opened the backpacks. Both of us put on our gloves.

'Quick! Dump the bones into the pit,' I said, mopping the sweat from my brow. Before I could finish my sentence, Charu was already at it.

Joining her, I threw Madhushree's clothes and her passport into the pit, after which I knelt to arrange the bones into the shape of a skeleton, my heart beating fast. In the deepening twilight, I must have looked as though I was readying the soil for the roots of a sapling, or so I hoped.

The moment I finished, Charu started shovelling soil over the pit. I marvelled at her commitment and love for me.

'What an idiot I've been! I don't deserve her,' I thought, as the two of us covered the pit with soil.

41

'The Evidence Is Undeniable'

We were quiet on our way home. The third day of the camp had been a massive exercise to boost the cult of Maharaj. In the morning, his devotees had been subjected to videos showing Maharaj engaged in various activities, ranging from rappelling down a hill to riding a horse, as though he was the manifestation of a man superior to all humanity. In the second half of the day, we had to tolerate his ambiguous discourses on the various issues plaguing the world. Yet, we could not help but marvel at the mesmerizing effect he had on all the disciples present in the hall. Except for us.

We each took a quick shower as soon as we reached home and then sat down to discuss the second part of our plan and set it in motion.

'So, what now?' I asked, feeling quite relieved that my life was returning to normalcy. At least I had a plan and Charu was helping me.

'I went to that place with only one purpose. I want that fraud God-man behind bars. I'm sure he has exploited innumerable girls and destroyed their lives,' Charu said angrily.

'The PM is visiting Hoshiyarpur next week. I'll be busy with the preparations whatever we do, we do it after the PM's visit.'

'Arjun, this is the best opportunity for us to pull up our plan. You can keep yourself stationed in Hoshiyarpur and feign ignorance about any raid on the farmhouse.'

'Do you think our plan will work?' I asked.

'Of course! You are the boss of this range. You control the outcome of the investigation of all criminal cases. You have already shared the video of Maharaj with an unconscious Sunidhi on various WhatsApp groups and it will go viral very soon. Now call Vikram.'

I looked at Charu's confident expression and picked up my phone.

'Hi Vikram! I hope you're alone. I need to discuss something very confidential with you. That's why I'm calling on WhatsApp,' I said.

'Yes, sir, I am alone,' replied Vikram.

'My wife and I have just attended a satsang organized at the ashram of Maharaj Saheb on the insistence of Ravi, my batchmate. As we left today, one of the ashram workers came to me. He was very scared and asked me not to reveal his identity and then told me some startling things about the misdeeds of Maharaj.'

'Sir, I wouldn't be surprised if those things turned out to be true,' said Vikram. 'I have always known that this Maharaj is a dubious fellow, but there was never any evidence. And of course, he's very well-connected.'

'This time the evidence is undeniable. A worker gave me a video showing Maharaj and his henchmen hiding a girl, I have just sent it to you. Call me after you watch it,' I said and disconnected the call.

In less than ten minutes, Vikram called me back.

'Sir, this is unbelievable. But will this be enough to implicate Maharaj? He can always claim that the video is fake,' said Vikram.

'You're right, but my informer told me that a few bodies have been buried in the ashram. You can search for them,' I said.

'Bodies? As in dead bodies?' asked Vikram incredulously.

'Yes, the ashram worker is sure that the bodies of one or two girls are buried on the premises. We have always heard that the ashram is a den of drug smuggling, and of course, many of the high and mighty go there to exploit young women too. I'm sure Maharaj must have had those who resisted killed in case they opened their mouths later. The latest case is that of a girl called Sunidhi who has been missing for quite some time. I don't think we've made any headway in that case,' I said.

Vikram was silent for a few seconds, probably trying to process what I had just told him. When he spoke again, it was with a note of acceptance in his voice. He had bought my story.

'Sir, this reminds me of a case from an ashram in Ahmedabad,' he said. 'That God-man is currently lodged in jail for the rape of a young girl. Unfortunately, I have no such victory to report here. Nothing came of our efforts to find Sunidhi. The ashram management simply denied the entire episode and we could not find any evidence of Sunidhi being taken to the farmhouse. I still can't look Sunidhi's parents in the eye.'

'Yes. We have to ensure justice on our watch. We cannot let down Sunidhi and possibly many other girls. You should raid the ashram immediately. I am sure you'll find quite a few skeletons.'

'Should I not get a search warrant?' asked Vikram.

'I know you're thinking about Maharaj's powerful connections. Don't worry. We don't need a warrant. The video will go viral soon and the public will be agitated. Nobody will dare stop the police then. No politician will risk the wrath of the public now, when the elections are due.'

'Okay, sir. You're right. I'll gather my forces and raid the ashram immediately.'

Vikram sounded really charged up. For the longest time, he had wanted to put Maharaj behind bars, but it had been impossible. Now, he had a good chance.

'All the best. Keep me informed. Oh, yes, I forgot to tell you. The informer told me that a body is buried at the back of the ashram. He said it is at a site where some tree plantation drive was held. Obviously, the drive was held to hide bodies without raising suspicion. Make sure you check that out.'

42

The PM Visits

'Sir, the PM's visit is on schedule tomorrow. We have made all the security arrangements. The SPG has already done the advance security liaison with the district police. We need about a 1000 more jawans to patrol the route in case the PM takes the road to the temple,' said Mukhtiyar, the SSP of Hoshiarpur.

The SSP was correct in his assessment. There was every chance that the PM's helicopter would be grounded due to inclement weather, in which case the PM would certainly arrive by road. I did not want any difficult situations on my watch, like the one some of my seniors had faced a few years earlier when the PM was stuck on a flyover for a good twenty minutes. It had the potential to become a huge vulnerablity in his security arrangement.

'Mukhtiyar, I will send you forces from all the districts in my range by the evening. I hope you have done the mock drill at least once. Also ensure that there is an alternate route for the PM to get to the temple. In this time of elections, many people will try to disrupt the PM's campaign. I will review our preparedness when I get to Hoshiarpur today,' I said.

I had deliberately planned the raid on the ashram for this time, since I would be away for the PM's programme and could avoid any direct involvement in the operation.

But I couldn't deny that with two such massively important events about to take place simultaneously, I was a nervous wreck.

Regarding Maharaj, I was anxious that things should go as Charu and I had planned and that Vikram would discover the remains of Madhushree's body. And then there was the PM's visit to Hoshiarpur. I had been a part of the operation that had thwarted a terrorist plan to attack the PM's motorcade just a year earlier. Now, the PM was coming to a district in my range again, but this time, as the IG, my responsibility was greater, and more importantly, direct.

The IB had constantly been sending us reports about an imminent attack on the PM. The PM had been sounded out by the NSA and the IB chief about the danger to his life but he was in no mood to give in to their fears. He had worked tirelessly to win the hearts of the people of the state and now was the time to reap the benefits of those efforts. The assembly elections were extremely important for him. There was no question of him cancelling this visit.

'It is your job to keep me alive,' the PM had clearly told the directors of the IB and the SPG.

* * *

'Surround the premises. Nobody should be allowed to enter or exit the ashram,' Vikram ordered the posse of police in his party.

It was a huge risk to raid the ashram of a powerful God-man, but Vikram loved risks. From a family of decorated army officers, he had grown up listening to stories of the valour of his kin. And as a conscientious, honest police officer, he had been waiting for an opportunity to end the misdeeds of Maharaj and his cult.

'I have a strong feeling we will recover enough evidence today to put Maharaj behind bars. After all, it was the IG who tipped me off. And the viral video will definitely put

Maharaj in a precarious position,' Vikram thought as he led his forces through the farmhouse gates.

'Sir, what are you doing? You cannot enter our premises,' protested Mehta as Vikram and scores of policemen drove up in police vehicles.

'*Chalo, jaldi*. Quick, check every nook and corner,' Vikram ordered his forces, ignoring Mehta completely.

'Sir, you are just inviting trouble for yourself,' said Mehta, pulling out his cell phone and tapping on a number.

Vikram snatched Mehta's phone from his hand and slapped him hard. The other ashram workers fell silent at once.

'DSP Saheb, tell some men to take shovels to the ground at the back of the building,' Vikram said, moving forward hurriedly. He had had the element of surprise to help him make a start and now he had no time to lose.

'*Yahaan khodo*, dig here,' said Vikram, pointing to the area where the plantation drive had taken place.

An hour later, a constable ran towards Vikram.

'Sir, sir, *ek kankal mila hai*. I have found a skeleton,' said the sweat-soaked constable.

Just half an hour earlier, when the police party had dug up nothing but saplings, Vikram had begun to get jittery, imagining the storm that would break over his head if he had to leave Mehta Farm with nothing useful in his hands. Now, he felt as if he had sprouted wings and he could fly.

He, the DSP and a few other policemen ran to the pit along with the constable. A semblance of a skeleton lay uncovered, the bones disjointed. The skull stared blankly at them. Next to the skeleton was a passport and some clothes.

'Call the forensic team,' Vikram ordered his DSP and looked at the passport. It was in the name of a Madhushree Bagaria.

* * *

'The PM's chopper has landed. He will go straight to an election rally in the district where he will address the gathering and then to the temple. We have put all the forces on alert,' said the SSP Hoshiarpur, calling me from the helipad.

'Good, Mukhtiyar, the weather gods have been kind to us. Now we need not worry about lining the route. Take care of the PM's security at the rally grounds and then escort him to the temple. Meanwhile, I will oversee the security at the temple premises,' I said.

I turned to the officers I was with.

'The PM's rally should take about an hour, so he should be here by 11.30 a.m. Reddy, have you checked the temple?' I asked Mukul Reddy, a young IPS officer who had been deputed by the police HQ for the PM's visit to Hoshiarpur.

'Yes, sir, we have thoroughly checked everything in the temple premises. The bomb squad has been deployed, all the priests and temple staff have been frisked, and we have checked the hotels and guest houses in the vicinity for any suspicious visitors,' replied Reddy.

'Sounds good. The SPG will take care of the PM's close proximity security,' I replied.

'I hope the visit goes well,' said Reddy, a tad nervous.

'I'm not worried about the rally area, though there will be thousands of people thronging the ground to hear the PM's speech,' I said. 'The PM will be at a sufficient distance from the crowd, separated by layers of barricades manned by the police. And he will be behind bulletproof glass. I am more bothered about his visit to the temple.'

'But sir, he will be in the temple only with the priests and his SPG guards. We have ensured strictly controlled access to the temple and removed everyone else from the premises,' replied Reddy.

'Did you look at the lane that the PM will take to the temple? The ancient temple is surrounded by hundreds of houses encroaching on the temple premises. The PM will have to move on foot for at least 500 metres after he alights from the car. He will be out in the open for about ten minutes,' I said pensively.

'You're absolutely right, sir. The PM's motorcade will have to stop on the main road. After that the PM will have to move on foot,' replied Reddy.

Though we had asked all the residents to stay inside their houses and ensured strict access control, the lane was a dangerous area.

Both of us took a deep breath, looking at the hundreds of policemen lined up along the path to the temple. I had also placed policemen on the roofs of the houses along the path. We had done everything we could to keep the PM safe.

* * *

This is amazing! We have actually found a skeleton at the ashram, Vikram thought.

'Come on, everyone. Spread out and look for more incriminating evidence. Turn this place upside down,' he ordered.

As the forces broke into teams and began their search, Vikram and the DSP looked for Maharaj.

'He must be hiding here somewhere. This is our chance to arrest him,' said Vikram.

'Sir, let's go to the poolside. That seems to be Maharaj's residence,' said the DSP.

As the DSP and constables entered the sprawling farmhouse, Vikram stopped in his tracks. This was where the video had been shot, he remembered. He took out his phone and played the video again.

The girl was being taken down somewhere here, he thought.

He stepped closer to the building, scanning the grounds. And . . . there it was!

An air conditioning duct barely visible to the naked eye, hidden behind a number of plants.

'Why on earth would someone have an AC at such a low level? There has to be a basement somewhere,' Vikram muttered.

He straightened up and turned to Mehta, who looked horrified by Vikram's discovery.

'How do we get to this underground room?' asked Vikram, glaring at Mehta.

Mehta hesitated for a second but opened his mouth the second he saw Vikram's bodyguard raising his hand.

'*Batata hoon*, I will tell you sir,' said Mehta, quivering like jelly on a plate.

He led them to the living room and removed a majestic picture of Maharaj from the wall to reveal a small opening that led to a staircase going down.

'Ohh-kay,' thought Vikram, taking a deep breath. 'This is it. This is where we will find all the evidence we need to put this so-called God-man away.'

He told his bodyguard to call the DSP. 'I'm sure Maharaj must be down here,' he said.

The basement was pitch-dark. Vikram switched on the torch on his cell phone and ran his other hand along to the wall to see if he could find a light switch. Suddenly, he banged his head on something hard. His cell phone fell down. He grimaced and moved his hands up to feel a glass wall in front of him.

When he picked up his cell phone and pointed the torch in front of him, he nearly stopped breathing.

A girl, almost in an unconscious state, was crouched in a corner behind the glass wall. The cubicle had a bed and a commode. It was clear that the girl had been kept captive for some time.

The lights suddenly came on. The DSP and some constables had entered the basement now and were equally surprised to see the nearly comatose girl.

Vikram opened the enclosure and carried the girl to the bed.

Patting her arms lightly, trying to comfort her, he finally saw her face properly and instantly recognized her from the picture her parents had shown him. Sunidhi! The missing girl. The one Maharaj had been taking away in the video.

The girl was in bad shape, clearly drugged and starved. She was babbling incoherently, her eyes remained closed. When she finally opened them, she began screaming.

'No more, please. No more. I can't take it any more,' she sobbed.

'It's all right, Sunidhi. It's all right. You're safe. We are the police. We'll take you home,' Vikram said, patting her back to try and calm her down.

He gestured to the lady constables to take care of the girl.

'Sir, you need to come here!' the DSP shouted from elsewhere.

Vikram ran to the other side of the basement where he found another room. When he stepped in, he stopped abruptly. One wall of the room was covered with a large white board. Pictures of the PM had been pasted on the board, the PM's schedule of meetings and rallies was scribbled beside of pictures. One date was circled. 26 June. That was today.

Vikram froze, beads of sweat flowing down his face. The PM was in Hoshiarpur right now.

He turned and ran up the stairs, bursting into the living room.

'Who was in the basement?' Vikram asked Mehta, a hard look in his eyes.

'I really don't know, sir,' Mehta said. He was shaking. 'Only Maharaj Saheb has access to this place. A few years ago, purely by chance, I saw Maharaj Saheb removing that portrait and going down the stairs, and that's when I learnt that there was a basement under the building. This is my farmhouse, but the plans were drawn up to Maharaj's specifications.'

Vikram looked at Mehta's frightened face closely and knew he was not lying. Any experienced policeman can largely gauge if a person is telling the truth simply by looking in that person's eyes.

'Mehta, help me find Maharaj or I will make sure you're finished for good,' threatened Vikram.

'Sir, he must be here. He was in the farmhouse when you arrived,' Mehta said, his voice shaking. Maharaj's time was definitely up. There was no point becoming a martyr to a lost cause.

The police team searched all the floors of the building, inch by inch, including the basement. But there was no sign of the God-man.

'Where the hell is he?' wondered Vikram, standing in the hall where Maharaj addressed his disciples.

He turned to his bodyguard. 'Ask DSP Saheb if we have checked all the bathrooms properly,' he said.

The team spread out on every floor, checking all the bathrooms thoroughly too. The policemen pulled out mirrors, cisterns and commodes, but no secret door or hiding place could be found.

Finally, only one bathroom was left. The walls were wet, as though someone had taken a hot, steamy shower just a little while earlier.

'Who the hell takes a steam bath when the police are raiding his residence?' the DSP muttered to himself.

He lifted a bathrobe lying on the wet floor. A pair of slippers lay in a corner of the bathroom.

'Why would anyone leave his clothes and slippers behind?' the DSP wondered as he returned to the bedroom.

'Maybe he saw us enter the compound and fled,' said an inspector.

'But there was no chance of running away. We came in too fast and surrounded the entire farmhouse. He has to be here somewhere,' said the DSP.

He returned to the bathroom, examining the walls.

'Odd,' he thought. 'Why is one wall made of wood?'

He looked at the wooden wall closely. Minute holes had been drilled into it.

Perplexed, he began knocking on the wall.

'There is a hollow behind this wall for sure. The sound is different here,' said the DSP to himself, slowly running his hands over the area to check for protrusions or anything else out of the ordinary.

He pushed a section of the wall hard and the panelling swung open, revealing a naked man behind it.

'What a shame! The legendary Maharaj Saheb crouched naked behind his bathroom wall. Jai ho Maharaj ki!' said the jubilant DSP.

* * *

'Why are the PM's pictures and schedule in that room in the basement?' Vikram asked Maharaj.

'Do whatever you have to do to me, but I won't tell you anything. All those who have sinned will have to pay with their lives,' replied Maharaj with a cold, steely resolve.

Vikram sat back, defeated for the moment. There was not much he could do to make the God-man talk. The man was not only very well connected but he also had a massive following of millions. There was no time for a sustained interrogation as the PM's programme was already underway, and the use of third-degree interrogation techniques was out of the question.

He returned to the room in the basement. There was no room for complications now. He had been given a rare opportunity to nab Maharaj and had excellent evidence against him that would convict him for sure. The skeleton of a woman, and even better, a woman who had been kept in illegal custody, had been recovered from the ashram with the God-man personally present on the premises. The video would be corroborated by Sunidhi herself. It had already gone viral and nobody could claim that it was fake.

Vikram returned his attention to the white board. The schedule encompassed six months of the PM's travels and visits across the country and included all the details of the routes and venues, particularly those in Punjab..

He turned away, looking around the room. There had to be something here to tell him what was going on.

Vikram rummaged through the room again, overturning everything in sight. As he threw out the contents of a drawer, he found a diary, a number of false beards and a few police uniforms. The beards reminded him of the encounter he had had with terrorists in Pathankot. He clearly remembered recovering false beards and police uniforms that day too. That encounter had taken place just a day before the PM's rallies and meetings in Pathankot.

He looked at the false beards and police uniforms again. There was no doubt that he was staring at a possible conspiracy to attack the PM. Or was he getting paranoid? If it turned out to be a false alarm, Vikram would become the laughingstock of the police fraternity. His career could also be derailed for his overzealousness.

He picked up the diary and went through its pages. It had codes very similar to the ones he had seen in the diary recovered from the terrorist's hideout in Pathankot. He remembered giving the diary to the IB in the hope that the code could be deciphered.

He flipped through the pages of the diary, still none the wiser, and stopped suddenly. One page appeared to have been torn out.

'What was so special about that page?' Vikram wondered.

As he touched the next page, he could feel the faintest of indents made by a pen on the paper. Vikram immediately took out his own pen and began shading the paper with it. As the ink spread on the page, an image appeared.

It was a drone.

43

View from the Roof

After performing the *aarti*, the PM stepped back, taking in the marvellous architecture of the centuries-old temple. I wondered if he was enjoying some me time in his otherwise extremely busy schedule.

'The PM is about to move towards the main road again. Please get the motorcade ready,' I directed Mukhtiyar on the phone.

I was quite pleased with how well everything was going. We were right on schedule.

I left the temple for the main road so I could escort the PM to the helipad, confident that Reddy and the SPG entourage would lead the PM safely through the 500-metre stretch from the temple to the road.

As I got into my car, my mobile phone buzzed. It was Vikram.

'Sir, we have recovered a skeleton from the grounds of the ashram and also the missing girl, Sunidhi. Maharaj has also been arrested, but sir—'

'Excellent work, Vikram!' I interrupted jubilantly.

'Sir, please listen, I have discovered a plot to attack the PM with a drone,' Vikram said frantically.

'What? What are you saying?' I asked tensely.

'I think the attack will happen any time now,' Vikram continued, almost shouting into the phone.

I opened the car door and scanned the congested area along the lane through which the PM was moving. The houses were chock-a-block, their roofs inter-connected. Swipers and policemen stood perched on the rooftops. Some policemen grew casual as the PM was about to depart. There was nothing alarming. Everything was calm. I was about to sit back in the car thinking that it was a false alarm that my eyes caught a flicker in the sky. I looked up, my eyes widening with horror at the sight above.

A drone hovered above the lane.

I ran to the lane, Bhajan Singh following me like a shadow.

'Reddy, there is a chance of an attack on the PM. Please alert the SPG and take the PM to the main road so we can evacuate him,' I shouted into my cell phone as I pushed past the crowds to the first house on the lane.

The drone was too high up to be shot from street level. I knew I'd miss it if I tried, and I didn't want to spread panic with the sound of a gunshot either. I had to get on the roof of one of these houses to take care of the drone.

'Please, God, please let this drone just be photographing or videoing the PM's programme,' I prayed, banging on the door of the house. It was unlikely, though. The district administration and police strictly enforced the MHA's drone policy that disallowed the flying of drones in secure areas.

The door fell open, the owner of the house raging. 'What are you doing?' he yelled.

I barged into the house, pushing him out of the way.

'Where are the stairs? I need to go up,' I shouted at the man.

A boy in the courtyard pointed the way. I ran up the narrow flight of stairs, stumbling a few times, Bhajan at my heels.

* * *

The PM did a final namaste to the temple priests and set off down the lane, accompanied by his bodyguards.

'Just around 300 metres to go,' muttered Shalin, the young SPG officer who headed the close protection team that was always at the PM's side.

The narrow, congested lane had been giving him nightmares ever since the PM's programme had been planned. It would be impossible to enforce security in this place, should something go wrong. 'These PM visits are terrifying,' he muttered to himself.

Just as Shalin laid eyes on the motorcade at the entrance of the lane, a thunderous blast rocked the area. It took Shalin a few moments to gather his bearings before he could arrive at the most logical realization—the PM of India was under attack.

* * *

For a few moments, Bhajan Singh and I were too shocked to react. Then, I ran to the edge of the terrace.

'Is the PM okay?' I yelled, my heart in my mouth.

Smoke rose from the mangled remains of a police car far from the lane. It was parked almost 150 metres away from the PM's car.

The SPG had been insisting on the use of a BMW 7 series car for the PM of late. The car could easily survive attacks from handguns up to .44 calibre magnum and most automatic weapons like the AK 47. The luxury ride also sported twenty-inch alloys with tyres capable of running even when flat. Even the fuel tank was self-sealing and the car also had an internal oxygen supply.

The PM's motorcade always comprises a minimum of five vehicles, including the VVIP car, a spare VVIP car and other mandatory vehicles like the advance pilot warning vehicle, a technical car and an ambulance.

The IED jammer that was part of the PM's security detail was capable of preventing the explosion of any remote-controlled IED in the range of up to 100 metres.

So, the police vehicle that had exploded had either been out of the IED jamming device's range, or it had been rigged with an IED using a timer, something that did not require a radio frequency to be triggered.

The blast had been massive, creating a crater around the car. Thick smoke engulfed the lane and neither the PM nor his security personnel were visible.

My heart felt like it would explode.

'Please, God, let the PM be safe,' I prayed, my mind a mess of myriad thoughts. 'If the PM of India was assassinated, it was under my watch. I am solely responsible for this fiasco. If only I had come a few days earlier to personally check the security arrangements. If only Vikram had called a few hours earlier . . .'

I clutched my chest; sure that I was having a heart attack.

* * *

'Sir, the girl Sunidhi, she said something. She's still incoherent, but I think the drugs are wearing off,' said the DSP.

'Could you figure out what she said?' asked Vikram.

'She keeps talking about some man. You must come here.'

Vikram left Maharaj in the custody of the other policemen and rushed out.

Sunidhi was sitting in a corner, covered with a shawl. She was hiccupping, probably an after effect of crying too much.

'She must be deeply traumatized,' Vikram thought, horrified by what she must have gone through.

'Please, save me from that man, please. I am so scared,' Sunidhi said, her hands folded in supplication. Her tears had dried now, but she still looked terrified.

'Who? The God-man? We have arrested him, don't worry,' said the DSP.

'Not him. The other man. He was all over me every night. He beat me, abused me,' said Sunidhi, her voice breaking.

'Which other man? Who are you talking about?' asked Vikram.

'I thought Maharaj was a bad dream but the last few days with the other man were terrible. That man was much younger and stronger, almost like a bull. His hands were as hard as rocks. He mauled me so badly,' Sunidhi was sobbing again.

'Can you describe him for us?' asked Vikram.

'I don't want to remember his face but I know I won't ever forget him. He had a squint in his eye,' Sunidhi said.

Hmm. This must be one of the god-man's VIP guests. That's why he brought him to the basement, thought Vikram.

'One more thing. He was hard of hearing,' Sunidhi concluded, burying her face in the shawl that still covered her.

Vikram stood still. There was something he remembered . . . something he had once seen.

He looked away from Sunidhi and began pacing the room, begging his brain to spit out the memory.

Hearing aids. That's right. There had been hearing aids on the counter in front of the mirror in that house in Pathankot. He had picked them up, he recalled.

And Kamran, the terrorist they had caught. Kamran had clearly mentioned a man with a squint during his interrogation by the JIC in Pathankot.

It all came together in a flash.

Sunidhi's tormentor was the fourth terrorist. The one who had escaped during the encounter in Pathankot.

* * *

The smoke had cleared a bit now. From my vantage point on the terrace, I glimpsed a man in a kurta pyjama and waistcoat. It was the Prime Minister of India. His head and shoulders were covered in dust, but he was upright. The SPG men were shielding him with their bodies, doing their duty.

I pulled out my phone and called Shalin.

'Shalin, take the PM to the safe house. Do not go to the main road. We don't know how many other cars are rigged with explosives,' I shouted.

'Right, sir, Reddy and I will take PM Sir to the safe house,' Shalin confirmed. His voice was shaking.

* * *

The SPG had come into existence by an Act of the Parliament with a single mandate: to protect the prime minister at all times, whether in India or abroad. As the head of the CPT, Shalin was directly responsible for the safety of the PM—and he had almost failed. His worst nightmare had very nearly come true.

His ears still ringing from the sound of the explosion, Shalin pulled himself together and stood like a rock in front of the PM, ready for any bullet or blast intended for the country's leader. It was his duty and he would lay down his life without a flinch. But he could not guarantee the PM's safety from the first bullet. He could only protect the PM from the second bullet. And what about explosives? And the drone that was still hovering over them?

* * *

Who triggered the bomb in the police car? And who is controlling the drone? I wondered, jumping the foot-high walls that separated the interconnected terraces of the houses on the lane, trying to find the person controlling the drone.

My phone vibrated. There were five missed calls from Vikram.

I called him back.

'Sir, sir! The terrorist is the fourth guy, the man we could not find during the encounter in Pathankot,' said Vikram, sounding almost delirious.

'What? What are you saying? I don't understand,' I said.

'Sir, the man with the squint eye, whose hearing aids I had picked up,' said Vikram after a deep breath. He described his conversation with Sunidhi.

It all came back to me. I remembered the entire Pathankot encounter with the terrorists vividly. We had killed one and arrested Timur Ali and Kamran but could not find the fourth one. We had managed to save the PM the last time but there was a clear and present danger right now!

I disconnected the call. Now at least I had an idea of who I was looking for.

44

The Room with the Mirror

'Hey, you, check every man in each house. Look for a man with a squint. Report any suspicious activity to me immediately,' I said to a subinspector stationed on the terrace of one of the houses.

'Jai Hind, sir! Absolutely clear,' replied the SI, saluting.

I looked around me. There were a number of police officers and snipers stationed on the rooftops of the houses and other vantage points above the lane leading to the temple. I shouted at a few snipers to shoot at the drone, but most of them looked too shell-shocked to react.

Bhajan Singh and I ran along the line of interconnected terraces, following the PM and his entourage who were running down the lane towards the safe house.

I looked up. The drone was hovering over the safe house marked for the PM.

I frowned. 'Who is operating this drone? Why is it over the safe house?'

A number of questions clouded my mind as I scrambled on to the terrace of the house that was almost at the end of the lane.

'This is the last house. If the attacker is not here, he must be hiding somewhere far off. Or does the drone work on artificial intelligence?' I thought, recalling the assassination of the Iranian general Qasem Soleimani in a US drone attack.

* * *

'The car exploded ahead of time. The timer did not work properly, I guess. The PM is well protected by the team now, so I have to wait till the SPG takes him to the safe house. That should be in a few minutes. The safe house is about 300 metres further down the road,' whispered the man manipulating the drone.

He was dressed in a police uniform.

He relaxed his shoulders, the expression on his face a strange combination of rage and sorrow. In just a few minutes, he would finally have his revenge for the deaths of his family and his children, on the fateful night of 27 March 2020, when elite commandos of the Indian Army had stormed the terrorist hideouts in Malalkot in Pakistan-occupied Kashmir.

The Indian commandos had been conducting searches for terrorists when they entered his house. It happened so suddenly that he did not have any time to protect his family, neither from the terrorists camping in his house nor from the Indian commandos. The terrorists used his wife, his father, his son as human shields and started firing on the commandos. The Indian forces had no choice but to retaliate. It was collateral damage they could not avoid, but for him, it was his family.

He shuddered as the memories overwhelmed him. Holding the lifeless body of his five-year-old son in his arms, his pregnant wife dying next to him. Memories of digging graves for his entire family.

As he'd dug their graves that day, he'd made a solemn vow. He would wage a personal war against the Indian state, particularly the prime minister who had ordered the surgical strikes.

The very next morning, he joined the Liberation Front. After training at the camps run by the Jaish-e-Mohammad, he had been ISI's blue-eyed boy, carrying out any terrorist attack that entailed the use of IEDs. During one such operation, an IED had exploded too close to him, resulting in the loss of hearing and damage to his left eye.

Last year, the ISI had sent him to India with Timur Ali to attack high profile targets and destabilize the ongoing peace process between India and Pakistan. But he and Timur had made it their personal mission to revenge themselves on none other than the Prime Minister of India.

* * *

'Suno, listen! Have you seen anyone carrying a remote or an electronic gadget on the rooftops or down in the lane?' I shouted at a tall, muscular policeman standing on the terrace with his back to me.

The man did not budge.

'*Sunai nahi deta, kya*, don't you hear me? IG Saheb is calling you,' Bhajan shouted.

I bent over, trying to catch my breath after sprinting across the rooftops.

The man did not respond to Bhajan. It seemed as though he was texting on his phone, but he was also looking up. It was strange.

Bhajan moved forward to confront him.

He turned towards us for a brief moment. Given our respective positions on the terrace, my eyes should have met his, but they didn't. Because the man had a squint in his left eye. And then I saw a remote control in his hand.

'Bhajan, stop him,' I shouted.

Bhajan hesitated for a moment, probably wondering why I was ordering him to nab a police officer. The next moment, the man had vanished inside the house.

I cursed and ran after him.

He thundered down the staircase and ran into a room across the courtyard. I cocked my Glock and went after him. The room was dark and empty. Where had he gone?

Bhajan arrived within a moment and switched on the torch on his cell phone. The whole room lit up, the torch reflecting off a large mirror in front of us, one that spanned the breadth of the wall.

I stilled, the Pathankot encounter flashing back in my mind. Then, I grabbed Bhajan and pulled him down with me.

The next moment, a burst of bullets sprayed over our heads.

Not an automatic weapon, a pistol, I observed mentally, my years of experience with weapons having turned into instinct.

'Switch off your torch,' I shouted at Bhajan, firing my Glock towards the mirror from my position on the ground.

Bhajan immediately placed his cell phone upside down on the floor, effectively blocking the torchlight and started firing at the mirror too. Within seconds, we heard a cry of pain.

For a very brief moment, Bhajan turned his mobile phone. The mirror had been shattered by our bullets and the man was clearly visible, his face shrivelled up with pain, blood oozing from his ear. When he saw the light, he raised his arm to shoot at us but was just a fraction of a second too late. As the 9 mm bullet from my Glock punctured his lung, he collapsed.

Slowly, Bhajan and I got up. Weapons in hand, we crept towards the shattered mirror that revealed the chamber within. The man was very obviously dead.

I smiled, slapping Bhajan on the back.

Ha! Charu and the armourer should have been here, I thought, pleased with my shooting skills with a small weapon. Then I snapped back to business.

I snatched the drone's remote control from the floor where the man had dropped it and ran back to the terrace. The PM had almost reached the safe house, and the drone was still in the air.

'Should I crash it? But I don't know if it's carrying an explosive,' I thought.

No. I had to bring it back to the terrace. I moved the joystick carefully, worrying all the while that the drone might explode.

It landed on the terrace, whirring noisily, and I rushed to it, seeking its power source with trembling hands.

There it was.

I switched off the drone. The whirring sound stopped abruptly.

45

'Congratulations!'

'Sir, the PMO has sent you a congratulatory note. A court of inquiry has been set up to look into all the lapses that led to the attack on the PM. And the NIA has taken over the investigation of the blast case,' said Vikram.

'Congratulations to you, too, Vikram,' I said. 'Putting someone like Maharaj behind bars is no mean feat. You deserve all the commendations possible for that daring raid on the ashram. And thanks so much for alerting me about the drone attack on the PM.'

'We were extremely lucky, sir. It was purely by chance that I discovered the terror plot when I found Sunidhi. It was she who gave me the description of the terrorist,' said Vikram.

I sighed deeply. To say I was relieved would have been an understatement. My life had gone through so many twists and turns in just a few weeks that even a Bollywood potboiler paled in comparison. My story had drama, romance, love, emotion, betrayal and action. It had everything. And it was all ending on a good note.

'There are still some unanswered questions, though,' said Vikram. 'I'm sure the investigations will reveal the answers, but I'd still like to hear your opinion on these mysteries. You know how much I admire you, and you are a national hero now, a role model for so many people like me.'

I smiled at the irony of Vikram's praise. I had become a hero from a possible zero. I had done so much wrong, ethically and professionally, that only some divine power could have come to my rescue.

'Please, Vikram. I'm not a role model. I am an ordinary human being and far from perfect. I just got plain lucky,' I said.

'You have always been too modest about your numerous achievements,' said Vikram.

'Stop embarrassing me. Just ask your questions, Vikram,' I said, my mood shifting to one of introspection.

I had been so proud of myself, so proud of being a person whom everybody admired. Then I had cheated on my wife, buried a murder victim and changed the course of an investigation to save myself. I didn't know if I could ever forgive myself. But life had to go on.

'Yes, sir. First question. Why would Maharaj keep Sunidhi at his ashram?'

'Come on, Vikram, what kind of a question is that! Surely the answer is obvious. Maharaj is totally debauched. He kept Sunidhi drugged and captive so he and his friends could easily exploit her for their pleasure. He isn't the only God-man in the country to do such a thing. Quite a number of them have been accused of abusing women and minor girls,' I replied.

'So why did he kill that singer, Madhushree?' asked Vikram.

I stared at the wall, gathering my emotional strength to be able to answer Vikram's question.

'He must have thought Madhushree had made the video to blackmail him. Later on, he would have realized that the blackmailer was really Madhav, so he had him killed too,' I said, reliving the entire chain of events in my mind.

'But why not kill Sunidhi too, since he knew that someone had made a video of him taking her down to the basement?' asked Vikram.

'That's a valid point, Vikram. He may have thought that since he had eliminated the two people who had been aware of the video, it would be safe to keep Sunidhi in captivity. Moreover, he was a very powerful man with influential connections. He probably never even imagined that an intrepid police officer like you would ever actually raid his ashram and arrest him.'

'Still. He must have been really fond of Sunidhi to keep her alive for so long,' said Vikram.

'Maybe. But I think he kept her alive for the squint-eyed terrorist. He must have been infatuated with poor Sunidhi. He tormented her so much for so long.'

'So who killed Madhushree and Madhav?'

'Ah! A source told me that it was some suspended subinspector of police, a guy called Atulkar,' I replied, thinking about that ghost-like man. Though I knew Atulkar had actually been the killer, I did not have any real evidence against him.

'Atulkar? Really, sir? He was such a celebrated cop in the ATS! They loved him for his trigger-happy ways and his ruthlessness. But where is he now? He has almost become a ghost! No one has seen him for a long time,' asked Vikram.

'I don't know,' I said slowly.

A chill ran down my spine.

Where is he? I thought.

46

Too much Whisky

'*Ek glass aur,* Munni, give me one more glass,' said Sood, his eyes glued to the TV screen.

'How much you will drink, saheb? Drinking too much is not good for you,' said Munni Lal, the cook.

'*Chal, bhaag yahan se,* go away,' shouted Sood, banging the glass table.

He looked at the TV one last time and switched it off. The news channel was airing the election results, and his party was being routed. He himself was trailing by a huge margin. The writing was on the wall. His political career was over, and it was a matter of time before the NIA linked him with the illegal activities of Maharaj Saheb.

'If that video had not been leaked, the police would never have raided the ashram and no skeleton would have been discovered,' Sood railed, flinging his glass against the wall.

'And why did Maharaj not get rid of that girl, Sunidhi? And how the hell was Madhushree's skeleton found in the ashram? Atulkar killed her in the hotel and personally checked her mobile phone. He did not find any video. Even Madhav died before the video was leaked. So how did the video get on social media?'

He paced the room in a drunken fury.

'I was the home minister. Yet I could not save Maharaj from the police. So Maharaj's followers have every reason to be angry and not vote for me. Without their support, my party and I are nothing.'

Sood looked at himself in the mirror. He had aged considerably in the last few days. He resumed pacing.

'Now that I'm out of power, I can do nothing to harm those two police officers. I want to destroy their lives the way they destroyed mine. Those bastards did not even give me an inkling of their plans. I could have stopped them if I had had any idea what was going on.'

Hands shaking, Sood poured himself another whisky and swallowed the drink in a gulp. His throat burned, but his fury flared hotter.

'Hopefully, I won't be linked to Madhushree's murder. There's nothing to connect me with her anyway,' he grumbled, thinking of his meetings with Atulkar, the Ghost. There was no way he could be linked to Atulkar either. He had been very careful in his meetings and WhatsApp calls.

Did Atulkar rat me out? No way. Atulkar was obsessed with his revenge. And I promised to drop all the charges against him and reinstate him in the police department if he did my dirty jobs, the way that inspector involved in the Antilla case was reinstated in Maharashtra, thought Sood.

The NIA will come after me now. But it will not have any evidence against me. Or maybe it will manufacture some. I don't know. I did not even know what Atulkar got from across the border. I just followed the Maharaj's instructions. I had nothing to do with the terrorist attack on the PM. In fact, the terror attack created a huge sympathy wave for the PM. He'll be back in power with a huge majority. Why the hell did Maharaj conspire with a foreign terrorist to get our PM killed?

Sood was thinking so hard, he was convinced his brain would explode.

'Munni Lal, pour me another drink,' shouted the former home minister of the state.

'Sir, you've had too many already,' said Munni Lal.

Sood glared at him. The cook did not say another word. He simply filled the glass to the brim.

As he was about to leave Sood's study, Munni Lal picked up a mobile phone lying on the desk.

'Sir, *kya main ye phone le loon*? Can I take this phone? It is quite an ordinary phone, not something befitting your stature. And it has been gathering dust on your desk for the last month,' said Munni Lal, looking hopefully at the phone.

'*Le ja*. Take it and get out. As though I care about some cell phone when I have lost everything,' Sood cursed, tapping his ring-laden fingers on his glass of whisky. He was too drunk to care about a phone.

47

'A Fresh Beginning'

'Come on, Charu, let's go. It looks as though it's going to rain,' I said, looking lovingly at my wife.

She still didn't speak to me much, but I knew she was trying to forgive me for my misdeeds.

'Why do you always forget your gun? The threat to you is even greater now,' she said, giving me my Glock and getting into the car next to me.

'I was paranoid once, with so many threats from criminals and dreaded terrorists. But now they're either dead or behind bars, and I am a much-relieved man. I just want to live a normal life now,' I said.

Charu did not reply.

'Charu, I'm sorry. I'm trying to make a fresh beginning. I know I've blundered, but I'm human. Please forgive me,' I said, with all the sincerity I could muster.

I don't know how I managed to talk to Charu like this, but I was pleased with myself for even trying.

The developments of the last few days had been extremely positive for me. I was being feted for having saved the Prime Minister of India, and the Madhushree case was being investigated by an SIT headed by Vikram, my protégé.

All the evidence points towards Maharaj. And he actually deserves to be behind bars for this because he is the one who had Madhushree killed, I thought, looking out of the window at the beautiful countryside.

'Bhajan Singh, play some romantic Kishore Kumar songs!' I said, reaching out to take Charu's hand.

Like a disciplined policeman, Bhajan Singh immediately complied, playing the hauntingly melodious duet *Tere mere milan ki ye raina*, sung marvellously by Kishore and Lata.

I looked at Charu's hand in mine. She was looking out of the window, her face turned away from me. But she didn't withdraw her hand from mine.

Happiness flooded my heart. Her attitude towards me was thawing. I had been delighted that she had even agreed to take a break in Shimla with me to get over the harrowing days of the week earlier and had resolved not to push her too fast. But now she was letting me hold her hand.

I let her hand go and began playing with her luscious hair, my fingers caressing her cheek on purpose.

She turned to look at me. 'Don't get any ideas,' she warned.

But there was a thin smile on her face. My joy knew no bounds and I hugged her immediately.

'Bhajan Singh and Pratap are also in the car,' Charu pointed out warningly.

'I don't care. I love my wife, and I have every legal right to show it,' I said, planting a kiss on her cheek.

* * *

'This is the place you thought of for a romantic getaway? Really, Mr One-of-the-Most-Brilliant-Cops-India-Has-Seen?' mocked Charu, referring to a particularly gushing newspaper editorial about me that had been published after the attempt on the PM's life.

'I'm so sorry. Google Maps led me astray. I genuinely typed Lovers' Point,' I replied, slapping my head.

'And your Lovers' Point turned out to be this,' sniggered Charu, pointing at a board next to our lovely cottage, one that read 'Suicide Point'.

'*Kya farak padta hai*, what difference does it make? Every lover commits suicide after getting married,' I said jokingly.

'You and your cheesy dialogues! Please stop watching those silly Bollywood romances.'

'And you stop watching those absolutely illogical suspense thrillers where the killer is revealed in the very first scene,' I replied.

We looked at each other and burst into laughter, guffawing madly. It had been a long time since we'd been at peace with each other. And with ourselves.

As I put my arm around Charu's shoulders, turning us both for a view of the valley below, my phone rang.

'I told you to put your phone on silent. Can't we have some privacy here at least?' protested Charu.

'It's Vikram. He must have an update about the progress of the SIT,' I said, looking at my phone. Charu made a face, but she knew the call was important.

'Yes, Vikram, tell me,' I said.

'Sir, you won't believe what just happened! I had been checking for activity on Madhushree's phone for days and today, I finally found it switched on! Quite a few calls were made from her phone,' said an excited Vikram.

'Seriously? Who was using it?' I asked, equally excited.

'We arrested one Munni Lal today. He had put a new SIM into Madhushree's phone. The cyber cell found him while monitoring the IMEI number of Madhushree's mobile phone,' said Vikram.

'Who's Munni Lal? I've never heard of him. Is he some big criminal?'

'No, sir. He is a simple cook, but he works for a big man.' Vikram sounded absolutely delighted.

'Big man? Who?'

'Yes, sir, a big man . . . Sood. Our respected former home minister.'

'Really? Are you serious?'

I was shocked beyond words. The former home minister of the state!

'Munni claimed he got the phone from Sood. And Mr Sood did not protest at all when we arrested him,' said Vikram.

'You arrested him already?'

I was so stunned that all I could do was repeat Vikram's words.

'Yes, sir. We have sufficient evidence to link him with Madhushree's murder. The present CM personally told me to fearlessly take action against anyone linked to Maharaj. Sood has been disowned by his party too.'

'This is amazing, Vikram! I'm so proud of you! Let's close this case as soon as possible. I'll come back tomorrow,' I said.

'But sir, you're on leave till the weekend,' said Vikram.

'That's all right. This is a very important case. I need to put all the missing links together so we have a watertight case against Maharaj and Sood. I would return today if I could, but Charu doesn't like travelling at night, especially on hill roads.'

'See you tomorrow then, sir. Jai Hind,' said Vikram.

'It was the former home minister who was behind it all,' I said, turning to Charu. 'Good that everyone involved in Madhushree's murder is behind bars.'

'Are you sure there was no one else?' asked Charu.

I thought about it. 'Was there anyone left to trace?'.

48

'Why Do You Always Forget Your Pistol?'

I looked at the valley from the kitchen balcony, waiting for Charu to come back with water from the cottage. The fall was very steep. No wonder this place attracted people with death on their minds.

Suddenly dizzy, I stepped back, only to see a fist coming at my face. There was no time to react. The blow came too fast and too hard; for a moment, I was stunned, my ears ringing.

'So, IG Saheb, you thought you'd get away with your fling with that singer in the hotel? I'm going to spoil this romantic holiday of yours today,' said a husky voice.

It was Atulkar, looking more menacing than ever.

'You! What are you doing here?' I asked, shocked to see my nemesis in my cottage.

'I was the one who killed your girlfriend. And now I will kill you and your wife. You destroyed my life. I hate you so much that I could kill you with my bare hands,' he said, reaching for my neck.

Though I struggled in his grip, it was useless. I knew I'd soon lose consciousness.

'Where the hell is Charu?' I thought, trying in vain to release his grip on my throat. He was much too strong for me. The only way I could get him to release me would be to hit him on a vulnerable part of his body.

I let go of his fingers, balled my hand into a fist and lashed out at his throat. It was a wild blow, but somehow I managed to strike his jugular vein. He fell back, clutching his throat and I stepped away from him.

'I know you feel you've been wronged, but that does not mean that you kill innocent people,' I gasped, barely in control of my breath.

'Don't give me this bullshit. I gave the police department everything and what did I get in return? I was imprisoned for killing a corrupt businessman who had bribed his way to wealth. I lost my family, I cannot see my only child. I have been treated as a pariah. And you expect me to forget it? I worked as a security officer with the same PM you saved when he was a minister in the state. But when I got in trouble, he disowned me. Even my mentor, Ravi Bhushan, did not help me. Only people like Maharaj, Sood and Timur Ali gave me reason to live, to seek my vengeance,' snarled Atulkar as he jumped at me again.

This time I was better prepared. I ducked and tried to hit him on his groin. But I missed and hit his rock-hard abdomen instead.

'You will die a horrible death, Arjun Kumar,' Atulkar shouted, hitting me with all his strength.

'But why? What is your issue with me? I was just doing my job,' I said, grimacing with pain and trying to fend him off.

'You just did your job. It's easy for you to say. It was you who implicated me in the case. You were the investigating officer. It's because of you that I went to jail, it's because of you that my family disowned me,' Atulkar shouted.

It was as though a pipe had burst above my head, dousing me in cold water. Suddenly, I remembered what had happened. I was the one who had found him guilty when I was posted as DIG CID. After that case, I had received a central deputation and forgotten all about him.

'If you knew I was responsible for your agony, why didn't you kill me earlier?' I asked, looking straight into my assailant's eyes.

'Oh, you were at the top of my hit list when I got out of jail. But you were so well protected, always surrounded by bodyguards. When I saw you with that singer Madhushree in the hotel, I knew I had a golden opportunity. I had to kill her anyway, but in doing so, I could frame you for her death and destroy you completely, professionally and personally. I easily found out your suite number from the reception and went upstairs using my old police connections with the hotel staff. I still don't know how you managed to wriggle out of that situation, but it doesn't matter. Now, you will die,' Atulkar hissed, moving towards me again, his deft fingers wrapping around my neck.

I could feel my strength slipping away, my mind and body growing numb.

'So, this is the end,' I thought.

I had imagined that my whole life would play before my eyes like a movie reel when I died, but the only thing I could think of now was Charu.

I called her name feebly and there she was. A little blurry, but there. A dying dream, I thought, my eyes slowly closing.

There was a sharp movement in the corner of my eye—Charu moved closer to the two of us, my Glock in her hands.

'Oy! Let go of my husband or I'll shoot,' said Charu in a steely voice.

Atulkar turned around, looking at her incredulously before he got a grip on himself.

'Madam! Welcome,' he said sarcastically. 'I would have let you live because I have no grudge with you. But now that you're here, I have no choice but to kill you too. Do you know, even that singer tried to shoot me. But do women even know how to use a gun? She didn't even know how to remove the safety catch.'

Charu did not bat an eyelid. In one swift motion, she calmly removed the Glock's safety catch and cocked the gun.

Atulkar turned pale. He knew now that Charu wasn't bluffing; this woman could shoot.

Pushing me out of the way, he ran towards Charu. Instinctively, I shoved my leg in his way causing him to lose his balance; he went scrambling for the balcony rail for support. But he had tumbled too fast. Between the speed of his fall and the bulk of his body, he crashed right through the wooden rail and off the cliff.

As the echo of his shriek died down, I stood up dizzily, my mind slowly processing what had just happened. I opened my arms to Charu.

'Why the hell do you always forget your pistol? And why do I always have to get it for you?' she snapped, slapping my chest in frustration before bursting into tears.

49

'I Just Got Plain Lucky'

'Sir, the NIA team is progressing very fast with its investigation. It has come up with quite a few revelations,' said Mukhtiyar, the Hoshiarpur SSP.

'Yes, the NIA is equipped with the latest gadgets and technology. And of course, our police team also helped,' I said. 'What did the NIA learn?'

'Sir, the terrorist's name was Altaf. He was an explosives expert and according to IB reports, he had been very active in Afghanistan. Though he was highly trained, he kept a very low profile. The ISI had assigned him and Timur Ali to carry out terror attacks in Punjab to rekindle the militancy by connecting him with our dubious god-man, Maharaj. But even the ISI did not know that he would go after our PM,' said Mukhtiyar, summing up the NIA report.

'If the PM had been assassinated, there would have been catastrophe. We would have had a war for sure,' I said pensively.

'The NIA says the car that exploded was the city DSP's official car. Luckily, the car was empty at the time. But the report so far does not mention how the terrorist planted the bomb in the car.'

'The terrorist must have had access to all the security plans for the PM's visit,' I mused. 'We assign all the police officers their duties well in advance. In any case, the city DSP has to be an integral part of the PM's security drill.

And it would certainly not be difficult to plant explosives in his car.'

'You're right, sir. According to the NIA, the DSP's car was blown up as a diversionary tactic. Altaf knew the car would not be part of the PM's immediate motorcade but blew it to create a commotion and divert the PM to the safe house,' Mukhtiyar continued. 'Then he planned to crash the explosives-laden drone into the safe house. It had enough RDX to blow up two or three such houses. But you saved the day!'

'Nothing like that, Mukhtiyar. I just got plain lucky,' I replied.

'Of course, sir. Luck plays a big part in any policeman's success. You have always said so,' said Mukhtiyar.

'Altaf must have planned this strike immediately after the PMO announced the visit to Hoshiarpur. The congested lane through which the PM had to walk was a nightmare for the SPG but a golden opportunity for any attacker.'

'Sir, but how did he manage to go to the terrace?' asked the SSP.

'He must have rented or even bought the house with the help of Maharaj. I'm sure the NIA must have found the owner of the house already. And it would not have been difficult for him to put on a police uniform and mingle with the other policemen deployed on the terrace,' I said.

'Absolutely right, sir. The NIA has already detained the house owner, one Sampat Ram. He is a staunch follower of Maharaj Saheb.'

The two of us pored over pictures of the drone that had been intended to attack the PM.

'It's a simple quad copter, not very difficult to procure. The RDX must have been smuggled from across the border with the help of his benefactors, of course,' I said.

'Sir, why would he not shoot the PM? Why use a drone instead of a sniper gun?' asked Mukhtiyar.

'It's not easy to shoot from a distance. The sniper has to adjust to a number of factors like the angle of the shot, wind speed and so on. Altaf already had a squint eye, so he must not have felt confident of his shooting skills. One miss and the SPG commandos would have formed a human shield and protected the PM with their lives,' I said, as I continued reading the reports.

'Maharaj Saheb had been getting a lot of funding from foreign-based terror groups to incite the local people to create unrest,' I added. 'The state home minister might not be involved in the assassination bid, but he must surely have assisted Maharaj and his followers in money laundering and drug smuggling. Sood definitely benefitted from the rise of Maharaj as the sect's followers voted en masse for Sood and his party.'

'Sir, the NIA will charge Maharaj for conspiring with Altaf to kill the PM. I'm quite hopeful that he will be finished for good this time. In any case, he will definitely be convicted for his crimes against women. Sunidhi's testimony and the recovery of that singer's skeleton will ensure that the fraud God-man is well and truly punished,' said Mukhtiyar.

'That singer's name was Madhushree,' I said, with a heavy heart. 'Your colleague Vikram is investigating those cases. I'm sure he'll make certain that the culprits are punished.'

'Sir, who was the police officer who provided Altaf with the information? He needs to be arrested too.'

'The NIA has already found out about him. His name is Vijay Atulkar. He was a subinspector of police, an encounter specialist of the ATS who was dismissed from service for a fake encounter. While in jail, he met the Liberation Front chief, Timur Ali. Atulkar was already disgruntled with the PM and Timur Ali added fuel to his hatred of the Indian government,' I explained.

'Through Timur Ali, Atulkar got in touch with Maharaj as soon as he got out of jail. It was Atulkar who provided Altaf with the smuggled RDX. The home minister must also have been in touch with Atulkar somehow.'

'Do you think there are any other people involved in the conspiracy, sir?'

'I don't know, but the NIA will find out, that's for sure.'

* * *

When Mukhtiyar left, I sat back in my chair. But I could not relax. I had some interrogation of my own to do.

I reached for the intercom. 'Gahlot, tell Pratap to bring the car. I need to go to Ravi Bhushan Sir's office.'

* * *

Traffic was heavy. It took us fifteen minutes to get to Ravi's office.

Inside the building, I watched Ravi through the glass walls of his chamber. He was reading a pile of files.

I took out my phone and dialled a number.

Ravi looked up, startled. He opened a drawer and took out a cell phone, looking curiously at the screen.

'He's probably wondering why the phone is ringing,' I thought bitterly. 'After all, he bought that cell phone for just one purpose. To call Charu.'

'Hi Ravi, no need to answer the call,' I said, pocketing my phone as I entered his chamber.

Ravi's face became absolutely ashen.

'It's not what you think, let me explain,' he said, his voice trembling.

'Did you think I wouldn't be able to trace the number you used to call Charu, huh?' I said, barely controlling my fury. 'Go on, tell me your pathetic lies. I'd like to see how much lower you can stoop.'

I would have loved to stretch the confrontation out, make Ravi squirm, watch him tie himself in knots trying to excuse his actions, but I lost control of my anger.

'Why the hell did you call Charu?' I asked, banging my fist on the table.

Ravi took a deep breath.

'Arjun, I'm so sorry. I gave in to jealousy. You have a great career and the best of postings. You have a great family. You have a lovely wife! And I have nothing like it,' he said.

'So?' I said furiously.

'When I got a hint that you might be having a fling with Madhushree, I deliberately called Charu to tell her about it. To make your relationship sour. I even instigated Madhav to WhatsApp you so would lose your mental peace,' said Ravi avoiding my eyes.

'I can't believe it. I thought you were my best friend. I never imagined you would try to destroy my life. You're disgusting,' I shouted.

Ravi's face crumpled. He began to weep.

'Don't waste my time with tears. Tell me: were you involved in Madhushree's murder?' I said.

'What are you saying, Arjun? You've known me for years. You know I wouldn't even dream of doing something so dastardly,' cried Ravi.

He was telling the truth. He'd always had a meek personality. He didn't have the guts to do anything bold, leave aside plan a murder.

'Do me a favour, Ravi. Don't show me your face again. Ever,' I said, as I stormed out of his office.

Epilogue

'Are you Mrs Rachna, wife of Vijay Atulkar?' I asked the woman who opened the door to the spartan, lower-middle-class flat.

'Yes, I'm Rachna, but I'm not Vijay's wife. I have no relationship with him,' said the woman sternly.

'I'm sorry if I offended you. I'm Arjun Kumar, IGP. May I come in?'

She stepped away from the door.

'Please come in, sir.'

'Is this your son?' I asked, looking at a boy who was reading intently.

'Yes. He's my son. Aditya.'

'Hello, beta, I'm an acquaintance of your grandfather, Head Constable Rajesh Atulkar. Your grandfather was the most honest and hardworking policeman I have ever known,' I said.

'I know,' Aditya beamed. 'I'm very proud of him.'

'Do you know what your grandfather's dream was?'

'Yes, uncle. He wanted me to become an IPS officer,' replied Aditya.

'Chalo, beta. Let's work together and make your dada's dream come true. I'll support you in this journey in every way,' I said, patting his head affectionately.

I heard a sound behind me and looked back.

Rachna was wiping her tears with the pallu of her saree.

*　*　*

'God-man convicted for the murder of Madhushree,' read the headline.

I felt at peace. Madhushree's killers had been brought to justice. Maharaj Saheb would be in jail for the rest of his life. His deputies had already started bickering amongst themselves over his throne. Sood, the former home minister, was also behind bars for money laundering and drug smuggling and the ED had attached his properties, after which his party had expelled him. And Atulkar, the Ghost, was dead. The NIA had encapsulated his role in the terror plot to assassinate the PM, connecting his meeting with Timur Ali in prison to his association with Altaf and Maharaj.

'Madhushree didn't deserve to die. Though I was not directly responsible for her death, I could never forgive myself for my part in it. I'll just have to live with the guilt,' I thought sadly.

I looked out of the window. Charu and our children were playing badminton in the garden.

'I'll live with the guilt, but I'll never let go of my family at any cost.'

The End

Acknowledgements

The last three years of my life have been extremely tough. I felt as if I was living a nightmare. I started questioning the world around me and pondered over the unfairness of life.

It was during this time I realized the importance of my family, whom I had taken for granted earlier. My wife Tanu stood by me like a rock. I really don't know what I would have done without her.

My son Aditya and daughter Aishwarya are priceless gems who inspired me with their resolve when they were going through turbulent times themselves. Their mere presence was so calming. And they are wise beyond their years.

My parents, my brother, my father-in-law were a constant support. My childhood friend Abhishek Bansal was like a sponge who absorbed all my frustrations and angst.

I would have almost dropped the idea of writing this book, but then my friend Ashema Mehta told me that this was my destiny. 'You'd get a lot of peace if you direct your energies to creative pursuits,' she said.

I want to thank Priyal Gulati for her wonderful insights and suggestions to improve the book. And, of course, I want to thank the young team at Penguin. Milee Ashwarya, Rachna Pratap, Nikita Dahiya, Saba Nehal and Gurveen Chadha have been outstanding with their inputs.

A shout-out to my friend Chetan Bhagat who has written a heartfelt foreword.

Scan QR code to access the
Penguin Random House India website